Maria Crofoot Bowling divides her time between writing, hiking, backpacking and adventuring in the areas around her homes in Flagstaff, Arizona and Radford, Virginia. Her portfolio includes numerous short stories, a novel, and a memoir on the backpacking life, all of which strive to show how human nature reacts and adjusts to the crooked paths life puts before us.

For
Jack Bowling and Phillip Stone,
who have faithfully supported all of my adventures.

Maria Crofoot Bowling

SHELTER IN PLACE

AUSTIN MACAULEY PUBLISHERS™

LONDON * CAMBRIDGE * NEW YORK * SHARJAH

Copyright © Maria Crofoot Bowling 2023

All rights reserved. No part of this publication may be reproduced, distributed, or transmitted in any form or by any means, including photocopying, recording, or other electronic or mechanical methods, without the prior written permission of the publisher, except in the case of brief quotations embodied in critical reviews and certain other non-commercial uses permitted by copyright law. For permission requests, write to the publisher.

Any person who commits any unauthorized act in relation to this publication may be liable to criminal prosecution and civil claims for damages.

This is a work of fiction. Names, characters, businesses, places, events, locales, and incidents are either the products of the author's imagination or used in a fictitious manner. Any resemblance to actual persons, living or dead, or actual events is purely coincidental.

Ordering Information
Quantity sales: Special discounts are available on quantity purchases by corporations, associations, and others. For details, contact the publisher at the address below.

Publisher's Cataloging-in-Publication data
Bowling, Maria Crofoot
Shelter in Place

ISBN 9798886930412 (Paperback)
ISBN 9798886930429 (Hardback)
ISBN 9798886930443 (ePub e-book)
ISBN 9798886930436 (Audiobook)

Library of Congress Control Number: 2023906362

www.austinmacauley.com/us

First Published 2023
Austin Macauley Publishers LLC
40 Wall Street, 33rd Floor, Suite 3302
New York, NY 10005
USA

mail-usa@austinmacauley.com
+1 (646) 5125767

A novel is a journey with many beginnings, twists, and turns. Countless friends and readers have helped me along the way, but I would especially like to thank my children Frances, Lindsay, and Matthew for always keeping life real; my late husband Jack Bowling, for supporting my dreams; and my partner Phillip Stone for bringing me nourishment, keeping me on schedule, and shuttling me hither and yon.

Invaluable feedback came through many writing groups, and I particularly thank Chelsea Adams, Piper Durrell, and Jessica Muller for slaving through so many drafts of this story.

This novel might still be unfinished if it weren't for the structure and guidance provided by the Mountainview MFA program at Southern New Hampshire University. Thank you, Craig Childs, for putting it on my radar, and thank you Ben Nugent for inviting me in. My mentors Hermione Hoby, Justin Taylor, Wiley Cash, and Rachel B. Glaser gave me spot-on insights and steady encouragement. Thanks also to Lydia Peele for her patience in many feedback groups, and a special thank you to Richard Adams Carey for sticking with me beyond the program and performing the final editing.

I am indebted to Dina Imbriani and the Mountain Shepherd Adventure School in Catawba, Virginia for educating me in wilderness survival techniques, and to Ted Koppel's book Lights Out for providing inspiration and crucial knowledge about the EMP threat.

Executive Summary

The Electro-Magnetic Pulse generated by a high-altitude nuclear explosion is one of a small number of threats that can hold our society at risk of catastrophic consequences. Virtually every aspect of American society is dependent on electronics. Electronics are used to control, communicate, compute, store, manage, and implement nearly every sector of United States (U.S.) civilian systems. When a nuclear explosion occurs at high altitude, the EMP signal it produces will result in long-term disruption of energy and power distribution, communications, shipping, and the flow of consumer goods. Air, rail, and travel by personal vehicle will be nearly impossible. The infrastructure necessary to address these problems will also be destroyed. The larger the affected region, the longer it will take to mitigate the damage. Power infrastructures may be lost for a year or more.

Part I

October 15

My name is Aurora McKenzie Scott, and I have left two homes in six months, one by choice and the second under duress. Luckily, I was somewhat prepared for both situations, unlike most people, who were taken by surprise and are marooned in dwellings that provide nothing more than a roof. The first home I abandoned was the townhouse in Arlington, which I bought with my late husband, about five years before the cancer took him. The second was an off-grid cabin on the edge of the George Washington National Forest in western Virginia. But that home, too, became unsafe. My present home is a tiny, octagonal hut with a slanted roof, hidden by thick undergrowth a few miles back in the woods. Peter and I designed it as our second layer of "bug out," a place to go if we had to give up the cabin he had so meticulously prepared. That was the plan before his death, just over a year ago. I have been in the woods for three months, since mid-July, when the strangers came, and I had to flee once more.

You might wonder why I have only now decided to tell my story. It does seem presumptuous to think that the person who eventually finds these words, perhaps long after my demise, will be interested in my story the way people have eavesdropped on others through the ages. If this nightmare ever ends, everyone left will have a story of equal hardship or worse. But perhaps I have grown too cynical. Perhaps the forces that started us down this path will ultimately lose, and there will be a way to restart America from the ground up. But it is hard to think that way anymore, and I find myself caring less and less.

So why? I can't say I really know. Just that my existence here has become overwhelmingly tiresome, and I know that something must change. I am becoming forgetful and wasting more and more time in a sort of peaceful listlessness. Sometimes when I wake up, I don't know where I am. I wonder why I don't hear the students starting breakfast, and I lie in my sleeping bag straining my ears for familiar camp noises. I have taken the pistol from under the pillow and placed it where I see it immediately upon waking. Firearms weren't allowed at the wilderness school where I worked. One look at the 9-millimeter, semi-automatic, and I remember quickly why I am here. Though I can remember most of what Peter taught me, my memories of him are also fading. But maybe by looking back, I can make some sense of what has happened and regain some sense of focus. Oddly, if he hadn't done so well preparing me, I wouldn't have the luxury of thinking about more than where to find my next meal. But mere survival isn't enough to keep me going anymore. So, I must look for another goal, another focus, an actual reason for living.

October 20

Chores have kept me too tired to write these last days, though I know that I should do better. But the snare I set on the west side of the mountain caught a young wild pig, and I have spent hours gutting, skinning, and cutting chunks of meat off the carcass. In early September, when I got my second deer, I set up a smoking area in a small cave a few miles from the hut. I don't have much in the way of spices, but I sprinkled the meat with some salt and hung it in strips along a rope I strung across the width of the interior. Late in the afternoon, I started a fire in the back of the cave, hoping that dusk would help cover the smoke. I blocked off the front of the cave by dragging brush across the entrance and spent most of the night and next day feeding semi-dry sticks onto the coals. Short on storage, I wrapped most of the meat in pieces of nylon tarp and buried it in the woods. So now I have been repeating the process with the pig. I have wasted a lot by hacking off just as many big hunks of meat as I could in a short time, worried that a bear or other pigs would come to challenge me for the food. With the deer, I have a decent store, though it wouldn't hurt to have more. Turkeys, squirrels, and other small animals I eat immediately, in order to postpone dipping into my winter supply for as long as possible.

At night, I worry. I have made a map of all my hiding places, but suppose I lose it or ruin it somehow? What if I dig up the meat only to find that insects and worms have gotten to it, or it has just rotted away? This is the gamble I am taking. Some days, I go by all the sites to see if they have been disturbed. As fall has come, I'm amazed at how different the woods look. With each visit, I reinforce my memory of each location. If I am not worrying about the food, I torture myself with the question of whether I should go back to the cabin. I tell myself that I should at least find out whether the strangers stayed. Perhaps they just took what they could find and left. I know this is what I should do. I think of all the hiding places where we stashed provisions. Surely, they couldn't have found them all. I know I should try, but the thought of seeing other people, and, worse, of being seen, is paralyzing. No one saw me leave that day, so no one knows there is anyone to look for back in these hills. My entire sense of security has come to depend on that.

October 23

Yesterday afternoon, the wind started to pick up. The skies had been overcast from the start, the morning air humid and close. Then the winds came careening through the tree branches, and by dusk rain was coming down in sheets. I lay in my sleeping bag listening and remembering backpack trips with Peter, before the cabin consumed our attention. I always felt safe with him, knowing that he had anchored the tent with the same methodical care with which he worked on the car or brushed his teeth. But for all his deliberation, he was far from predictable. On every trip, he would do something to surprise me, like hiding frozen steaks and beer in his pack when I was expecting freeze-dried camping meals or rigging up a hand line and catching a couple trout while I was off exploring. Without him, the roar of the wind took on a menacing tone, and I was struck again by the uncertainties of being totally cut off from the outside world. Was this a passing storm or the edge of a hurricane? I had no weather forecast to ease my mind. This morning the wind abated a bit, but the rain did not, so I'm prepared for a day inside, digging into my stores of instant coffee, reading from our store of books, and adding to this record.

Where to begin? Five years ago, Peter and I were a somewhat atypical couple living in a townhouse in Arlington. I say "atypical" not because there was anything particularly strange about us, but because of our jobs—his at the NSA doing I'm not entirely sure what, and mine as a counselor for at-risk teens at a wilderness school in the Appalachian Mountains near Charlottesville, Virginia. His job occasionally took him away for short stints of time, while mine required me to be away for periods of four to six weeks, with breaks of two to three weeks in between. We'd been married for about three years when Peter began to talk about buying or building a cabin. I was a bit surprised at first. Peter was a planner and somewhat frugal. Though we made enough money between us for a comfortable life, he had always emphasized saving over spending. So, for him to suggest laying out the cash to buy and maintain a second dwelling seemed out of character. But I was an easy sell, as I too frequently complained about the culture shock of coming home to the congestion of Arlington after several weeks in the woods. It would be a place where we could go to recharge, he said.

At first, spending weekends on road trips exploring leads we got online seemed a lark. Often, we'd camp in state parks or stay at rustic motels, and our outings felt like adventures. But, as time went on, Peter became more and more specific about the land we looked at—the sun had to be just so, there had to be a creek on the site, or better yet, a spring. The nearest town must be several miles away, and the land had to be nearly surrounded by woods. Then he began using words like "off-grid" and "self-sufficient."

Over lunch that day in some West Virginia diner, I asked him why it was suddenly so important that we be off-grid and said that it seemed like a lot of trouble to go through for the occasional power outage. "I camp pretty off-grid all the time," I reminded him. "I don't mind having some amenities when I'm not working. Are you thinking we won't be able to afford a little electricity?"

I threw in the last question as a joke, but as he slowly stirred his chili, I knew he had something serious on his mind.

"But it could be more than a little power outage," he began. Our eyes met across the table. "It could be something much more drastic, and it could last a long time. Like months, maybe even years."

I glanced out the window beside the booth. It was early spring, and daffodils were nodding along the fence line at the edge of the parking lot.

"Do you know something?"

"Know? Nobody knows…But there are possibilities and capabilities that people have…we call them 'unstable actors.' Remember that cyberattack on Lehman Brothers? That's nothing compared to what could happen."

"Is this classified stuff you're telling me?"

"No, no. Not at this level of detail."

His eyes were down in his chili again, but his mind seemed to be far away.

"It just wouldn't hurt to be prepared—shelter, food, water. A way to get more if it lasted very long."

"Hmm…so you want us to become preppers, like those crazy militia people."

"More like the Mormons…just some common sense readiness…and, if nothing major happens, we'll still have a nice little getaway."

Not long after that, we found the place, a stalwart-looking, craftsmen-style cabin with deep front and back porches and wide dormers above each porch. The land was a thirty-acre plot surrounded by national forest with a driveway that was just an overgrown dirt track. Beyond our driveway, the forest service road climbed for a while and then dead-ended a couple more miles up the hollow. Built in the 1950s, the cabin had most recently been the retirement home of a couple from Martinsburg, West Virginia, but by the time they'd passed, their children were scattered too far to want to make use of it.

"Just make an offer," the real estate agent said. "The heirs have been squabbling for years over the property taxes, low as they are."

A couple months later, we arrived for a long weekend with cleaning supplies, an air mattress, and a few coolers of food. Peter had taken care of the nitty-gritty details of the house purchase while I was at work, and we'd just closed the day before. My school term had been complicated by a new student who came with more than the usual emotional baggage and who spent the first two weeks pitting the other girls against each other. Adding to everyone's misery, the weather stayed cool and rainy for weeks. It took most of the three-hour ride from Arlington to decompress, but by the time we drew close to the last turnoff, I was ready for our first weekend at the new retreat. I couldn't wait to get rid of the old-person-shut-up-house smells, and Peter was anxious to see what needed to be done, first to make the place livable, and then to repurpose it for off-grid survival.

We'd agreed to have the electricity turned on until the solar was up and running, but we hadn't done it yet, so that first weekend was like indoor camping. The weather had finally turned warm, and I was happy to run around opening windows and peeking in closets.

The cabin was laid out so that from the center of the front porch, you walked into the left end of the living room and opposite the doorway to the kitchen. A few feet from the doorway was a woodstove and brick chimney. Directly behind the wall, in the kitchen, was another wood-burning cook stove, a white and green porcelain model from back in the 1920s. There was a propane gas stove, too, but the wood stoves would be more than sufficient for heat. With a little cleaning up, they would both be in good working condition. The eat-in kitchen was the same size as the living room, with its own door to the back porch. To the left of the kitchen doorway, a hallway ran down the center of the house with a bath and small bedroom on the right, and a larger bedroom and the stairs on the left. Peter had pulled the car around back and was lugging in a cooler when I opened a door between the kitchen and bathroom.

"Ah...a cellar," I called. "Have you been down there? I thought it was a closet."

"Yeah, when I came for the inspection. It seemed pretty dry, no mold or anything." He walked down the hall to look over my shoulder. "I think we should put a floor in here, though."

My blank look conveyed that I was not following him.

"You see...if we make it into a closet and put in a trapdoor, we can cover the door with a rug or some old linoleum, and no one will know it's a cellar. We can block off the cellar windows so that from the outside, it'll just look like a crawl space. That way, if someone breaks in, they won't take whatever we have down there. And, we can use the closet as more pantry space. Let me show you something else."

I couldn't help smiling at his excitement as he led me through the kitchen and out the back door, grabbing two headlamps off the counter as he passed. One of the plusses of the house had been the weathered barn that was situated just a couple hundred feet to the back right of the yard. Peter headed straight for it.

"Remember the root cellar under the barn?"

He led me to a set of stone steps that was situated about halfway down the right wall. From a distance, the weeds hid them from view.

"This entrance is pretty obvious, but if we filled it in, it wouldn't take long for the weeds to take over and no one would know it was ever here. Then we could cut a trapdoor in the floor of the barn and park that old tractor on top of it. Presto! Hidden root cellar."

"Wow," I said, "You've been giving this a lot of thought."

"Well, I had some time to spend after the inspection."

"And you really think that all this secrecy is necessary?"

"Ay," he said, using his pet name for me, "If we lose electricity for a long time, there will be no food shipments, and people will be desperate for their next meal. Even out here in the country."

He led me down the steps and pushed open the heavy, wooden door at the bottom. We pulled on our headlamps, and he picked up a broom he'd left by the door. Batting at cobwebs as we went, he showed me three separate rooms: a large outer room with waist-high bins that we figured were probably used for potatoes and other root crops, a smaller room to the right with a sand floor—maybe for crops that needed a drier environment—and a last room to the back left that was lined with deep shelves. I tried to imagine all that space filled with food. It would be enough to last a very long time.

"We'll need to buy a couple of thermometers and something to measure the humidity. Then we'll know what we can store down here the best," Peter said, peering into a corner. "I haven't seen any mice droppings, so it must be sealed pretty well."

"Hmmm…So, now we need to become food storage experts," I said, as we emerged into the warm sunshine.

It was a relief to be out in the fresh air. While Peter fiddled around in the barn, I headed back into the house and started hauling our duffels, sleeping bags, and air mattress up the stairs. The second floor was more like an attic, a huge room that ran the length of the house, divided in the middle by just the chimney. I laid out the air mattress against the chimney on the front side, so we'd be able to see out the front dormer, and attached the air pump. While the pump whined behind me, I gazed out the window. Looking south, I could barely discern the break in the canopy made by the forest road. The town of Wagner was out of sight, far to the west. I imagined the woods and road crawling with desperate people looking for food. It was then that I realized that I'd been focusing much more on the idea of the cabin as a getaway, something I really needed, than as a survival home, something Peter seemed more and more convinced was necessary.

That night, as we lay on the air mattress and basked in the moonlight falling through the window, I broached the subject.

"You know, we talked about having this place as a retreat and a haven from catastrophe. But I'm not sure that it will ever be a place where I can relax if all we ever do while we're here is prepare for some kind of Armageddon. Are you sure you're not just being paranoid?"

Snuggling up to my side, Peter reached an arm across my chest and pulled me closer. "Ay, if you knew what I knew…" he said. "I can't tell you specifics, but there are countries that want to bring us down, even at unimaginable costs to their own people. But I promise, we'll make this a place we can both enjoy, and I can do most of the work while you're on your teaching stints. It'll be a lot more fun than hanging around the townhouse by myself on the weekends. And if you want me to ease off on the project when you're here, I can do that, too. You don't have to do anything you don't feel like doing."

"Well, when you put it that way, it sounds better, even though it makes me look kind of lazy."

"Ay, you are anything but lazy, and you know it. Hey, let's take a picnic lunch and explore up the creek tomorrow," he suggested.

And that's what we did, and we had a great time, finding several waterfalls, a few frogs, and even a little snake that came swimming across a little pool toward us. And, of course, I didn't even notice that while we were goofing off, Peter was probably thinking about where he would put this little hut.

October 24

After writing yesterday until my hand was too sore to go on, I reheated some oatmeal with dried apples that I gathered last month. Luckily, just about all of these hills were at some time farm land, so it's not unusual to find overgrown orchards in seemingly unlikely places. Pigs and apples are the legacy of generations of hardy, Appalachian mountain farmers, and I'm thankful for all they've left me. Unfortunately, the wild blueberries and huckleberries that I gathered in July are sitting in tins in the root cellar back at the cabin. I usually gathered the apples at mid-day, hoping that the bears would be napping, and used my largest backpack to haul them back. I often saw deer scavenging the windfalls, and piles of bear scat everywhere, though I never actually saw one. Near the smoking cave are some large stone slabs where I spread the apple slices on tarps to dry. This was a tedious process, and sometimes the weather turned rainy or humid, and I had trouble getting them to dry.

Peter built this hut from a gazebo kit that he modified to suit our needs. It has a double floor with the bottom platform sealed to keep out moisture, insects, and rodents. Between the two floors, eight inches of storage space hold the majority of my food in airtight tins. Rice, beans, biscuit mix, instant milk, instant potatoes, Tang, sugar, coffee, honey, spices, tea bags, dried eggs, nuts, raisins, canned chicken and tuna, and some real luxuries—freeze dried meals that Peter made himself by cooking extra stews and crock pot meals and then drying them in a dehydrator.

For the inside framing, Peter used two-by-eights, which left about four inches of exposed stud after he finished the interior walls. Between the studs, shelves at various levels provide more storage area. At eye level, an eight-inch window runs around most of the interior except for the few feet directly behind the woodstove. The window is coated with a non-reflective substance to make it harder to see from outside during the day, but I still feel like I'm in a fish bowl at night, so I close the blackout curtains and use as little light as possible. This hasn't been a problem during the long days of summer, but I wonder if I will go a little stir crazy when the cold weather and short days set in. Two vents near the ceiling and two near the floor provide for cross ventilation and can be closed off in the winter. The bed platform is about two feet off the floor and stands against the wall opposite the woodstove with the area underneath providing yet more space for storage.

You may be wondering how Peter got all this stuff up here. I helped him sometimes, but he often invited a friend or two when there was a lot of heavy lifting. The hut is about four miles from the cabin, behind the crests of two more hills, and maybe nine hundred feet higher in elevation. The forest road goes about halfway up, but then the route turns left up a hollow, over the ridge to the northeast, across the next hollow and halfway up another hill to a small knob. Peter hid the hut in a dense rhododendron thicket just over the crest of the hill. A spring-fed creek flows down the crease below the knob, about a five-minute walk downhill. Renovations around the cabin took about a year, but as we started our second summer there, Peter was already hauling up the building supplies for the hut. Though he camped here many times during the building process, by early fall it was enclosed and ready for our first night here together.

Since Peter put the windows so high, I must stand to see out. Yesterday, as I was swallowing down my lukewarm oatmeal, the rain seemed to pick up and pounded against the walls with new ferocity. It came in waves from the southeast, unusual for this area where most of the weather comes from the southwest. When I rose to look out, the window was plastered with bits of leaf, twigs, and other debris that made it almost impossible to see through. Even on a good day, the thicket limits the view. Yesterday all I could see were the leathery leaves of the rhododendron, slapping against the glass.

Curious beyond my better judgement, I pulled on my raincoat and pushed open the door. Heavy as it is, made of two by sixes, the wind nearly pulled the knob from my hand. I pushed myself out and closed the door behind me, holding onto the knob for support. With my other hand clamped to my head to secure my hood, I looked toward the top of the ridge, where an assortment of oaks, maples, hickories, and pines stuck out above the brush, waving wildly. They seemed to me like sentinels of the forest, warning of danger and calling, "Go back! Go back!" I stood, transfixed, rain pouring down my pants and into my boots, when a loud "CRACK!" sounded from behind me to the right, and I turned to see the upper third of an oak break and topple toward me. Its branches made a sound like bright static as they crashed into other trees on the way down. *Damn!* I thought, though I quickly realized that the crown of the tree would fall a good thirty feet short of me and the hut. As the tree came to rest, I looked around at the other trees in that direction. Though they continued to dance and gyrate, I didn't think more than a couple of them were close enough to pose a threat. Glancing at the downed tree once more in disbelief, I pushed open the door and thrust myself back into the precarious safety of the hut.

The wind and rain began to die down in the early evening, and I woke this morning to a light cloud cover that has been coursing over the mountains as though in slow motion. I emerged from the hut after breakfast to a world of downed branches and debris with a half-full chamber pot in hand, really a one-gallon plastic paint can with a close-fitting lid. Periodically, I dig a trench near a fallen tree about a foot deep and a few feet long. The soil is soft, so it is more a matter of scraping than digging. This becomes my toilet until it is half full. Every time I add to it, I sprinkle on some of the leaf meal I've scraped away to cover the smell and help the excrement decay. After a week or so, I refill the hole and dig a new one. I rinse my bucket with plain urine or used water from my dish washing, but I've found that the lid is tight enough to keep in the stench, so I don't attempt to sanitize it.

After toilet duty, I took the water bladder to the creek for drinking water. The rain filled the rain bucket with a couple of gallons that I will use for cooking, but I prefer creek water for drinking. I've given up on purifying it since the source is so close, and it hasn't made me sick yet, though sometimes on a sunny day I leave the bladder in the sun for a few hours to catch some ultraviolet rays. The container is as clear as any jar I have, so I'm confident that the sun can do its work. Filled to the brim, it weighs about twenty-four pounds, but I can fit it into my backpack and it still weighs less than the usual thirty-plus pounds I carry on backpacking trips.

These daily chores are probably the reason that I have kept my sanity, such as it is. Though chaos may reign elsewhere, life in these woods is reduced to its simplest directives—get water, get food, maintain shelter. There is no thinking about when to repaint the townhouse, how much to put in the savings account, or whether it's time to put new tires on the car. Procrastination affects my life immediately, so I do what needs to be done. No firewood—no cooking; no water—no beverages, cooking, or washing (though I do still put off the laundry sometimes). I basically have three changes of clothes, plus fleeces, a down jacket, a warm base layer, a rain suit, and a few extra pairs of panties. Just downstream from where I take my water is a little pool where I wash my clothes in a small, plastic tub, using just a few drops of biodegradable soap. I try to change my undies at least every other day, but I admit, it's not much of a priority. Most of the time, I just string the wet clothes around the inside of the cabin; they seldom dry outside in one afternoon, and then I'd have to bring them in at dusk, anyway.

My toilet and water chores were done by mid-morning, so I moved on to cooking, which has been my biggest challenge. During these hot months, starting a fire in the woodstove is pure torture, so I've made myself a little cooking area in a small clearing north of the hut. Although I know that someone could see the smoke, I tell myself that I have no choice. Though the air had dried out since the storm, the temperature was still mild for late October, so I hauled my Dutch oven full of soaked pinto beans to my cooking site and got a fire started under the grill, which we took off the Weber kettle grill we had on our porch in Arlington. I keep a little camp chair hidden under a tarp in the brush nearby, along with a small pot for heating water. Cooking beans is a long-term project, and I can't walk off and leave them for more than a few minutes for fear that the fire will get out of control, so I brought my notebook, pen and sketch pad. By late afternoon, the beans were getting tender, and I added more water, some rice, and a few dehydrated carrots and peas. The final result wouldn't win any awards, but it was tasty enough and would last through several reheatings. I finally dug in at around six, leaving myself just enough daylight to haul everything back to the hut.

October 26

Yesterday was a lost day. That is what I call the days when I let myself get caught up in a bout of malaise and melancholy. There must be an inner clock that regulates these moods because they usually come when I have nothing pressing to do, so they haven't impinged upon my survival thus far. I worry that this may change, though, and that one day I'll find myself unable to crawl out of my sleeping bag to do more than pee. I did manage to get up, though, and spent the day wandering in the woods, finally arriving at a certain rock a few miles along the ridge where I have gone before. I am amazed by how long I can just sit there and allow thoughts and feelings to wash over me. Most of the feelings center around Peter, images that come and go—his posture as he stood in front of the mirror to shave, the way he patted his pockets before going out the door, his smell when he kissed my neck. Inevitably, these images lead to more disturbing memories—IV lines sticking out of his arm, hospital gowns open in the back revealing an unfamiliar, emaciated body, a pale face against a pale pillow. But his eyes never changed, and I hold onto the memory of his gaze. I've learned that there is no point in trying to fight these moods. The most I can do is call a kind of truce, acknowledge them, and wait. Eventually, they recede enough for everyday life to break in, sometimes in the form of some necessary bodily function—hunger, thirst, exhaustion. After such an interlude, I'm likely to feel drained for as much as a day before I regain some energy.

So, I am not feeling totally back to myself as I sit on the sleep platform against the wall and take up my pen. When I think about what to write next, I am overwhelmed by what I've yet to convey, little details and the big story of what it was like on the day everything ground to a halt. It's odd how removed I feel from that person who suddenly realized that the big disaster was imminent. Looking back, she seems at the same time confident and naïve. Of course, we were all naïve to varying extents. But, at any rate, this is how I remember it.

On the morning of April 1st, I had just stepped out of the shower in Arlington when the NPR news broadcast on the bedroom radio caught my attention. A cascade of computer glitches and irregularities had struck Wall Street just after the opening bell. Data simply disappeared from the computer systems of the major traders, and their operating systems were behaving erratically. At first, the industry suspected some sort of elaborate April Fools' hoax, but efforts to identify and fix the problem had gone nowhere. Trading was suspended for the day, and trading houses were desperately trying to figure out what had happened. An anonymous spokesperson for one of the brokerage houses reported, "It's as though someone took a magic eraser and wiped out all of our files." Commerce Secretary Abraham was urging the public to remain calm. At the moment, everyday banking systems did not appear to be impacted; however, many banks were choosing to shut down their computer systems out of an "abundance of caution."

As I stood towel-drying my hair, I tried to digest the news and wondered what was going through the minds of millions of Americans. Would they panic? Start a run on the banks? If the bankers were smart, I thought, they'd all close their doors immediately. I pictured fist fights at ATMs and streets snarled with traffic. Perhaps people would just sit still and wait. Wall Street's problems might seem far enough removed that middle America wouldn't understand the possible ramifications of the announcement. Or they'd have blind faith that the problems could be easily fixed.

You might think I'd have remained glued to the news, but speculation was the last thing I wanted to hear, so I switched over to the classical music station, knowing they would interrupt the program if there was an important update. To tell the truth, I felt a little detached, part of me just wanting to ignore what I was hearing and its possible implications. But in the back of my mind, I knew that this could be the start of something big, the big "it" that Peter and I had been preparing for since we'd bought the cabin. Without thinking, I started throwing clothes into a duffel—my favorite jeans, hiking boots and the fleeces that I kept with me most of the time. I was halfway through a two-week break, so I could afford to disappear for a few days. My electronics and chargers…What else? I'd been meaning to make a bug out list, but I'd gotten lazy since Peter's death.

Back in the bathroom, I was pulling all of the over-the-counter medications from the shelves and dumping them into my toiletry bag when I saw Peter's aftershave. In the months since his death, I had left the little blue bottle right where he had left it, occasionally sprinkling some on my nightshirt. I dropped it in with the medicines and went back to the bedroom for the gun.

In the kitchen I packed the bread and some food from the pantry into reusable bags and took them out to the pick-up. I brought in a cooler, dropped in some ice packs and all the ice from the ice maker. The milk, butter, cheese, some vegetables, a few condiments, and several packages of meat from the freezer came next. I looked around the refrigerator shelves at the containers of leftovers. I couldn't take it all, but it would surely rot if the electricity went off. And if it went off for a long time, that would be the least of anyone's problems, I thought. But, in spite of myself, I pulled them out, dumped them down the garbage disposal and tossed the containers into the dishwasher. I'd turned the downstairs radio to the same NPR station, and I could feel my own panic rising as the music lilted on. Then the music was interrupted by that high-pitched tone they use for testing the emergency broadcast system.

"This is not a test," a male voice began. In addition to the breakdown of the computer systems at Wall Street and several major financial institutions, there were reports of a major power outage on the west coast, affecting the grid from just north of San Francisco south to the Mexican border. The president had been briefed and was expected to make a statement within the hour. In the meantime, people were encouraged to remain calm, and if it was feasible, to return home. Metropolitan areas were being encouraged to follow storm evacuation procedures as though a winter storm or other natural disaster were imminent. The goal was to get workers and students home in as orderly a manner as possible. The term "abundance of caution" was repeated several times, but no details were provided about what the threat might be.

Just go, I thought, as I turned the radio off and the dishwasher on. But what was I forgetting? Keys. Which to leave and which to take? I pulled both sets of truck keys from the kitchen drawer and dropped them in my purse. If you've ever tried to get new keys for an antique pick-up truck, a 1966 Ford F-250, to be exact, you can appreciate how carefully we kept track of those keys. I left the second set of my car keys in the drawer. My neighbor, Linda, already had a key to the house. In the garage I took three cases of powdered milk and set them in the back of the truck. Also, three empty gas cans, in the hope I could fill them on the way. I looked around. There was nothing left to take that we didn't have at the cabin. I pulled the truck out of the garage and stopped it in the driveway. Up and down the street of townhouses, everything seemed quiet.

As I got out of the truck, Linda's door opened and she stepped out onto her porch, her six-month-old, Annie, perched on her hip. Linda had also taught at the wilderness school until she'd gotten pregnant, and had alerted us when our unit came up for sale. Her husband, Steve, was an engineer in the Army, stationed in Iraq on his second tour.

"Hey, I was just coming over to talk to you!" I called.

"Have you heard?" she asked, as I walked up.

"Yeah. I was just heading out to the cabin," I told her. Steve and Linda had been up there once, just before Peter got sick. Steve had marveled at the solar panels, water pumping and storage systems, and massive food supplies we'd squirreled away.

"Do you want to come with me? There's plenty of room in the truck."

Linda, a slight blonde who'd had a hard time with both her pregnancy and labor, hugged Annie to her chest and looked down at me doubtfully.

"No. I think we'll be okay here."

"How 'bout your mom's? Maybe you should head over there." Linda's mother, a seventy-five-year-old widow, lived about two hours west in Frederick.

"I don't know. They said to stay home, and this is home for me."

"Are you sure?"

Linda nodded.

"Well, hey, let me give you something." Returning to the truck, I grabbed a case of powdered milk and took it back to Linda's porch.

"This might come in handy." I walked up onto the porch and set it on a chair. Annie squirmed and smiled at me, and I tickled her neck. "My car keys are on the counter. And you can help yourself to anything I left, okay?"

I rubbed Linda's shoulder.

"You think it's bad, don't you?" she asked.

I shrugged. "Too soon to tell. But be careful. Who knows, I may be back in a few days. And, oh, water. Be sure to store up as much as you can. Seriously, like garbage cans full, tubs…in my house, too."

"Okay, I get it. I'll try to be ready for…whatever…"

I asked her one more time if she was sure she wanted to stay. She nodded, and I gave them a quick hug, not wanting to make it seem like the final goodbye I thought it might be.

Hopping back into the truck, I waved as I pulled out of the driveway and started down the street.

Turning out of the development, I immediately found myself in bumper-to-bumper traffic. At the first corner, cars waiting to pull into the Wells Fargo had backed up onto the street, and the parking lot of the drug store and Walmart was full. I figured people were getting cash and milk in one stop with their debit cards, and I wondered whether the stores would have thought to impose limits. Peter had insisted we keep a few thousand dollars at the cabin and a couple hundred in the truck, though I'd argued that cash probably wouldn't do us much good in an apocalypse. I was kidding at the time.

For a while, I'd kept the radio on, but the constant re-hashing of what had already been announced was only feeding the rising panic that I was struggling to keep at bay. I turned it off and tried to concentrate on something practical. You should call your mom, I thought, or at least Aunt JoAnn.

One of the things Peter and I had had in common was that we'd both been born late in our parents' marriages, and we'd teased each other about being accidents. His parents had died in their late sixties, his dad of a heart attack, and his mother of a stroke not long after. His brother, Greg, was fifteen years older and worked for a tech company in California. Likely, he was in the midst of the power outage.

My own parents split when I was in college, when my mother was in her third year of battling lupus. The way Mom described it, Dad had done his best to ignore her condition by spending more and more time in the basement of our house in Worcester, Mass., watching his model trains go round and round. As part of an experimental treatment, Mom's thymus had been removed. I was still finishing my junior year at George Washington University in D.C., and she insisted I stay at school. When Aunt JoAnn brought Mom home from the hospital, Dad and the train set were gone. Soon after, Mom sold the house and moved in with Aunt JoAnn, who helped her as best she could until Mom decided that she was too much of a burden and moved to a senior facility on the outskirts of town. I'd made it a point to visit several times a year, but after Peter and I married, our jobs kept us around Washington most of the time. The last time I'd visited, right after Christmas, she'd seemed even more confused than usual. Memory loss is common with lupus, but so are blood clots, and I wondered if she might have had a mild stroke. We sat in the sunroom where we could look out onto the snow-covered lawn.

"So, how is Peter?" she'd asked every time there was a pause in the conversation. The first time, I said, "Peter died, Mom, remember? It was cancer."

"Oh my, I'm so sorry." She reached for my hand, and we held hands awkwardly over the arm of her wheelchair.

I looked at the wrists protruding from her thick robe. They seemed puffier than last time, and I wondered how her kidneys were doing. Then I changed the subject, but a couple minutes later she asked again, "So how is Peter?"

At the next stoplight, I brought up Aunt JoAnn's number. After three rings, an automated voice came on the line, saying "All circuits are busy. Please try your call again later."

"Fuck," I said and dropped the phone on the seat, thinking, *Why didn't you try sooner?*

Heading west, I weaved my way along secondary roads until I came in sight of the I-95 interchange. Traffic was at a total standstill on the overpass, and everyone waiting at the on-ramp seemed to be shouting into their cell phone. I continued under the highway and circled around to the north of Quantico where the traffic thinned, and I continued angling west-southwest, heading in the general direction of Harrisonburg, Virginia.

Every half hour or so, I turned on the radio to see if there were any new developments. The statement from President Browning had been postponed, and even the news anchors at NPR were repeating rumor and speculation. One story was that Pakistan had launched the cyberattacks out of revenge for the new sanctions. Another was that North Korea, backed by China, had issued an ultimatum—include them on the U.N. Security Council or face a crippling of the economy. Every time I turned off the radio, I tried to reach Aunt JoAnn and got the same recorded message.

Once outside the metro area, traffic settled down. The shopping centers and strip malls were still busy, but none of it had the frenzied feel there had been in D.C. After a couple hours of meandering, I reached Route 340 and headed south along the east flank of the Blue Ridge, past woods and farms and the occasional deserted crossroads. The brush on the mountains was starting to bud out, giving the hills a reddish hue, though the trees were a long way from sprouting their leaves. Winter wheat had turned the valley floor green, contrasting with the dull grays and browns of winter, all details I would normally have treasured if I hadn't had a pervading sense that I was being tailed by a mythical demon that might overtake me if I didn't hurry, hurry, hurry.

After skirting Harrisonburg to the east, I turned west on several county roads until I crossed under I-81. Just past the interchange, I came to a gas station where we'd frequently stopped on the way to the cabin. If I could fill the truck and the extra containers, I'd be in good shape to leave the area if I should need to. But as I pulled in, the first thing I noticed was that the gas handles were all covered in plastic bags. Disappointed, I parked the truck and went into the store.

The owner, a middle-aged man from Lebanon, stood behind the cash register, straightening the drawer. He glanced up briefly and then looked down again, his thick fingers pulling each bill flat as he laid them in their respective slots.

"Hello, Eessa," I said, surprised that I hadn't gotten the usual friendly greeting.

"Have you sold out of gas already?"

He glanced up briefly and mumbled that the police had told him to shut off his pumps.

"Really? Why?" I asked.

He glanced out the storefront window and leaned slightly toward me.

"I am the only station with a generator in the area. I am to save my gas for emergency vehicles if the power goes out."

"And they think that's likely?"

He shrugged. "They are being cautious, they said, just in case."

"Hmm. That's too bad. I was hoping to at least fill up my truck." A stuffed tiger on the floor behind the counter reminded me that he had an extended family under his roof. "How's your granddaughter?"

In spite of himself, he broke into a smile.

"She is fine. She and my daughter are waiting at home. My son-in-law will come to take over for me soon," he told me.

"Why not just close up?"

"My neighbors may still come for food. It will help make up for not selling the gas."

"Yeah, I guess so. But if the power does go out, you should make it look like you're closed. Maybe lock up the food you have left or take it home. The power might not come back for a while."

"How do you know this?"

He looked genuinely startled, and I thought maybe I should have kept my mouth shut.

"I don't know anything, but it is better to be safe. If there's food on the shelves, someone might break in." I gave him the gentle version of what could happen, knowing I'd already alarmed him enough.

"Yes, perhaps," he mumbled.

"Wait a sec," I said, and I walked back out to the truck. In my head I could hear Peter saying, Are you sure you can afford to do this? But I ignored him and grabbed one of the two remaining cases of instant milk out of the bed. Back in the store, I plopped it down on the counter. "For your granddaughter," I said. "Just in case."

"That is very kind. Let me pay you. I am very sorry about the gas."

And he did look sorry and a little overwhelmed as I turned toward the door.

"Don't worry about it. It's a gift. I hope you all remain well."

With just under half a tank, I knew I had plenty of gas to get to the cabin, but not much to go anywhere else should the need arise. The stations back near Arlington had been packed, and I'd gambled on being able to fill up closer in. But then I reminded myself that the stations in the next town would probably still be selling since, as Eessa mentioned, his was the only station with a generator for miles.

October 27

This morning I woke up with more energy than I've had in days. The temperature had dropped overnight, and I'd pulled the sleeping bag up over me, so I awoke in a warm cocoon with cool air washing over my face. The leaves have started falling, and their scent has freshened the air. Fall has always been my favorite season; at the wilderness school it always seemed to have a calming effect on the students. Chores weren't as sweaty, we could put hot comfort foods back on the menus, and we could spend clear nights around a bonfire, which always served to put the girls in a good mood.

I decided to take advantage of my energy to clean up a little and get to work on the laundry. After a quick breakfast of leftover beans and rice, I gathered my soap, washbasin, and clothes in a sack to haul to the stream. There wasn't much—a pair of jeans, some sweatpants, socks and T-shirts, a bra, a few panties, and some rags. The sun was already baking the oak leaves as I swished through them and angled my way down into the hollow.

A few minutes later, I stepped into the edge of the pool, placing my feet carefully so as not to stir up the sediment. Soon after moving up here, I chopped off my auburn hair, trying to reduce it to about a half an inch all over. The result was an uneven, spiky mess, what you might imagine would happen if you let a three-year-old go at you with a pair of kindergarten scissors. When I raised the hand mirror to survey my work, I was shocked at what it did to my eyes. They appeared rounder and larger and had the expression of a startled cat. The up side was that it now took only a few drops of soap to wash, and I could rinse it with a fraction of the water, which would come in handy when the weather turned cold.

After bathing and dressing in my last clean clothes, I stooped by the water and washed the rest. Hefting the sack of wet clothes to my shoulder, I noticed something flapping in the rhododendrons across the creek. I already had my boots on, so I walked upstream to cross on the rocks. As I got closer, I could see a dark blue bandana with a black, paisley print hanging evenly over an inner branch, as though it had been placed there to dry.

Damn, I thought. I turned slowly and looked hard into the tree line. Someone's been here. I stood for several minutes, waiting for my heart to slow so that I could listen for out-of-place noises. A squirrel flitted up a maple across the creek. Farther up the bank, a woodpecker tapped its staccato rhythm. A gnat found me and began assaulting my face and eyes. I swatted at it and came out of my trance. If someone was watching me, it wouldn't do any good to stand there. And if they'd seen where I came from, how hard would it be for them to find the hut?

I re-crossed the stream, retrieved the sack, and started back, tramping upstream for a while before circling around toward the hut. Just over a small rise, I stopped behind a tree to listen. Random rustlings. A few bird calls. Nothing that sounded human. When I drew close to my thicket, I tried to survey the area with the eyes of a stranger. Leaves had gathered in the crooks of the branches, adding another layer of camouflage to the hut. The rhododendrons, being evergreens, had kept their leaves. If I looked hard, from this vantage point I could make out a few inches of window frame and a foot of the upright that made up one corner. As before, I thought that a person could come quite close without noticing the hut at all, if they weren't looking for it. But that was the catch.

Hanging around just fed my paranoia. It was all I could do to wring my wet clothes and hang them inside before I had to get out. I'd become sloppy about keeping my gun with me, but no more. I hadn't reset any snares for days, so armed with the 9mm and a fixed-blade buck knife, I set out in the opposite direction of the creek. Twenty minutes or so took me to a clearing where I'd seen a flock of turkeys before. With the arrival of cooler weather, I thought they might come back to soak up some sun. I spent an hour or so rigging nooses where I thought they might come walking. Then I went into the woods and inspected fallen trees for signs of squirrels. Peter had taught me that they would habitually sit in the same places to eat acorns. All you had to do was search the trunks for nut shells to figure out their paths. So far, his advice had netted me more than a dozen.

By the time I'd set five squirrel snares, I was beginning to feel less panicked, so I sat down on a log to eat some nuts and think things through. I hadn't seen the bandana when I went for water the day before, but that could have just been oversight. I hadn't seen any other people signs, either, like wet spots on the rocks, but they might have dried before I came, and I didn't cross the creek much anyway. I decided to assume that the bandana couldn't have been there more than two or three days. So, who left it?

The most encouraging answer was that it was just someone passing through. If they were spying on me, they would have been more careful. Maybe they'd stopped at the creek for a while and headed on. They could be miles away.

As much as I wanted to believe that, I had no evidence one way or the other. So, suppose the person was still in the area? Did they know I was here? Could they be looking for me? Maybe one of the friends that helped Peter with the hut was trying to find me. That was a thought I'd entertained before. With no electricity, no clean water, no food, and absolutely no law and order, the city was probably the most dangerous place a person could be. I thought of Charles, nerdy, dumpy-looking Charles, with his egg-shaped body that hid an amazing reserve of old-fashioned gumption. But that was stupid. If a friend was close enough to leave the bandana, they'd have shown up at my door by now.

Which left the more obvious possibility, the one that had been lingering in the back of my mind for months. Why wouldn't the group who drove me out of the cabin try to find me? The solar panels were no good if you couldn't figure out how to connect them, and Peter had set up the system with all kinds of dummy wires and hidden switches. Without electrical expertise, they'd probably just conclude that the system was broken. But to come looking for me, they'd have to have a reason to think I was here and that I could fix it, wouldn't they? In which case, why would I have left?

What to do, what to do? Take a backpack farther into the woods and watch the hut for a few days to see if anyone showed up? Go looking for the owner of the bandana? Pretend they were gone and just go about my business?

That last option was just wishful thinking. I knew I couldn't pretend I was safe if someone might be that close. Surveilling the hut would be almost as bad. It seemed I would end up exactly where I'd been before, trying to decide whether my home was worth killing over. I could hear Peter in my ear again, saying, *Yes, it is, yes, it is. This is your life we're talking about!*

Finally, I decided that my only option was to gather more information. So, tomorrow, I will cross the creek to look for a campsite or other evidence that can tell me whether the danger is real. Tonight, I will sleep as best I can on a pad next to the woodstove with the pistol and rifle within reach. If anyone comes through the door, I will have the woodstove as cover.

October 28

I passed last night in varying degrees of discomfort and dread, starting awake every time a twig or acorn tapped on the roof. For dinner, I'd made just a small fire in the woodstove to heat water for oatmeal, letting it go out so as not to roast overnight, but I'd also left the vents open so I could hear better. The result was that I got quite chilly in my summer sleeping bag, but I was up and ready to go just as the woods became light enough to walk. In addition to the pistol and knife on my hips, I carried a small set of binoculars, a bag of nuts and raisins, two bottles of water, and the headlamp and first aid kit that seldom leave my daypack.

Heading straight to my bathing pool, I settled myself on the slope about twenty yards above the creek in a place well hidden by trees and brush. A quick look through the binoculars told me that the bandana was still there. I sat for a long time, rising occasionally to stretch a bit, but mostly scanning the woods and waiting to see whether someone would come for water.

By mid-morning, I was feeling somewhat encouraged and launched into the second phase of my plan, which was to walk the area across the creek in a series of half circles. I started by walking upstream for ten minutes or so. The going was slow, and I was trying to be quiet, so this probably took me only a half mile up. I crossed to the other side and started to walk a wide arc that would take me back to the creek at about the same distance below the pool. I walked quite slowly now, staring out into the woods in all directions, looking for any sign of disturbance.

My first pass yielded nothing except that I noted a grove of shagbark hickories with their green-husked nuts thick on the ground and quite a few still in the trees. Under better circumstances, I should return with my backpack. At the creek, I turned upstream to tighten my arc by about a hundred feet. About a third of the way through my second pass, I heard a loud rustling off to my right. Since it didn't sound very close, I merely stepped behind an oak, put my hand on the butt of the gun, and watched. Within seconds, a lumbering, black shape appeared through a break in the brush. It was my favorite kind of black bear, not too large, a safe distance away, and heading in the opposite direction, perhaps toward those hickories. I might have given you the impression earlier that I am afraid of these creatures, but that is not true. What makes me so wary is the knowledge of my circumstance. If I were to startle a bear into attacking, step too close to a copperhead or rattlesnake, or merely cut myself badly gutting a squirrel, I would be on my own. There would be no ambulance, no blood transfusions, and no antivenom. I have a few bottles of antibiotics Peter put in the first aid box, but no way to get more. An accident, even a small one, could kill me.

The bear disappeared into the brush, and I continued my arc, coming to the creek a little faster this time, turning downstream for a bit and then launching off again. At this point, I was feeling pretty good about the chances that the bandana belonged to someone who was now many miles away. But I continued looking into the woods to either side, scanning each chunk of new territory carefully before moving forward another thirty feet or so. Walk, repeat, walk, repeat.

At about the farthest point from the creek on that third pass, I spotted a large patch of green through the trees. Too uniform and bright to be an evergreen, it crouched motionless a long stone's throw away in the direction of the creek. I lifted my binoculars to my eyes. There was no doubt. I was seeing fabric, probably the side of a tent. I froze, trying to digest the idea that someone had been this close to me for—how long? Then I looked slowly around, imagining the gaze of hidden eyes. I even scanned the lower branches of the bigger trees, but everything was as silent and still as a patch of woods can be.

Step by step, I moved closer, raising the binoculars at regular intervals. Soon I noted the tent brand on the corner of the rain fly: Coleman. The fly was unzipped and one side hung loose. Then I was close enough to see that the tent sat at the edge of a little clearing, and beside it someone had made a fire ring of just a few water-smoothed rocks, probably hauled up from the creek. At a distance of forty feet or so, I circled around the tent to see if I could see inside. But even with my binoculars, the gray netting veiled the interior so that all I could make out was a dark pile of something that could be a sleeping bag. I raised my gaze again toward the trees. From this angle something else appeared—a yellow nylon bag that dangled from a tree branch well into the woods on the other side of the clearing. A food bag?

When I was sure there was nothing else to see, I carefully retreated to where I felt hidden but could still watch the open tent flap. I backed my way into a bush and hunkered down to ponder what I'd found. People who hiked as a hobby tended to buy more upscale tents, MSR, Big Agnes, North Face, and the like. A Coleman was more likely to belong to a hunter or someone on a budget. Of course, that was in the old world where you could choose such things. Back at the cabin, I still had the three-person Marmot that Peter and I had used and a two-person Big Agnes. At least this person wasn't camping in one of my tents. He or she had some experience, though, for they knew enough to hang their food bag away from the tent and out of reach of bears. The tent was out in the open, not secreted in the rhododendrons or other brush. This was encouraging, too, because it meant that the owner wasn't worried about being found.

I watched the tent for a long time. The day had warmed up; it was probably near seventy. A person could be inside sleeping, but more likely they were out doing something, perhaps hunting or exploring. I waited another half an hour. Nothing changed. Finally, I circled stiffly back to the creek, crossed over, and observed the bandana for a while. Again, nothing.

Heading back to the hut, I approached slowly, alert to any movements or irregularities. I was no longer in a panic, just cautiously optimistic that whoever was camped across the creek had an agenda of their own that didn't include me.

Later in the afternoon, I checked my traps and found a squirrel, flopped unnaturally over the side of the log where I'd attached my snare. I carefully loosened the noose—these smaller ones being made of florists' wire that I could reuse indefinitely—and tied the carcass to my belt. The turkey snares had been knocked off of their branches by animals or the wind, so I reset them. Halfway back to the hut, I gutted and skinned the squirrel on a fallen tree, a process I've become surprisingly used to, considering the way I grimaced the day that Peter first taught me.

All seemed normal as I came to my thicket, but still feeling uneasy, I hauled some water, my Dutch oven and a few other ingredients to my cooking spot and started a stew. I fought the urge to go back to the tent after I ate. Instead I cleaned up and returned to the hut to record my day. I have already set a good fire in the woodstove and plan to sleep on my sleep platform with my gun by my shoulder, as usual. In the morning, I will go back to the tent.

October 29

I write tonight from my usual spot on my sleeping platform, but part of me feels that I am being callous in doing so, and that I really ought to be sleeping in the tent or at least somewhere near. As difficult as it has always been to determine what exactly we owe to other people in our lives, be they strangers or not, it is even more difficult now that survival is so precarious.

I returned to the tent this morning, this time after the sun was well up and the day had warmed. I took my empty water bladder and two full bottles to drink, thinking to fill them on the return trip. For some reason, I didn't expect to see anyone. In the back of my mind, I suspected that the tent had been deserted, even though the food bag was hanging in plain sight. I approached with the same caution as yesterday and noted the food bag hanging exactly as before, even to the height that I remembered. Peering through the binoculars from a safe distance, the lump of sleeping bag or whatever seemed also about the same, and the rain fly hung open, all of which fueled my hope that the camp had been abandoned.

So I crept closer, still trying to stay under cover and crouching a bit as I approached. Every time I stopped to listen, all I heard was a soft stirring of leaves in the breeze. Finally, I was right outside the tent flap, peering in at the lumpy sleeping bag. I reached up for the tent zipper, a big curved L, and had started pulling it down when something moved inside the tent and emitted a soft whine, sounding so much like the mew of a kitten that I pulled back on my heels, totally confused. Then the smell hit me, something fetid and rotten.

"Who...?"

It was a mere trace of a word, weak and wispy. A female voice, I was sure.

"Are you okay?" I asked, trying to assess the danger, knowing that the whole scene could be a trap.

The answer was another muffled sound, maybe an "I," but it trailed off into nothing.

As I stood there, the smell became stronger, and I thought that no one would voluntarily stay in that stench, and that was what finally gave me the courage to unzip the tent, and with one sleeve up against my nostrils, crawl in.

Several moments eked by before my eyes adjusted to the eerie green light. I first made out a head at the top of the sleeping bag, surrounded by a tangle of stringy, brown hair. A pale face with half-closed eyes fixed in my direction. A pair of blue jeans wadded up between the sleeping bag and the tent wall, and a bloody T-shirt seemingly thrown against the other side of the tent. In addition to that first horrible, rancid smell, I could also smell urine, but I still couldn't place the source of that first smell. I looked back at the girl's face. She looked to be about fourteen. Confused, I opened my mouth to question her, but I couldn't figure out where to begin.

Then her mouth moved and she uttered three clear words, "I lost it."

As she said it, she turned her face away and started kicking feebly at the sleeping bag, as though to push it off.

Still kneeling, I reached over to help. The bag wasn't zipped, so I grabbed the free side and lifted, not really thinking about what she was doing or why. As the sleeping bag came away, she turned toward the wall, and the smell became almost unbearable. I saw that her naked back side was covered in blood, and the sleeping bag where she had lain was soaked with dark, jelly-like globs and most of it was black but some was bright and fresh.

"Did you hurt yourself?" I asked.

She shook her head and said again, "I lost..."

"You lost a baby," I said.

The back of her head bobbed slightly.

"Okay. I think I can help. Would that be alright?"

Again, the slight nod.

"Okay. I need for you to drink some water. You've lost a lot of blood, and I think you've been here for a couple of days, right?"

As I spoke, I shrugged out of my pack and pulled out a water bottle. I covered her up, pulled her gently onto her back, and lifted her head like an infant's in the crook of my arm. She had enough strength to tilt her head slightly as I poured some water past her lips. She swallowed and I poured in some more and then some more until she'd gotten down about eight ounces and let her head go limp in my arm. I put down the bottle and pressed the back of my hand to her forehead. She was hot, but not dangerously so. Lowering her head back down, I pulled my bandana out of my pack, soaked it, and wiped her face. Then I soaked it again laid it on her forehead.

"I'm going to give you some Tylenol. Do you think you can swallow it?"

Another nod.

I reached for her wrist and found her pulse. It was a little weak, but mostly steady and not too fast. I laid her hand back down.

"I'm Aurora. What's your name?"

Though she was lying very still, her eyes followed all my movements, and she made good eye contact.

"Edie."

"Nice to meet you. Here." I lifted her head again. "Open—" I dropped two Tylenol on the middle of her tongue and raised the water bottle to her lips. She took a big gulp and nodded.

"Do you need to go to the bathroom?"

"No, but I…" It seemed like she was embarrassed about having an accident, so I interrupted.

"Don't worry about it," I told her. "I know you must be really uncomfortable, but I don't have what I need to clean you up right here. I'm going to prop you up a little, just so you can drink some more. Then I'm going to go get some supplies. The less you move, the less likely that you'll bleed. Okay? I'll be back in around an hour. Hey, by the way, does anyone know you're here?"

"No. No one knows anything," she mumbled.

Hurray, I thought. No one would show up looking for her, which I suppose was sad for her, but much better for me.

On my way back to the hut, I made a mental list of what I needed: clothes, rags, water and something to put it in, a bucket, a heavy sleeping bag, meds, and food. I still had my Jetboil and a box of propane canisters that I was saving for emergencies. But what would I do about the bleeding? I hadn't yet run out of tampons, but I didn't have any pads, and I didn't want to ruin another sleeping bag. Lying on a tarp would be pretty uncomfortable…When everything else was stuffed into my backpack, I found a rain jacket of Peter's, along with a couple of his T-shirts and boxers, and brought them along, still not exactly sure what I would do with them.

I spread the rain coat on the inside of the clean sleeping bag and eased Edie onto it. Then I cleaned her with warm water and rags that I made from the T-shirts. She kept her eyes closed during the process but helped a little as I rolled her and shifted her weight. I folded and pinned more rags inside some old bikini bottoms I'd been using as panties and slipped them up her thighs. Her legs were long and spindly and brought to mind pictures of undernourished children I'd seen on TV. She'd probably been skinny even before the blackout and hadn't had enough to eat for a long time. Once I had her reasonably dressed in a T-shirt and boxers, I took the raincoat outside, wiped and dried it, and brought it back in. I told her that I needed to tie it around her waist to protect the sleeping bag, and she lifted her hips compliantly. The coat was big enough that I could zip it up the front like a skirt, and it had side zippers that I opened for better ventilation.

"You a nurse or something?" she asked as I propped her back up, using her knapsack as a pillow.

"No. But I've had a lot of first aid training. Do you think you could eat something?"

She nodded.

I spent the rest of the afternoon spooning ramen soup into her mouth and encouraging her to drink. I'd concocted a weak beverage made from powdered Gatorade and Tang in the bladder of my Camelback and clipped the drinking tube where Edie could reach it. Then I gathered the bloody clothes and her sleeping bag and took them outside. Standing by the fire ring, I held up the T-shirt and jeans to see whether they might be salvaged, but there was so much dried blood that I dropped them onto the charred sticks in disgust. That left the wretched sleeping bag, which I knew already was a total loss, but I couldn't help myself from unrolling it on the ground. Globs of dried blood like old pudding, some as big as my fist, stuck to the flannel. I couldn't make out anything that looked like an embryo or fetus, and I wondered whether it was buried under the blood somewhere, but I'd seen enough, so I rolled the bag up again and laid it gently on top of the clothes in the fire ring.

Before I left, I helped Edie onto the bucket to pee and fed her a little more ramen. The rags between her legs were mostly clean, the amount of blood about the same as a woman would expect a few days into her period. I'd been waiting to see whether she would throw up, but so far, she'd kept everything down. Her forehead felt cool but not clammy, another good sign. Finally, I gave her another dose of Tylenol.

"Are you allergic to antibiotics?" I asked.

"No, I don't think so," she answered.

Peter had been obsessed with trying to get antibiotics that we could store at the cabin and hut, but it was difficult to do. The bottle I brought to the tent was one of three that I had at the hut. I shook out two tablets and placed them in Edie's hand. She took them with some Gatorade.

"If you have to throw up, try to use the bucket," I instructed. "I'll be back in the morning."

She didn't reply, just rolled over and burrowed into the sleeping bag.

I re-attached the rain fly, zipped it up tight, and left.

So now I sit here against the wall, pen in hand, and wonder why it was so important to me to come back here to sleep. I tell myself that Edie will be fine and that I have done enough. If she started to hemorrhage badly overnight, I wouldn't be able to stop it anyway, and, besides, she seemed pretty stable when I left. But I know it is more than that. It is a compulsion to maintain distance between myself and others, a trait that has always been part of my personality and that few people have managed to get past. Staying would have meant commitment, and I don't know how far I want to take this unexpected relationship. It is too early to tell, I think, so for now I will just concentrate on getting her on her feet. The bigger questions can wait.

October 30

Back at Edie's tent this morning, I made us both oatmeal with a few dried apples, adding some of my precious sugar to Edie's for the extra calories. She seemed a little stronger and was awake in the tent when I arrived. The Gatorade mixture was about half gone, meaning she'd drunk about twenty ounces, and there was fresh urine in the bucket.

I changed the rags in the bikini bottoms and made us each a mug of tea. She hadn't bled much overnight and reported that the cramping had mostly stopped. I gave her another dose of meds and a vitamin and said I'd be outside if she needed me. By this time, I was full of questions, but I didn't want to upset her, so I postponed them until she had more fully recovered.

After cleaning up, I decided to check out Edie's food bag. I released the knot in the rope where she'd tied it to the tree and the bag dropped like a stone. Back at the clearing, I dumped it onto my raincoat. Considering it had been seven months since the blackout, she had more food than I would have guessed: six packs of ramen, four granola bars, a small container of peanut butter, about three cups of rice and several packets of EmergenC. Coincidentally, or perhaps not, it was the same tangerine flavor that Peter and I had at the cabin. As a matter of fact, everything in Edie's pack could have come from my own pantry except for a little cub scout pan, a plastic cup and some cutlery.

Huh, I thought and just sat there amazed, sipping my tea and waiting for the implications to sink in. Had she broken into the cabin on her way up here? Maybe she'd been living there. But she'd probably have more meat on her if she had access to all of my food. But then again, not if she hadn't found the cellars. And where was the guy who'd gotten her pregnant?

I finished my tea, stuffed everything back into the bag except the granola bars, rolled and snapped the top, and hung it back in the tree, which took several tries since the carabiner attached to the end of the rope was so small and light. She should have stolen a heavier carabiner, I thought, but without any real conviction. I'd been avoiding thinking about the lives of those surviving elsewhere, and I knew I could never blame anyone who was just trying to survive, as long as they weren't harming anyone else…

When I stuck my head back into the tent, Edie was lying with her back toward me. I crept over and felt her forehead, which was warm and dry. I laid the granola bars within reach and backed out.

What I really wanted to do was wander around the woods until I could figure out how to handle this new information. But I'd said I'd be there, and I didn't want to wake her up, so I ended up just going down to the creek, filling the water bladder, and staring at the water for a while. There was a calm eddy on that side, and water striders were scooting around on top of the pool like erratic figure skaters, darting this way and that with no apparent purpose. Then I noticed some tiny tracks in the mud, shaped like little hands. I knew they were raccoon, but they looked so human that I couldn't help thinking about the baby that Edie had lost and wondering how far along it had been. Probably less than twelve weeks, I concluded; I hadn't seen anything substantial enough on the sleeping bag to make it seem otherwise. And all I really knew about her was that for some reason, she had chosen to take off into the woods rather than stay where she was.

When I got back to the clearing, I decided to go ahead and burn the bloody sleeping bag, rags, and T-shirt. I enlarged the fire ring and got a good-sized fire going. Then I fed the sleeping bag into the flames, starting at one corner. Most commercial sleeping bags are treated with flame retardants, but this one seemed to have missed the treatment, or perhaps it had been washed out, because the fabric caught fire easily, and I soon had a larger blaze than I expected.

"Wow."

I heard Edie's voice behind me. She was kneeling at the door of the tent, and I could see that she'd pulled on the sweatpants I'd left at the foot of her sleeping bag.

"I got up to pee and got dressed. I'm hardly bleeding at all now. Do you think it's okay for me to stay up for a while?" she asked.

"I think so." I helped her to her feet and guided her to the camp chair. I'd stuck another one inside the tent, more of a folding stool, really, and I retrieved it and a fleece jacket to put around her shoulders. We settled a few feet from the fire, and I handed her a water bottle and urged her to drink.

I told her about emptying her food bag and said I was surprised that there was a place where she could get ramen and granola bars. She said that her Uncle Ray had been scavenging food from abandoned houses or houses where the people had died.

"He never brings home too much at a time, though," she said. "He says we have to ration, and he's afraid we'd eat it all up if he brought home a lot. But I think he keeps a lot for himself and trades some of it for other stuff, like booze."

"Is your father around?" I asked.

She looked off into the woods and said, no, he had died a few weeks after the blackout. He'd been a dialysis patient and also diabetic, and the dialysis center's generator had only enough fuel to run for a couple weeks. He'd run out of insulin, and she and her mom had had to push him a mile to the dialysis center in a wheelchair. At the end of the second week, he told them not to bother. Then he sat on their porch, drinking and smoking and waiting to die.

I didn't know what to say to that other than "Hmm."

Then she surprised me by asking if I was the lady from the solar house.

"What solar house?" I asked, trying to sound like I didn't know exactly what she was talking about.

"The house the Bensons used to own. On the forest road," she answered.

She said her uncle had been real excited when he'd first gone out to it, said maybe they should move there, but when he couldn't get the electricity going, he'd changed his mind. Said there was no point to being that far out when they had a perfectly good wood stove where they were.

"I didn't think he was serious about moving away from town, anyway," she finished. "He likes being top dog too much."

I got up and poked at the fire, still digesting the idea that "Uncle Ray" had been to the cabin. There wasn't much left of the sleeping bag but the zipper, which I might have ripped out if I had thought of it. Since she seemed to be opening up a bit, I thought it was a good time to bring up some more important questions, so when I sat back down, I asked her outright, "Edie, do you know who the father of the baby was?"

All she did was shrug.

"Were you raped?"

Another shrug. She stared at the fire.

"Why did you leave?"

Finally, she turned her head and looked me in the eye. "I couldn't let anyone know."

"Not even your mom?" I asked.

"Especially not my mom," she answered.

After a lunch of instant chicken soup and granola bars, I offered to wash her hair. She put on Peter's raincoat and tilted her head back so that her hair hung down over the back of the chair. I heated water in the Jetboil, dumped it in a water bottle, and cooled it down by adding more water. It was a slow process and used a lot of fuel, but I knew from experience that getting clean was a sure way to raise one's spirits. At the wilderness school, we would take small groups out on backpacking trips ranging from one night to five. When we returned and the girls had a chance to clean up, they'd seem almost high from the experience of surviving the trip and being clean and well-fed. I didn't think about it this way then, but now I see that we were teaching them to appreciate the small things in life, probably one of the most important survival skills there is.

As I poured water through Edie's hair, I was reminded of the times I spent with Linda after the baby was born and Steve had gone back to Iraq. I would bring her supper and spend the evening, breaking up the monotony of being home alone for both us. I remembered Annie's bath times, and how delicately Linda cradled Annie's head in her hand as she ladled warm water over her fine, coppery hair, the water lifting the suds gently, the surprised look in Annie's eyes when an errant drop trickled down her face. Where were they now? But that was just one more question that I couldn't answer.

By the time Edie's hair was clean and combed, she was getting tired, and I was getting restless, so I helped her back into the tent for a nap. "I've got some stuff to do, but I'll bring back something good for dinner," I promised, straightening the sleeping bag under her legs.

It felt good to be alone as I climbed the hill in the direction of the hut. I'd always been aware of this contradiction that rules my life, the need for companionship that never seems to outweigh my need to feel strong and independent. Working at the wilderness school had turned out to be the perfect match for this personality quirk—I could be a leader and help the students through difficult times, but I would always be someone they moved on from rather than a permanent fixture in their lives. Peter had somehow understood all that, but now he was gone, too.

I circled around the hut but didn't go in as I passed. Nothing looked disturbed in my little thicket, so I continued up to check the traps. The squirrel snares were undisturbed, as were all of the turkey snares except one. The ground around this one was all torn up, as though some creature had been clawing and writhing around in the dead leaves. This was typical, snaring animals by choking them to death is not in any way humane, but I feel it necessary for two reasons. One is that I don't have enough bullets to use them up hunting; the second is that shooting a gun back here is the surest way of broadcasting my presence. I often hear the far-off crack of a rifle but never close enough to be alarming. Eventually, a hunter is likely to come through, but I'll cross that bridge when I come to it.

Glancing around the disturbed area, I tried to figure out what had happened to the noose, but all I found was the length of rope, shortened by a foot or so. It looked like whatever had been caught had chewed its way through. Coyote, was my first thought. Fox, maybe. Deer just thrashed until they choked, and turkeys weren't smart enough to try to peck the rope. If it was a coyote, he'd have scratched the noose off in no time once he was free. Imagining his panic made me sad, just as I was a little sad every time I caught something. No wonder the Native Americans treated their prey with such respect. Killing innocent creatures is hard.

For dinner I took a bona fide Mountain House dehydrated lasagna meal back to the tent, and I fried up a couple of corn cakes in the fire ring, using just a bit of self-rising cornmeal. The lasagna is an old favorite; the cheese in the packet is real mozzarella that gets gooey and stringy and sticks to your spork as real cheese should. Edie was appropriately impressed.

After dinner, she asked me if I had any books. I still had my Kindle, which I could charge with the little solar charger I used for backpacking, but I didn't want to give her that. In the hut I had my Wilderness Medicine manual and a book of edible wild plants. Peter and I had liked to read to each other, so he'd stuck some books in with the games, and I was always re-reading books that we assigned the girls from the Virginia high school curriculum. In fact, I was pretty sure that I'd dug Maya Angelou's I Know Why the Caged Bird Sings out of the bottom of my pack when I arrived at the hut. I told her I'd look around, made sure she had water for the night, and retreated to my own space.

The days have been getting short, and I've been forgetting to adjust my schedule. In normal times, the clocks would be changing soon, but, of course, the actual time means nothing to me. It was almost dark when I came to my thicket, though, and I felt conspicuous as I ducked into the rhododendrons. The temperature dropped rapidly with the sunset, and I got a little fire going to warm up the hut before climbing into bed. Edie would be plenty warm in Peter's winter sleeping bag, I knew, but I still experienced a pang of guilt at having an actual "house" to go to while she slept in the tent. For some reason, though, I just wasn't ready to bring her here. It was that commitment thing again. If I showed her this place, I'd have to share it.

October 31

The weather has turned, and the day started out gray and much colder. I doubt the temperature rose above fifty by noon. Then a cold drizzle began to fall. Edie started I Know Why the Caged Bird Sings as we sat in front of the fire after breakfast, but before she could get too engrossed in her reading, I tried to get some more information about Ray and his gang.

"Has Ray always been an opportunist?" I asked.

"I don't know," she answered. "But he and Daddy never got along, and I'm pretty sure it's because of my mom."

She went on to tell me that Ray hadn't been around when she was younger. He'd gone off to Oklahoma to work for a fracking company. She could remember maybe one or two Christmases when he'd shown up with a skinny wife and a stepson who never did anything but play video games on a tablet.

"He and Daddy were hardly ever in the same room together, and grandma, that's Grandma Horton, would barely speak to my mom. It was really weird. But once I heard Mom and Dad fighting. I think maybe Mom had dated Ray for a little while before he dropped out of school, and Dad said he was still 'carrying a torch' or something like that. Back then, I didn't know that that meant he wanted to be with her."

Ray had come back to town alone after his mother died and the fracking wells had been played out, but he'd continued to keep his distance from Edie's family until after the blackout. Then he'd shown up with food, beer, and cigarettes and sat on the porch with Edie's dad for those last few days before he died.

"I was inside putting some water on the woodstove to heat," Edie said, "and I remember Ray pacing back and forth on the porch, telling Daddy how he didn't need to worry because he was going to take care of us. Daddy just sat there, and then he finally told Ray to sit down and shut up. 'You won,' he said. 'So just leave me in peace for a goddam minute, will ya?'"

"I guess Ray just saw his chance and took it," I said.

"Yeah," she said. "And he's been taking it ever since."

I got up and poured some more hot water into our mugs and then it started to rain. Edie moved into the tent, and I left her with a thermos of more tea with some Tang mixed in for extra calories. Her bleeding and cramps have all but stopped, and there are no signs of infection, though I'll keep up the antibiotics for another day or two. But I have to admit that her story sobered me, and I am glad to have had the rain as an excuse to come back to the hut and get some distance.

I have tried not to think of what happened to people I know back in what used to be the civilized world of cities and towns. But I can't help thinking about my own mother, and wondering whether there could be the slightest chance that she and Aunt JoAnn are still alive. Just after I found gas at the last town on the way to the cabin, another announcement came over the radio. The FAA had grounded all domestic flights and was landing incoming international flights in other countries. Trains were emptying their passengers at the nearest towns. It was like 9-11, only worse because the nature of the threat was so vague. The word "precaution" was being repeated over and over, but no one was being told what the precaution was against. A few miles short of the cabin, I finally got through to Aunt JoAnn. I told her that I thought something very bad was about to happen and asked her to bring Mom back to her house. At first, she said that the nursing home should be prepared for emergencies and Mom should be fine.

"No," I told her. "She won't. Remember Katrina, what happened in the nursing homes when the electricity went out? I think something is about to happen that could be a lot worse. Do you know what an Electro Magnetic Pulse is?"

Of course she didn't, and I admit that I even sounded crazy to myself as I explained that the entire electric grid could be wiped out for over a year if someone detonated nuclear bombs in the upper atmosphere above the United States.

"Wouldn't the radiation kill us?" she asked.

"No, Aunt JoAnn, but everything that uses electronics will be useless. Peter explained it to me, and he would know. All the big transformers will fry, and since they come from overseas, it will take months, even years, to replace them. Planes will literally fall from the sky, and there will be no deliveries of food, gas, medical supplies, or anything else for a very long time. Think about it—no supermarkets, no heat, no running water…"

"And it will just affect the United States?" she asked.

"I don't know. It depends where they explode the bombs," I told her.

"Where are you, dear?" she finally asked.

"I'm on my way to the cabin. I'm in Peter's truck. It's an antique, and it probably won't be affected. That's why he's been keeping it up so well. Kept it up, I mean."

"Well, I'll see what I can do. I guess it wouldn't hurt to bring her home and see what happens," she said. "She can't use the stairs, but I guess I could put her in the downstairs parlor."

I could hear her getting used to the idea. I only hoped she grasped the urgency of the situation. "Thanks, Aunt JoAnn. Just, please, do it now."

"Don't worry, dear," she said. "I'll take care of your mother."

But it was just a few minutes later that I saw a small flash of light arc from an electric line at the top of a wooden utility pole on the side of the road. The arc struck the top of the pole, which emitted a quick puff of smoke but didn't ignite. I was still trying to digest this when I came up behind a small SUV drifting toward the shoulder. As I drove around it, I noted the look of confusion on the face of the driver, a man with grizzled hair poking out from under a baseball cap. Around the next bend, another car, a white Honda sedan, sat halfway off the other side of the road, facing me. Two more vehicles were sitting at a stop sign a mile farther. The drivers, a young woman in scrubs and a middle-aged man, stood talking on the grassy shoulder, while the woman punched numbers into her cell phone. I drove by, suddenly feeling so sick that I thought I'd have to pull over to throw up. *It's happening. It's happening right now*, I thought. And there was no way Aunt JoAnn could have gotten to the nursing home that fast.

Not long after, I finally reached the gravel lane to the cabin. When I jumped out of the truck to unlock the gate, I was in such a panic that I almost fell to my knees. My mind was churning and telling me that I had to hurry, hurry, but there was nothing to hurry about. I fumbled with the padlock and pushed the gate wide. Pulling the truck through the opening, I tried to concentrate. *What's next?* I asked myself. *What was the plan?* I went about fifty feet before hopping back out to close and lock the gate. Lying parallel to the driveway were a couple of saplings and some small boulders. *We'll use these to block the driveway, just in case someone else has a working vehicle*, Peter had told me. *It won't stop anyone, but it'll slow them down.* I tugged at the saplings until I had them in place, and then I rolled the rocks onto the drive behind them.

The cabin looked peaceful and still as I pulled the truck around back and entered through the kitchen. Everything appeared as I'd left it on my last visit in the fall: French press in the dish strainer, dish cloths hanging on the refrigerator door, and a half-gallon of RV antifreeze sitting on the counter from when I'd winterized the drain traps. With the flip of a couple of switches in the cellar, I soon had running water and electricity. I unloaded the truck, arranging condiments, cheeses and frozen meats in the refrigerator, as though I'd just returned from the grocery store, and tried not to think about what other people might be doing. At first, I didn't turn on the radio, although I knew that some stations could use generators to stay on the air for days. After starting a fire in the kitchen woodstove, I used a bit of precious propane to reheat some taco meat for a taco salad, which I ate mechanically, staring out at the back yard toward the barn. Safe and warm and fed, I switched on the radio that we kept on the kitchen counter and searched the AM dial.

The reception was sketchy, but I managed to catch a station out of Charleston, West Virginia. A woman's voice reported that most of the cars on the road had stalled, and although a few of them could restart, disabled vehicles were blocking most of the major roads and highways. Traffic lights had gone blank or had defaulted to blinking mode, and the gates at some railroad crossings were stuck in the down position, causing more congestion and confusion. Millions of people were stranded in the mid-Atlantic region alone, and sparking electric poles and blown-out transformers had caused hundreds of fires. The reporter's tone was grim, yet determined, as she chronicled tales of small emergencies that someone seemed to be giving her in no logical order: a car fire here, some looting there, cars stranded in the Baltimore Harbor Tunnel and on Interstate 77 where it crosses under Walker Mountain. Finally, she cycled back to the main thread: a series of nuclear devices had been detonated above the continental United States, and the resultant Electromagnetic Pulses had disabled all three regional power grids, namely, the Eastern, the Western States Coordinating Council, and the Electric Reliability Council of Texas. (I recalled saying to Peter, "You mean Texas has its own fucking power grid?") As these grids also cover Canada, electricity was out over the entire North American continent. It was believed that the weapons had been fired offshore from four to six locations in the Pacific, the Atlantic, and the Gulf of Mexico. The government was endeavoring to find out who was responsible, but the degree of uncertainty had so far prohibited a retaliatory strike.

The announcer continued to say that the President was in a safe place and in constant communication with intelligence and military resources. People were strongly advised to stay at home and shelter in place.

As the broadcast turned back toward the more local aspects of the story, I thought back to everything that Peter had told me would happen in this scenario. He'd tried to get me to read the various government EMP vulnerability reports, at least the ones that were public, but I had steadfastly resisted. The cars that were still working properly would soon run out of gas. The majority of gas stations would be without power, and no one would have access to fuel. The refineries would shut down, and the natural gas pipelines would malfunction and even explode, making any type of refueling impossible. This was because their automated monitoring and control systems, so reliant on electronics and microchips, would fry, and it would be impossible for them to operate safely. Most significantly for American society, the extent of the damage to power plants and transformers would be catastrophic, as the transformers are manufactured abroad, are individualized to their locale, and take years to replace. Banks, unable to access funds wirelessly or keep records, would not reopen.

From the announcer's tone, it seemed that total chaos had not yet broken out. The people stranded on the roads weren't thinking beyond the need to get home, and those already there probably hadn't realized yet that they were in for a long-term reversion to the days before electricity. It would be just a matter of days before food began to run out in the cities, while those used to living farther from the grocery store might have a few extra days. But before long, folks would begin to understand that their lives had been profoundly transformed, and that no one was coming to help.

I wished I had some way of knowing whether Aunt JoAnne's car was still operational and whether she would even have made it to the nursing home if it were. The chances of getting a call through were almost non-existent, but in a day or two, the mere fact that people couldn't charge their phones might improve my chances. Of course, by then Aunt JoAnn's phone would be dead. Parts of the telecommunications network might run on backup systems for a while, but before long, we'd all be cut off from each other. And when it got to that point, would the government, such as it was, be able to function at all? I tried her number, got a busy signal, and hung up.

Staring out the window, I watched as the wooded hill behind the cabin became veiled in twilight. The kitchen was getting hot, so I made a cup of tea, grabbed a solar camping lantern from the windowsill, and headed upstairs. Tomorrow I would try to gather my thoughts and figure out what needed to be done. But I was too tired and confused to do anything more productive that night, and I hoped I'd done enough just getting myself where I needed to be.

The one decision I did make was about lights. Using them indiscriminately would only advertise that I had electricity. The town of Wagner was several miles to the west, but anyone wandering the hills or coming up the road might see them, thus my decision to use the solar lamp. The shades upstairs were closed as I'd left them, the familiar down quilt was stretched taut across the bed, and the latest gear issue of Backpacker magazine sat on the night table. The woodstove had chased off the spring chill, but it was still too early to try to sleep, so I tried to distract myself by flipping through the magazine from cover to cover, reading descriptions of high-tech camping equipment that people would need now more than ever but that they could no longer order.

October 31, continued

After writing until midday, I realized that I was getting behind in some chores. The rain had let up some, so I took my little folding saw and wood satchel up into the woods above the hut to gather some firewood. I'd seen a dead maple about five inches in diameter leaning against an oak about a week ago, so I spent the rest of the afternoon sawing it into chunks and hauling them back to the hut. Peter always said that there was no such thing as too many tarps, and I've come to believe him, as I am currently using about four camo-colored five by eights to protect all the wood I've been stacking around the exterior of the hut. With that accomplished, I gathered some rice, bouillon, and dehydrated chicken and got ready to go feed Edie. At the last minute, I added some dried peas to the rice, making a mental note to teach Edie about complementary proteins, one of our standard nutrition lessons at the school.

As we sat in front of the fire waiting for the rice to cook, I asked Edie how her mother had been doing since her dad died. She said that she thought her mom was just trying to forget about it.

"And how about you?" I asked.

"I don't know," she said. "It's kind of strange. It feels more like he just went away. My mom wouldn't let me see his body, and then Uncle Ray and his friends took it off and buried it somewhere."

I was curious about what they'd been doing with all the dead bodies, so I asked. Edie said that folks were supposed to write out a paper about what happened and put it through the mail slot at the town office so that there could be some kind of official record, but she doubted that most people bothered. Otherwise, it was just up to folks to bury their own.

Then she told me that her uncle and a few of his friends had appointed themselves to "check in" on folks that lived on the outskirts of town. "According to Uncle Ray, there's been a lot of heart attacks, on top of all the people dying because their medicines have run out, or they got sick, or they haven't been getting enough to eat," she said. "It seems weird," she continued, "but there's no one to do those autopsy things like on TV, so who knows? If there's no kin nearby, anyone who wants to just walks in and takes their stuff. And you won't believe what the sheriff is doing."

I raised my eyebrows.

"Guarding cows!"

She explained that the Mennonite dairy a few miles west of town had herded most of their forty-some cows into town when they realized that there wouldn't be any electricity for milking.

"It was so funny!" she said. "It looked like a cattle round-up from a Western, only the herders were wearing those funny clothes. The cows kept stopping in people's yards, and everyone came out of their houses to watch. The Mennonites said that they wanted to donate the milk to whoever wanted to milk the cows. So, the sheriff has been trying to keep the cows safe on the fields at the elementary school and keep some kind of schedule for who can get the milk. The cows still belong to the dairy, and the milk is more valuable than the meat, the sheriff says, but not everyone agrees, so some people have been deputized just to guard the cows."

"It's about the only thing in town that's half working," Edie went on, "and there's not much the sheriff can do about anything else. I guess you could call it the honor system, 'cept there's not enough honor to go around."

That thought seemed to sober her.

"So, you aren't thinking about going back then?" I asked.

"I don't know," she said. "I thought about hiding out in somebody's barn, someplace that's been abandoned, but Uncle Ray and them are still taking stuff from the houses. He'd probably find me sooner or later." She shrugged.

When I left Edie for the night, she assured me that she'd been plenty warm, and she didn't mind sleeping in until the day warmed up. "Besides," she said, "I can get the fire going myself in the morning if I need to."

Then she asked, "Is your tent very far?" and I realized that she had no idea that I was living in relative splendor compared to her.

Thinking back through our conversation, I'm struck by how typical Edie is in some ways. Behind their façades of shrugs and evasions, I've found that pretty much every teenage girl hopes to find that one person who will really listen to both what they're saying and what they're leaving out. Tonight, Edie told me, however indirectly, that law and order have pretty much broken down, that people are dying mysteriously, and that there are those who go around doing whatever they want, including "Uncle Ray." In spite of all she's seen and been through, however, she seems remarkably composed, as though her current hardships are merely the continuation of a life that has already taught her the importance of limiting her expectations.

November 1

I could kick myself, or worse.

This morning I took my time getting ready to check on Edie. I stoked up the woodstove and heated some water for oatmeal, threw in some nuts and had a leisurely hot breakfast. Through my narrow windows, I could see bare branches shaking against a gray sky, and I realized that November was just a day away. A large hemlock that had escaped the woolly adelgid outbreak reminded me that Christmas would soon follow, and I wondered what it would be like to be alone in my hut during the holiday. But it didn't have to be that way, I thought. I could bring Edie here, and then I would at least have some companionship, and she would be safe, or at least safer than she'd been in town. The provisions would go faster, but she could help gathering fruit and nuts, setting traps, and performing all the other chores that have been keeping me focused.

I continued my meditations as I crossed the creek and headed up the hill on the other side. I was so lost in thought that when I entered the clearing it took me several seconds to register the fact that it was empty, and Edie was gone.

I say "empty," but that's not entirely true, since she'd left an assemblage of my possessions by the fire ring: the Jetboil and cookpot, the folding stool and camp chairs, and, wrapped carefully in Peter's rain jacket, the book.

I don't know why it hit me so hard, but I found myself sinking into one of the chairs with the book in my hand. Damn, I said quietly, but then it sounded so good that I said it again, louder. Damn, damn, damn!

After a while, I found myself turning the book over in my hands and wondering whether Edie had finished it. The folded post-it note that I'd given her as a bookmark stuck out about three-quarters of the way through the book, between pages two-forty-eight and two-forty-nine. I glanced over the pages and saw that she had underlined one of my favorite parts. "At fifteen, life had taught me undeniably that surrender, in its place, was as honorable as resistance, especially if one had no choice." I unfolded the post-it note and saw, written in loopy cursive, the words, "Time to go back to my cage. Mom needs me. Thanks, Edie."

Peter and I never intended to have children; his job made him too aware of the United States' multiple vulnerabilities, and mine convinced me that trying to provide someone with an unblemished childhood was nearly impossible in the world of cyberbullying, sexting, and drugs. Better to spend our efforts trying to help and protect those who were already here. But Edie was already here, and her mother, as dependent as she was on "Uncle Ray," was about useless, as far as I could tell. I sat for a while, thinking about how I had failed Edie. Perhaps all it would have taken to change her mind was an invitation, the one I'd been withholding out of what? Selfishness? Yes. That was it, selfishness. My own particular brand that compels me to avoid the burden of being closely bonded to someone else.

I continued to sit as my feet got cold from inactivity, the light seeped from the sky and the wind began to push at the branches. Scattered raindrops pelted my head and shoulders for several minutes before I roused myself from my stupor. I put on Peter's jacket, stuffed the cooking supplies into my backpack and gathered the folding chairs under my arms. Balancing it all was awkward, but I was too stubborn to make two trips, so I ended up slipping in the creek and soaking my right leg up to the knee. It serves you right, I told myself, as I stumbled the rest of the way to the creekbank.

Back at the hut, I accomplished no more than stoking the fire in the woodstove and getting out of my wet clothes before I sprawled on my sleeping bag and buried my head in my pillow. I hadn't felt so much like crying since Peter died, and the funeral home handed me the cardboard box that held his ashes. What are you doing here? I asked myself. *What makes you so special that you get to survive out here all alone while other people get hungry and sick, or hurt, or raped? And what the hell do you think you're surviving for?*

In those moments, I hated myself more than I ever have. And I hated Peter, too, for making me promise before he died that I would be vigilant and keep myself safe. A stupid promise that he must have thought would give me a purpose to go on. But he was wrong. It isn't working. It isn't working, and it isn't ever going to. So now what?

November 3

I woke yesterday feeling a bit hungover from the pain of losing Edie and my fruitless soul-searching. The hut was chilly, and when I went out for firewood, I could see that the leaves were weighed down with little discs of ice. Winter would be here before I knew it, I thought, and if I happened to decide that survival was worthwhile, I needed to do some more preparation. I spent a lot of the morning inventorying my food and trying to decide what I could allow myself to use over the winter and what I should save for as long as possible. I decided to go ahead and use the four jars of peanut butter, maybe at a jar per month, because of its good fat content and because it might go rancid. The game I was catching would become leaner and leaner toward the end of winter, and essential fatty acids could become a problem. To supplement them, I should gather hickory nuts and acorns, both high in protein and fat. According to my wild edibles book, hickories are also high in some B vitamins. I was more worried about vitamins and minerals than protein. We'd stocked both the cabin and hut with jars of vitamins, but they wouldn't last forever and would become less effective as time went on. I decided that a vitamin every third day and a couple of tablespoons of Tang every week would keep me from any major deficiencies. The Tang would run out by spring; I only had three containers, but then I would be able to find other sources of vitamin C. From here on in, the vegetables that we'd freeze dried or put into meals would be a bit of a delicacy. If I allowed myself just one freeze dried meal a week, they'd last me into February, and then they'd be gone for good.

Dried beans and rice could be stored indefinitely, so I should be careful with them. The same for the cornmeal. The nuts I already had should be eaten before they could go bad, and I'd be out of oatmeal by December unless I severely slowed my usage.

What else? When the instant coffee, tea, and cocoa run out I will be truly sorry, though I ought to be able to make my own tea in the spring. Instant coffee, cocoa, and mashed potatoes are my special treats, but I doubt I have the willpower to make them last through the winter. I guess we'll see.

That afternoon, I checked my traps and found a turkey. As I approached the snare, I at first didn't see the bird, and the soggy leaves dulled the sound of my footsteps. I took hold of the rope, followed it into the brush, and was startled when the bushes started to thrash. It was as though a cyclone of dark feathers had suddenly spun up from the earth. I backed up to a safe distance and gently pulled on the rope. I'd never found anything alive in a trap before, so I was just going with my gut. As soon as the bird cleared the bushes, it hopped and jumped toward me, flapping its wings and trying to fly, although I could see that it had injured a wing in its struggles. Instinctively, I dodged, pulled the rope taut, and gave a sharp yank, which landed the turkey on its side. It looked like a large, feathered fish that someone might land on a river bank. My jerk on the rope had broken its neck, and after a few moments of sporadic gyrations, it lay still.

For some reason, the whole episode left me feeling embarrassed, and I couldn't help but glance around, as though someone might come out from behind a tree and scold me for my cruelty. But I was quite alone, and after beheading the turkey and letting it bleed out, I took it back to my cooking site to pluck, butcher, and stew.

You probably wonder how I manage to eat from the same stew or pot of beans for days without refrigeration. I doubt that my method would pass muster with a food safety expert, but it's worked so far. After I take my meal from the pot, I put the lid on and let it simmer for a few more minutes, just to be sure that all the bacteria are killed and the lid is also sterilized. Then I remove the pot from the heat to cool. My thought is that the lid will act as a seal, however imperfect, to keep out most germs. I heat it again with the lid on and always let it simmer for a few minutes before I eat from it again, eradicating any bacteria that have started to grow. As long as I know that the food has heated thoroughly and it doesn't smell or taste funny, I don't have any qualms about eating it. If you picture the swinging cauldrons that were attached to fireplaces in the colonial days, you can imagine that our forebears used pretty much the same process. Anyway, it seems to be working, since I haven't gotten sick since I left the cabin.

Today I hiked back up to the hickory stand with a hammer, a two-quart pot, and a cloth bag. After filling my water bottles at the creek, I climbed the bank on the other side and angled off to the southeast. The day had remained cool and gray; I'd broken out my thick, wool socks and wore one of my heavier fleeces under my rain jacket, which I use more often as a windbreaker than for rain. It was good to be out walking; the climb out of the hollow warmed my muscles, and I strode along feeling strong and purposeful, aware of the crunch of my footsteps and the musty smell of the still-damp woods. I took a deep breath and let it out slowly, musing on how all the strategies we'd used on our students at the school were becoming lifelines in my new existence. Exercise, good nutrition, plenty of sleep, and ample opportunities for accomplishment were the foundations of our curriculum. But it had seemed much simpler when I was the counselor and teacher, not the one in need of reprogramming, and I wasn't so sure that a high degree of mindfulness would be sufficient to cure what ailed me. What was that catch phrase? Necessary, but not sufficient. Yeah, that was it.

When I felt that I was getting close to the right place, I slowed my gait and proceeded cautiously, remembering the bear I'd seen nearby. I considered yelling and stamping my feet but thought that if a bear was particularly happy with his or her foraging, it might not be run off so easily. The grove, really a clump of trees about fifty feet in rough circumference, was situated on a gradual, north-facing slope. I scanned the tree trunks and listened carefully for a minute or so before I deemed the coast to be clear. Judging from the split husks littering the ground, I was arriving a little late in the season, but rummaging through the leaves still yielded a good number of the green-hulled nuts, so I dropped my backpack and got out my supplies.

Before long, I had a couple gallons of nuts in my sack. The next step was finding a decently flat rock for the hulling. I could have taken them back to the hut for this step, but I preferred to leave the husks where they would normally be left by the squirrels. Sitting with the rock on the ground between my outstretched legs, I hammered each nut on the stem end, pulled the hull off, and dropped the shiny inner nut into the pot. If the nut had an obvious worm hole or looked moldy, I threw it back under the trees. Lastly, I poured water from my water bottle on top of the nuts in the pot. This was the easy internet solution for sorting bad nuts. With about four inches of water in the pot, about a dozen or so nuts floated to the surface. These were the bad ones, and I fished them out and tossed them away. What remained seemed a paltry amount so I went through the process two more times in order to get what I hoped would be about two weeks' worth of snacks. I should have started back when the nuts first started falling, as the supply would probably run out before I had enough to last me all winter, but I made a vow to come back frequently until then and, if I was still around, do better next year.

Back at the hut, I put the nuts in a shallow pan on the woodstove, just to give them a head start on the drying process. After a week or two, they'll be ready to shell.

As I write tonight, I struggle to put into words what I feel now that I am again alone. Melancholy, malaise, listlessness…Edie's absence has turned into a dull ache, a reopening of the wound left when Peter died. Although I feel good about what I've accomplished these last two days, the ache insists on sifting into all the empty spaces of the day, especially these quiet evenings after the gray turns to dark outside my window and I close the curtains to hide myself from imagined eyes. If I only had a plan or goal…When I was teaching, occasionally a student would come to me with the attitude that everything in her life sucked and that there was no reason to expect anything to ever get better. Knowing the student's background, I sometimes secretly agreed. But what did I say? I remember my words clearly. *Think of your life as a story. You're only in the very beginning. You don't know where all this is going to end. Try not to judge. The story isn't over yet. It could still have a happy ending. Don't give up after chapter two.* I wonder now, was it all just bullshit? And if it wasn't, why is it so damned hard to follow my own advice?

November 5

Since I wrote last, I've been back to the hickory grove twice to gather nuts, and today I spent a good part of the afternoon wandering east of the creek, broadening my knowledge of the territory. The sky was clear for a change, and the mass of damp air that's been anchored here for the last week or so has finally moved on. I didn't find anything of note except for another little creek, which I followed uphill to its source, a basin about the size of a soup bowl under the roots of a beech tree. Finding another water source was quite satisfying, and when I returned to the hut, I added it to the map I've been constructing since I started burying my winter meat.

I am trying my best to focus on one thing at a time, whatever chore presents itself at the moment, and spend the rest of the time planning my next activity or distracting myself with food and reading. I know that I have been putting off the telling of those first few days at the cabin. Describing requires reliving, and I am hesitant to bring back all of the images that came to mind as I tried to imagine what was occurring elsewhere. But I said I wanted to make sense of it, right? Isn't that why I'm writing this? So, I will force myself to look back.

That first day at the cabin, I tried to call Aunt JoAnn at least once an hour. When I managed to get out at all, I got that same "all circuits are busy" message I'd been getting most of the day before. By early evening, I couldn't even get that. Peter had explained why this would happen, that the telecommunications system's emergency response depended on re-routing data from downed areas through areas that were up and running. It all worked quite well if the problem was local or even regional, but a country-wide blackout was beyond the scope of any contingency plan. Not to mention that the systems that did the re-routing would themselves be compromised.

I left the radio off and focused on the chores that needed doing outside. The first order of business was to hide and disable the truck. At edge of the woods, Peter had created a large brush pile using the branches of trees he'd cut for firewood and small saplings he cleared from the perimeter of the yard. Behind the pile was enough space to park the truck. Though the weeds had grown up considerably over the summer, they were still mostly dead from the winter, and I drove the truck in easily. Then I removed the battery and used a wheelbarrow to haul it back to the barn. The next step was to take out the coil wire so that if someone managed to replace the battery, the truck still wouldn't run. Finally, I covered it with a large, brown tarp and heaped brush all over and around it. By the time the weeds grew up again, I hoped that it would be almost invisible, or at least appear long abandoned.

Of course, hiding the truck like that made it impossible to use for a quick getaway. Peter and I had debated this decision. His main point was that after the fuel ran out, thieves would be out looking for any vehicle that could still run. In addition, hiding it would make it less obvious that the house was occupied. As for me, I couldn't imagine wanting to go anywhere anyway, except possibly to Worcester to get my mother, and I knew that there wouldn't be nearly enough gas to get that far.

Once I was satisfied that the truck was well hidden, I walked back to the barn to store the battery in the root cellar. This took several steps, since I couldn't move the tractor off of the trapdoor without using a come-along, which was tedious, to say in the least. But I finally got the door propped open and struggled down the stairs with the battery. Peter had wired each room of the root cellar with a single light socket, so when I flipped the switch all the shelves jumped into view with the garish, white light of a strong LED bulb.

Plastic containers and tubs lined the shelves and floor, filled with pasta and rice, beans and canned meats, oatmeal and Cream of Wheat. There were pickles and flour, sugar, honey and agave sweetener. We'd tried to use cans only when absolutely necessary, since they'd be hard to dispose of, but we'd loaded several shelves with jars of tomato sauce. Two large tubs held bags of coffee, enough for well over a year. Spices, teas, bouillon, dehydrated meats, and, of course, instant mashed potatoes. It was an embarrassment of wealth, financed by years of tax refunds. In the second room were dried fruits and vegetables: nuts, apricots, apples, raisins, prunes, and coconut. Dried peppers and tomatoes, onions and sweet potatoes. In the last room, we'd stocked canning jars and lids, cases and cases of them, and seeds: herbs, lettuce, peas, string beans, spinach, chard, cucumber, peppers, cabbage, squash, cantaloupe and melon.

I walked through the rooms, soaking in their earthy smell, wondering whether I'd be there long enough to put a dent in all those supplies. I don't think it was a premonition, just a lingering sense of disbelief that everything Peter had predicted, as crazy as it had seemed when he'd first shared his fears, could actually have come to pass. While the rest of the country was in panic mode, I was standing amid a great storehouse of almost everything I could need for many months. Who else out there was this lucky? The Mormons, maybe, minus the electricity. And a few hundred die-hard preppers, scattered around the country.

When I went in for lunch, I tried the radio again. I couldn't get the Charleston station, but I managed to get the NPR station out of Charlottesville, Virginia. The announcer was a man this time, Winston Bennett? I couldn't be sure. But he said, "Here are more details about what is happening Day One, Post-EMP." Funny, they'd already decided how they were going to name the days. He reported that air traffic control had been taken out by the pulse, but most commercial traffic had already landed. Of the few planes left in the air, it was believed that most had crashed. But since the passenger lists were all kept electronically, there was no way to access them. The airlines weren't even able to give out flight numbers. The planes that somehow didn't lose all of their electronic controls landed by sight, though there had been a couple dozen mishaps on the taxi ways, including a major collision at Hartsfield-Jackson in Atlanta. There was no official word from the government other than the repeated message to "shelter in place," and also no word about possible secondary attacks, which was the elephant in the room, as far as I was concerned. Would whoever did this be content with just bringing America to its knees? Or would Russia or China soon arrive at our doorstep, eager to "help?"

As I speculated on possible future threats, the reporter finally identified himself as Richard Blevins. Richard who? I thought. Then he announced that the station would be going off the air until four p.m.

"In an effort to conserve power, we'll be back on the air for twenty minutes every four hours from 6 a.m. until 10 p.m., unless there is a major announcement," he said. "Until next time, be safe."

Huh, I thought, as I switched off the radio. For most people, that would be a tall order. By now I supposed that looting must be in full swing in the major cities. Unless their emergency plans had accounted for a lack of gasoline, police departments would soon be patrolling on foot, if they weren't already. Even with emergency generators, water wouldn't last for more than a few days in the big high rises. And then the shit would really hit the fan, so to speak.

I thought about Linda and Annie and decided to try a call.

"All circuits are busy," repeated that irritating, mechanical voice.

I wasn't surprised. I knew it wouldn't be long before there was no voice at all.

November 6

Today was another low-energy day. I woke again to clouds and an outside temperature of just around freezing, judging from how quickly my hands got chilled when I went out for wood. Breakfast was reheated turkey stew over rice, with a cup of mint tea. After breakfast, I made myself empty my waste bucket and cover over the trench. I'd already decided to dig the new one alongside the oak that fell during the storm, so I dragged my shovel over and scraped a new trough in the fresh leaves near the lower end of the trunk where the branches wouldn't get in the way.

The energy required to dig the trench was just enough to warm me but not enough to chase away my dark mood. The sky seemed to have lowered as I worked, so that by the time I headed back to the hut, I felt the grayness closing in on all sides. Though I could see a good distance through the trees now that the leaves were down, I felt more secluded than ever. I put it down to the successive days of gray and decided to hike up to my view rock where I could at least see the surrounding mountains.

What I call my view rock is actually a place where a bare shelf of sedimentary rock keeps the forest at bay, creating an overlook about fifty feet long and maybe half that in depth. I'd brought my folding stool and sketchpad, so I took them out and got comfortable. The lookout faces northwest, and I was immediately aware of a breeze cooling the left side of my face, so I turned more toward the north as I started to sketch. Before me the tree-covered hills stretched away, gray upon gray upon gray, until they were lost in a sky that was just a shade lighter. The only relief points were patches of evergreens, which showed as black clumps scattered randomly on the hills. I spent a long time sketching the slopes, trying to reflect the gradients of light with a No. 2 pencil. When I was somewhat satisfied with the land, I started on the sky. I was wearing my fingerless, knit gloves, but still my hands were becoming stiff as I tried to convey the subtle variations of the clouds. Frustrated with my efforts, I pressed harder on the edge of my pencil and before I knew it, I had turned the sky into a swirling mass of clouds that swarmed above and between the hills as though in pursuit of invisible prey. Damn it, I thought. This was not what I'd intended at all.

I started to rip out the page, intending to destroy it, but then I stopped. I had plenty of reasons to be angry, I knew. But this was getting me nowhere. Somewhere there were people who remembered me. Who knew who I was and liked, even loved me. Even though I could climb the highest mountain and look in every direction and see no one, they were out there. I couldn't really be this alone. I looked down at my sketch. It hadn't turned out as planned, but I would keep it. As was my habit, I wrote the date in the lower right-hand corner: November 5, two years since the diagnosis of Peter's cancer.

November 7

I woke this morning feeling somewhat better, as though a fog had lifted and though not quite out of sight, permitted some weak sun to filter through. As I walked back to the hut yesterday, the pewter clouds began to produce light flurries that floated and danced on the breeze that continued to strengthen from the southwest. They didn't amount to anything by dusk, but by this morning, the ground had collected a thin coating of dry flakes.

My first chore was getting water, so I scuffed through the leaves and snow down to the creek, where I immediately noticed that the snow on my perching rock had been disturbed. Mostly it was trampled and melted, but heading downstream were tracks about two inches in diameter with clear claw markings at the top of each pad. The claw prints told me immediately that they were dog tracks, not feline, since bobcats and mountain lions retract their claws when travelling. Cool, I thought. I'd heard coyotes yipping in the evening, usually off to the east, but I had yet to see one. I wondered if it might be the same creature who chewed its way out of my turkey snare. The clans were territorial, I knew, so if it wasn't that same one, it was probably related.

As I climbed back to the hut, I felt a familiar tightening over my uterus that signaled that my period might be coming, and I wondered whether my bleak moods might be explained as PMS. When Peter was alive, I used an implant in my arm for birth control. They last for three years and, in my case, reduced my period to irregular spotting. But the term of the implant had run out a couple months after he died, and I hadn't seen any need to replace it, though I surely would have if I'd known I'd be living in the woods within a year. At any rate, before long, my periods had returned with a vengeance, and while I had plenty to be depressed about, it could be that these moods that felt like a black hole opening in my heart could be partly biological. The thought comforted me because it presented the idea that all I might need to do to keep my sanity was to hold on for a few days each month.

On my second day at the cabin, or Day Two Post-EMP, as the radio would call it, I continued to take stock, rolling back the area rug that hid the cellar stairs, pulling the wind-up radio off the shelf, and locating batteries that I hoped I wouldn't need. Peter had installed a water storage tank just to the left of the inside of the barn, and I checked to be sure it looked intact, though as long as I had electricity, the well pump could supply all my water. The tank could be filled from a pipe that Peter had run from the creek and just added a layer of redundancy to our water resources. Everything seemed to be in good working order. It was a shame I couldn't have grabbed a few laying hens on my way out of town, I thought, as to the right of the door was a stall that had been turned into a chicken coop. The one freeze-dried food I could not stand was eggs, and I knew I'd miss my omelets dearly. And cheese…One consolation was that we'd stocked several cases of red wine, mostly for me, and a pretty good stash of Jack Daniels.

The day was dazzlingly sunny, though brisk, and I spent some time just sitting on the front porch, sipping tea and wondering what was happening in the rest of the world. I hoped I had made a strong enough impression on Aunt JoAnn about how long this could last. Worcester was proud of their water system, with its multiple reservoirs and state-of-the-art filtration plant. During an ice storm about ten years ago, their back-up generators lasted for all eleven days of the blackout. But the system was monitored by the same kind of computer system that controlled the power plants and oil refineries, a system full of electronic components that had almost surely been fried by the EMP. Could their back-up generators work without them? If not, the pumping system wouldn't be able to fill the storage tanks or pump water to the majority of the citizens outside of the few gravity-fed neighborhoods. And even if the generators did work, they would eventually run out of fuel. I pictured hundreds of people trying to get water directly from the reservoirs, camping on the grassy banks and in the nearby woods, and defecating just yards away from their water source. Then I pictured Mom, a few weeks down the road, sitting in her wheelchair in JoAnn's living room, hungry and dirty. Before long, the logistics of taking care of just one disabled person would be overwhelming. But better that than leaving her in a nursing home where she might be totally abandoned.

Distressed by these thoughts, I tried to divert my attention to matters a little less personal. Peter and I had discussed food scarcity, and I had said that at least people in the country would have an easier time since they were more likely to have woodstoves and maybe some livestock. That was true, Peter said, but then he reminded me that a lot of that livestock was kept inside electric fences. If there was no other way to contain them, soon there would be cows and horses, goats and pigs wandering around everywhere. Some might stick around out of habit and the enticement of hay or other feed, but that would eventually run out, too. With people growing hungrier, it would be finders-keepers. And, he pointed out, without reliable food from their owners, the animals would go foraging, with many starving, falling prey to predators, or becoming feral.

"Don't you think people will try to help each other? Without refrigeration, there wouldn't be much reason to try to hoard a whole cow," I pointed out.

"Some will, I'm sure," he replied, "but a lot won't."

As I sat on the porch that day, the sun dipped toward the woods on my right, where it became wrapped in an orange haze that I realized after a few moments must be smoke. The wind was still, and I wasn't particularly worried that the fire would spread toward me. I went back inside to fix supper, using the last of the eggs to make a ham and cheese omelet and wishing I had bought more from Eessa.

At six, I turned on the radio for the promised broadcast. The same station came through, and the same announcer began to speak, but this time his voice came in fits and starts as he struggled to maintain a professional tone.

"This is Richard Blevins of NPR, reporting on April second, or Day Two, Post-EMP. I am not sure what we can report to you this afternoon…Due to the power outage and other circumstances, we are no longer receiving transmissions from any official government sources or, actually…from any of our stations. Um, we have a few bits of news…but it has come to us through ham radio operators, who also tell us that the official emergency channels on their networks are not broadcasting. These unofficial sources report major fires in New York, Chicago…uh, Atlanta, and San Diego. The causes are unknown…sorry folks, I'm kind of winging it here…they say among the possibilities are gas line explosions, house fires, and arson, though I guess the power line fires are also a factor. There is also an unsubstantiated rumor that we have launched a strike against Iran…but, again, these are rumors. It is unclear whether emergency management services are being mobilized anywhere…as travel on the roads around the larger cities and towns has become quite dangerous. I am sorry that we have no more to report…We are hopeful that we will receive some official news before our ten o'clock broadcast. Please, folks, if you feel safe where you are, stay there."

Nothing in the broadcast surprised me, though I wondered how the ham radio people were getting their news out to NPR. But the tone of the reporter was downright frightening. The man was obviously having trouble keeping his wits about him. It must be difficult to try to do your job when society seems to be crumbling around you, I thought. It was amazing that he was still trying. And this was only the second day. Everyone has been through power outages, but I suppose that the magnitude of this quickly drove people to panic. Before there had always been the promise of FEMA and the National Guard, of supplies being trucked or flown in from somewhere else. Already, it seemed, people were realizing that this was disaster on an unprecedented scale. Without fuel or electricity or a single region that could function normally, there would be no help coming.

The evening was still young, so I stacked my dishes and decided to climb the mountain behind the house to see if I could get a better view toward town. Sunset would be shortly after seven-thirty, but I should have time to climb up about halfway. I pulled on a light fleece and grabbed a flashlight before heading out the back.

I headed up the hollow to the right, past the barn and the place where I'd parked the truck. After a few minutes, I turned and started angling my way up in the opposite direction. Before long, I was breathing deeply and taking in the smell of dead leaves and damp earth. The bushes were just budding out in little bursts of color that looked as though they'd been dabbed on by an artist's brush. There were no paths here, so I was "bushwacking" my way along, being careful not to trip on fallen trees or rocks hidden by last year's leaves, heading in the general direction of a little outcropping I'd seen from the forest road. When I looked back, I could see the house down below to the east, which was reassuring; I'd have no trouble finding my way back. About thirty minutes later, I rounded the flank of the mountain and found myself below the rock cliff that was my goal. A five-minute scramble, with the help of some roots and saplings, and I came out on top.

A couple miles off to the west, down in the hollow, I could see the white, clapboard house at the corner where the forest road turned off of the county road about two miles away. The road itself was hidden by the trees and the top of the road bank. Scanning farther to the west, the county road also disappeared in the trees and the hills. Another three or four miles along the road lay the town of Wagner, too far away to actually see. Peter and I had driven through twice, just out for a drive, but it was west of where we always turned off to come to the cabin. I could picture a garage, a couple churches, some brick storefronts, and the Dollar General on the far side of town. I wondered whether looting had already started and whether there might be an attempt by someone to keep things under some semblance of control. Curiosity sparked my imagination. Maybe I could sneak over for a look sometime. Peter would disapprove vehemently of any such plan, I knew, but the idea stayed in the back of my mind for weeks.

I turned my attention to the sky, where the sun was descending in a blaze of orange that reached out in all directions. The haze hid the sun itself, and the effect was as though the sun had chosen this day to melt along the horizon, spreading its brilliance like spilt syrup above the silhouetted earth. I would have liked to stay and watch the rest of the light show, but I'd seen enough to convince me that there was no great fire coming my way, and I needed to start back before the woods were too dark.

As I retraced my steps along the side of the mountain, I remembered how cautious, even paranoid, Peter had been about the possibility of intruders coming to the cabin. Not only had he taught me how to shoot the 9mm and the AR-15 we kept under the bed but we'd discussed evacuation plans, which usually involved his creating a distraction while I got away. Of course, as he became sicker, he realized that he wouldn't be here to help if it ever came to that. The main thing, he always stressed, was to get out before anyone knew I was there. That still seemed to be the most logical thing to do, but I wondered how I would even know that someone was coming. That part had always been a little vague, as though Peter believed he would magically sense the impending danger.

I tried to think it through as I came up behind the house. I always locked the doors at night, so anyone trying to get in would have to break a window or break down the door. That would certainly wake me, but then I'd be trapped upstairs, though I supposed I could climb out on the back-porch roof. And then…what? Jump off the roof and run into the woods? And they could always show up in broad daylight. I could look out one day and see people coming up the drive or out of the woods. What then?

By the time I entered through the back door, I was feeling pretty nervous. I loaded up the wood stove and made a cup of tea, wishing we'd put blackout curtains downstairs, too. Up in the bedroom I reviewed my bedtime procedures. I usually slept in a T-shirt and undies, but that night I started leaving my jeans across the foot of the bed where I could reach them quickly. My boots and socks I placed an arm's length from the right side, where I still slept. Peter had built desks in both dormers; his was the one that faced out the back. I hung a thick fleece and a black down jacket over the back of his chair, and I stuck a headlamp in one pocket. Finally, I reached over the desk and pulled up on the window frame, but it stuck fast, giving me a chore for the next day. On my way back to the bed, I grabbed a notepad and pen off of my desk. Then I settled in, took a sip of tea, and began my bug-out list.

November 8

After a hard frost last night, I hung around in the hut for most of the morning, reorganizing my food stores and making space for all the hickory nuts. I'd been saving all my resealable pouches, and I'd emptied a few tins of oatmeal. Even so, I had to put a couple gallons of nuts in an extra pillowcase. But not enough storage is a better problem than not enough food, so I felt pretty content as I rummaged around and repackaged calories.

When I finally went out, the air had warmed and the sun was casting sharp tree shadows up the hill. I'd decided to go up to my snares and move them closer to the hut. I haven't trapped a squirrel for a while, and I thought maybe I'd have better luck elsewhere. That last turkey I'd snared was a tom, and since they generally travel alone, I had no reason to believe another would happen by. Females tend to band together with their young, and I'd have caught one by now if they frequented that clearing. On the way back, I would look for a clearing near some oaks where they might look for acorns.

The sunshine was welcome after so many gray days, and I felt good as I tromped along, peering through the trees and catching sight of little outcroppings and caves I'd never noticed before. As I came close to the clearing, I slowed my pace. A sound like a cross between a grunt and a growl reached me from the bushes on the other side, not loud enough to be a bear, I thought, but I wasn't sure, so I put my hand on the pistol and gingerly withdrew it from its holster.

The growling continued, and after a minute I ruled out pig, and it certainly wasn't any kind of fowl. That didn't leave much that would be big enough other than bobcat and coyote. A light breeze was coming down the hill from the north, so whatever it was hadn't gotten my scent.

My curiosity grew as I stood there, and I was confident that I could scare off whatever it may be, so I edged my way west, keeping behind the brush, and then slowly headed toward the noise from beyond the western edge of the clearing. By now I could hear several distinct growls and an occasional yip, and before they came into view through the leaves of the rhododendron, I had figured out that it was a band of coyotes, but I wasn't quite prepared for the rest of the scene.

One of my snares had caught a doe, and she lay on her side with her hooves toward me and her head twisted back as though it were looking over its shoulder at some noise though, of course, its eye was fixed and glassy. Beyond the carcass, a full-grown coyote sat, her face stained dark brown, while along the belly of the deer, four half-grown pups, maybe four or five months old, lunged and ripped at the deer's innards. Most of the stomach was gone, and two heads periodically disappeared into the body cavity while the others tugged at the neck and flank. But most surprising was the sixth animal, a dun-colored dog with pointy ears that tore at the deer alongside the pups. She was about three-quarters the size of the full-grown coyote and skinnier, with a sharp snout and a white chest. I assumed it was a "she" because I couldn't imagine a coyote family taking in a male. I watched for several minutes, and though, at one point, the mama lifted her gaze and looked straight at me, she showed no reaction. Had I somehow blended into the brush? Or did she not care that I was there? Maybe she'd seen and smelled me before and decided that I was no more a threat than the little dun colored dog.

Scenes like this play out routinely in nature, and it wasn't like I didn't know it, but I guess I've always spared myself the gory details. I wasn't particularly shocked or even especially grossed out, just in a funny way, respectful, as though I'd accidentally eavesdropped on someone else's private ritual. The dog was a surprise, though, and it confirmed what Peter had predicted about people's pets becoming feral. Thinking about it as I headed back to the hut, it almost felt as though I were witnessing a blip in evolution where the trend toward domestication was taking a step backward as pets and livestock were released into the wild.

November 9

Yesterday I went back up to the traps. The deer carcass was completely gone; perhaps the coyotes had dragged it into the brush. At any rate, I felt totally alone as I gathered up my nooses and headed over to the east side of the hill.

The air was crisp and dry, and the temperature was mild for November, maybe somewhere in the mid-60s. My route took me below the cave where I did my smoking, so I detoured a bit to see whether it was still usable, meaning that no creature larger than a mouse had moved in. I cautiously peered through the brush I'd left at the entrance and didn't see anything in the dim interior, so I pulled a few branches away. Save for the pile of ashes and a bit of wood I'd left, the cave was empty. Great, I thought. I'd be able to use it again if I caught something big enough to preserve.

After that I spent a couple hours inspecting little clearings that might draw turkeys, downed trees where squirrels might pause to eat, and barely discernible deer paths. By late afternoon, I'd set ten traps and headed back to do some laundry and water chores.

The work of the day wore me out, so instead of writing last night, I sat on my bed and sketched a portrait of Edie. Drawing from memory was a challenge; I mostly wanted to capture her sharp nose, the slight wave of her hair, and the way her eyebrows rose in the middle that gave her a sort of perpetually skeptical look. I'd always loved doing portraits; when I was still in grade school, I would copy pictures of my favorite singers and actors, family members and friends. My practical side led me to double-major in Psychology and Education, but I filled my electives with art classes whenever I could. I remember one day when I was in third grade and my mom asked me why I wasn't using my chalkboard anymore.

"I can't," I replied. "I drew a horse that I really like, and I don't want to erase it."

That was when my mother started buying me drawing pads, pencils, and paints and letting me sign up for art classes after school.

It all worked out pretty well, since art therapy was a technique we used with the girls at the school. Even the ones who swore they couldn't draw a circle made progress, and being absorbed in their work took them totally out of themselves, at least for a while. I remember one girl, Grace, who came at the beginning of a summer term. When she finally realized that no one was going to judge her efforts, she began drawing quite detailed still lives and household scenes with almost Rockwellian qualities. But if you looked closely, each work contained a hidden detail, like a wilted flower, or a child crying outside the window. I remember one particularly, of a bedtime scene where the mother was reading a story to a little girl. When I looked closely, I could see that the curtains seemed to be dripping, while the shadows on the moon outside the window suggested an angry frown. One day, I drew caricatures of the girls as they worked, and I managed to catch the intensity of her concentration. When I gave it to her, she seemed shocked, almost as though she didn't quite recognize herself, but then she smiled, a rare expression that made me feel that I'd managed to do something good.

Peter was always enthusiastic about my art, too. At first it was a little unsettling to have him looking over my shoulder, but he was so admiring of my work that I came to enjoy his presence. In the last few weeks before he died, I would often sit beside him on the bed and sketch simple nature scenes on postcards that I would send to our friends as thank-you notes. He thought my drawings were amazing, but to me they were an excuse to sit with him when he was too tired to listen to me read or even speak much. It was a quiet time, and not as sad as you might think. Just a time to cherish all the moments that he wasn't in great pain and we could still be together.

The picture of Edie turned out okay, and I pinned it to the edge of one of the two-by-eights. I have some pictures of Peter and myself in a box under the bed, but I haven't been able to bring them out, and I have no pictures of my mother or Aunt JoAnn here. You could say that Edie is my one connection to the outer world, and perhaps having a daily reminder that she's back in Wagner, trying to survive in a harsher place, will inspire me to keep going.

On Day Three Post EMP at the cabin, I went to work on my evacuation plan. First, I took some sandpaper and worked on the edges of the window behind Peter's desk until I could slide it up and down quite easily. Then I took the screen out and practiced climbing out the window. My first idea was to kneel backward on the desk and reach one foot at a time over the windowsill, easing back until I could feel the roof of the back porch, about thirty inches below. But the windowsill itself was sharp where I'd taken out the screen; there was no way I could kneel on it, and it scraped my thighs as I tried to wriggle backward. So, then I pulled my feet back in and tried to go out sideways, keeping one knee on the flat, inner part of the windowsill as I reached for the porch roof with my outer foot. That worked much better. With my hands gripping the frame of the windowsill, I felt that I had plenty of control as I reached down with my foot and turned to plant the other beside it. Out and in, out and in, I practiced a few times until it felt automatic. Then I sat down on the roof of the porch to think about the next step.

The edge of the porch roof was at least fourteen feet off the ground. I could lower myself with a rope, but that would be awkward, and I'd have to leave the rope hanging there when I left. Of course, I could just lay a ladder on top of the roof. Then it would be there when I needed it, and I could lay it down against the back of the house when I got down or even slide it under the porch. Peter had inspected the roofs and the rain gutters after we bought the house, so I knew that there was a pretty long ladder in the barn.

After dragging the ladder across the yard, I leaned it up against the porch and practiced stepping from the roof onto it and climbing down. Then I climbed up and tried to pull the ladder onto the roof, but that was nearly impossible because the weight of the ladder threw me off balance, so I ended up hauling it into the house and up the stairs. Once I had it laying on the top of the porch, I started worrying whether a strong wind could blow it off, so I fetched a couple of big rocks and an old towel and anchored the ladder by laying the towel over one of the uprights and weighing it down on both sides with the rocks. That all looked and felt pretty silly, but it made me feel better, so I guess it was worth it, even though when the intruders came, I ended up going out through the back door, so this part of my plan was all for naught.

The next thing I did was to prepare my backpack. If I had to leave in the middle of the night, I might not want to try to get all the way to the hut. In fact, it might be better to go in a different direction until I was sure I wasn't being followed. So, I prepared my pack for an overnight or two, just to be safe. I'd packed for so many overnights, I could almost do it without thinking: headlamps, fire starters, first aid kit, water filter, Jetboil and fuel, tarp, hat, gloves, rain poncho, rope, lightweight sleeping bag and pad. Spork, bowl and food: granola bars, jerky, a couple pouches of chicken and ramen. When I had it all packed, I took the backpack to the far side of the wood pile, where I set it on some wood to keep it dry and covered it securely with the back side of the tarp that was already there.

Those first couple weeks, I felt a little nervous every evening as dusk settled in. Most nights, I'd take a cup of tea upstairs and sit at my desk for an hour or so, watching out the front dormer for lights in the woods between the house and the road. If I sat in bed, I could only see the tops of the trees nearest the house. I took the AR-15 up to the hut, thinking that it would be unwieldy to climb out of the window with it and the pistol. Otherwise, I mostly read and hiked, often finding myself back up on the outcropping, looking toward town and wondering what was happening there. Once in a while, I heard what sounded like a gunshot in the distance, and on the fourth day, a small plane buzzed over, heading southeast. I imagined its passengers as a family that had a little puddle jumper and was using their last fuel to head someplace they thought might be better. Someplace like…like nowhere I could imagine.

I guess that was the hardest aspect of my life at that point, all of the wondering about what was happening elsewhere and the knowledge that everyone I knew and loved was experiencing hardship and uncertainty like nothing they'd ever known. No heat, no cooling, no water, no plumbing, no food, no refrigeration, no medication refills. Dark, dark nights and days without hope. Peter had left a printout of the government EMP Risk Report in his desk, and one night I took it to bed and started to flip through the pages, just to see whether it offered the smallest bit of encouragement. But after skimming through the chapters on the electric grid, food supply chains and emergency response vulnerabilities, I put it back down. There was no good news there, just detail upon detail about how interdependent our systems were, and how, if they all were damaged at once, there would be little anyone could do to get things started again. A few islands of hydro, wind and solar power might get going, but even then, the distribution systems had all been destroyed. Repairs take experts who need transportation and communication and supply deliveries, all of which were gone. The United States, or should I say, the entire North American continent, would be helpless for many years without a major rescue from abroad. And this thought led to another: what if other countries had been hit, too?

November 10

Writing is a challenge tonight, but I'll do my best until I get too uncomfortable. I had a crazy, stupid accident this afternoon out of total lack of attention and overconfidence. I was out at my cooking site and thinking how nice it would be to have some sort of table out there. As I sat on my stool eating a bowl of ramen, I looked around for a solution. It was another crisp, sunny day, which I supposed added to my general sense of well-being and confidence. Before long, I spied a downed tree, about 20 inches in diameter at the base, with a root ball that held the bottom of the trunk about three feet off the ground. The trunk slanted at a slight angle, and I got to thinking that I could cut a chunk out of the side of the tree maybe two or three feet long to make a level surface.

The thought of a new project excited me, so I went back to the hut and got my saw and axe. I figured that I could cut grooves into side of the trunk at intervals of a couple inches and then use the axe to chip out the wood between the cuts. I wanted the surface to be a little over hip high, so I started cutting where the center of the tree was about that high and made my deepest cut first. That cut took the longest, but each successive cut was a bit shallower until I reached the part where the top side of the trunk itself was at the desired height. Then I started chipping from the shallow end, and I was surprised at how fast I progressed back down the trunk.

Wrapped in the excitement of creating my table, I worked with vigor, ignoring the fact that I hadn't thought to grab my gloves or think about what precautions I should take before I started chipping away. And, of course, that was when a wood chip flew into my left eye.

If there was anyone around, my presence wasn't much of a secret after that because you could probably hear my screams of "Fuck-fuck-fuck-fuck-fuck!" for miles. I held my hand over my eye and danced around like a marionette for a minute or so before I could calm down enough to start thinking in a near-rational way. Then I sat down on the far end of my table-log, still cupping my eye with my left hand, and tried to think of what to do. Tears streamed down my cheeks, and the pain and stinging were close to unbearable. And I couldn't stop moving my eye, even when I closed both of them, which made the pain even worse.

"Just sit," I said aloud. "Sit and try not to move. Gentle breaths, in and out…"

I followed my advice and tried not to even think for a few minutes, during which my eye continued to weep. With both eyes closed, I could manage not to blink, but I was obviously going to have to move eventually. At least it was still fairly early, maybe around two, so there was no rush to get back to the hut.

After a while my usual coping strategy of stoic resignation kicked in, and I began to think about what I needed to do next. My eye was so irritated, there was no way of knowing by feel whether a splinter was still embedded there. Maybe I could tell using the hand mirror back at the cabin. All of the counselors at the wilderness school are required to maintain Wilderness First Responder certification, so I knew, in theory, what I needed to do, which was to flush my eye with clean water. I had some water in my pack and also a syringe in my first aid kit, but the water probably wasn't super-clean, so I decided to wait until I got back to the hut and could boil some. By then I was feeling comfortable enough that the thought of getting up and walking back was quite unappealing.

Nevertheless, I forced myself to stand and looked around with my good eye. The axe was lying next to the table-tree, and the saw was over near my pack. What I wanted to do most was to make a patch for my eye, just to keep it from blinking until I got back, but that would require digging the first aid kit out of the depths of my pack and then putting everything back in. So instead, one at a time, I took my tools over to the tarp where I hide my grill and chair and shoved them under. I only took my hand from my eye long enough to shrug into my pack, turned my head to take a last look around the clearing, and headed home, walking gingerly through the dead brush.

Even using my Jetboil, it took a lot of time to heat and cool the water, and I downed some ibuprofen in the meantime, just to feel like I'd done something. Flushing the eye started it stinging and tearing again; I pulled water from the Jetboil with the syringe and held my head sideways over a wide, shallow pan and cursed some more as the water hit my eye and ran off my temple. I tried to be aggressive with the flushing in spite of the pain. If something was stuck in there, the water might be enough to dislodge it.

Finally, I held my eye open and examined it in the hand mirror.

A bright red splotch about the diameter of a pencil sat on the outside edge of the iris at about the seven o'clock position. With my left eye blurry, it was hard to discern whether there was something in it or not. Bracing myself, I pulled the lid down over the eye, let go, and then opened it, but everything was still so irritated, it was hard to tell what I was feeling. Without a definite answer, I flushed the eye some more and then patched it with gauze and medical tape. Although the manual says that patching isn't necessary for an abrasion, it felt better having the eye kept closed. The next textbook procedure says, "If unable to remove the object or discomfort persists, evacuate the patient." Yeah, right. I suppose that within a day or two, it will become more obvious whether there is still a splinter there. In the meantime, my next worry is infection. As prepared as we tried to be, one item missing from the first aid kit is any kind of eye drop or saline solution. Sterile water will have to do.

So, here I sit with my patched eye, trying to write somewhat legibly and record my stupidity for the wisdom of the ages. I guess sometimes we just have to relearn things, even the really obvious ones like to be extra careful when you're working alone, especially after an apocalypse.

November 11

I've mostly hung around the hut these last two days, examining and flushing my eye and otherwise trying not to move it. Reading and sketching were out, and I've been pretty minimal with my cooking. Even walking down the hill to the creek yesterday felt risky, but I needed water, so I went along slowly with my good eye on the downhill side. This afternoon I managed to check my traps and found a nice, fat squirrel. But I didn't trust myself to skin it with just one eye open, so I tossed it into the woods. The temperature has hovered around fifty degrees, but it was quite pleasant in the sun, and I sat in my camp chair in the cooking clearing for quite a while both days. This evening the eye feels somewhat better; I'm pretty sure it isn't infected and that the splinter is gone, so I'm giving writing another try.

With so much inactivity, my thoughts have turned back to Edie and little bits of our conversations. Since she knew about the "solar lady," Ray must have been to the cabin at least once. Was he one of the ones who came that night? It seemed quite possible. How would he have known that it was a woman alone that lived there? Most likely by the clothes I'd left: panties, a couple bras, feminine hygiene products. I should have left more of Peter's things there instead of bundling them up and giving them to Goodwill or throwing them away. All I'd kept were some T-shirts and wool socks, a fleece jacket, and one bottle of cologne, just to remind me of how he smelled when he wanted to dress up. But then, what difference does it make that they knew a woman had been living there alone? Probably not much, since no one had challenged them when they arrived.

My existence at the cabin from April to July has taken on somewhat of a fairy tale quality in my memory, although there were periods when I tortured myself imagining what might be happening to my mother and Aunt JoAnn, Linda and the baby, my friends, Peter's brother, and the group at the wilderness school. How would the school's administrator have reacted to the directive to return home? Would they have tried to evacuate the girls? The ones in camp could go easily, but there was usually a group out backpacking that might be two or three days away. The head counselor with them would have received a message by radio about what was happening. I tried to imagine what that would be like—hurrying the girls back to a deserted camp and trying to get enough of a cell phone signal to figure out what the hell was going on. If I were in charge, I would have sent everyone home as quickly as possible, just leaving behind a van for the backpackers. And hopefully, that van would still start...and have enough gas to get back to Charlottesville. Which counselor was likely to be out backpacking? Megan? Sylvie? I hoped it was Sylvie; that woman was as badass as they come.

When they really got going, my speculations took on a life of their own, ricocheting through possible scenarios, most of them disturbingly bleak. Other days, I managed to push the disaster back into a dark corner of my mind, and I lived as though I was on a protracted R and R, and Peter was back in Arlington working and not ten months dead. Those are the days that slipped by like a dream. Though I knew I was fooling myself, I didn't care. I had what I needed, and it seemed fine to drift along pretending that the outside world didn't exist. But there were practical days, too. Days when I knew exactly where I was and why, and I kept a tight rein on my thoughts and feelings, and planted some vegetables and picked berries in the woods and looked over my shoulder a lot. Luckily, it was on one of those days that the looters came.

November 12

This morning I woke to another hard frost, and when I tossed off my sleeping bag, I realized that I hadn't stocked the woodstove before I went to bed. My breath came out in puffs, even as I stirred the coals and threw in a few sticks. With just my little saw and no splitting axe, I've gravitated toward saplings about five to six inches in diameter. I definitely need some thicker pieces that will last longer through the night. So far, hot coals have been enough to keep the hut comfortable, but that luxury will probably expire as true winter arrives.

When I emerged from the hut with my bathroom bucket, the sun was already shining on the frost, creating a landscape glittering with splashes of pink and orange. The effect was so brilliant that my eyes immediately began to water, and I noticed that my injured eye felt only mildly irritated. When I got back to the hut, I took off the patch to see how it would fare, and when I found that I could function without being constantly distracted by it, I left the patch off. I feel as though I've dodged a bullet with this first injury, and I hope that I prove smart enough to heed its warning.

As I went about my other chores throughout the day, I thought back that mid-July night when the strangers showed up at the cabin. I still question my actions, wondering if Peter would agree that the threat was serious enough to warrant giving it up. He would have done more to defend it, I think, but he also would have wanted me to be safe. I think he always envisioned making a heroic stand while I hid in the woods. But it turned out that the decision was only up to me. Hide, fight, or flee? It was all a matter of what I was willing to do to stay.

After the day when I hid my backpack in the wood pile and put the ladder on the roof, I thought a lot about what else I should do to be prepared. It was possible that someone might come innocently, just looking for food, but such an "innocent" person could also be a decoy, so I was determined to be vigilant. I wore the 9mm in a shoulder holster, even though it was awkward and also hot, as spring melted into summer. If someone did come, I wanted it to be unclear whether the cabin had been occupied recently, so I unplugged the refrigerator and only cooked enough for each meal, washing the dishes immediately. The calendar in the kitchen remained stuck on April. I didn't dust, and I never left clothes in the washer or hung any out. I dumped my coffee grounds immediately each morning and tossed them and other organic waste in the woods daily. Once in a while, the toilet got so gross that I broke down and cleaned it, but not often. I didn't mind the weeds growing up in the yard, even though we had one of those old-timey mowers without a motor, and I tried to walk on the walkways and not make paths through the grass.

Most of my evenings were spent on the front porch reading, playing card games on my phone, which I could still charge even if its function as an actual phone was useless, and sometimes playing Scrabble against myself. This brought back memories of the times Peter and I had spent there before his diagnosis. I even pretended that he was my opponent, praising him for words that I made and gloating when I beat "him." All the while, I periodically scanned the edge of the woods below the house and listened for unusual noises, perking up at rustlings that turned out to be deer and starting at sudden bird shadows on the yard.

At dusk, I would go up to the bedroom and continue reading in front of the desk with my feet up on an open drawer, facing toward the road so that I could look out for lights through the trees. When the weather turned hot, I kept a fan blowing air out of the east end of the house and pulling in the breeze from the west, and I'd stay at the desk until the house started to cool. Then I'd go down to the cellar and turn off the electricity. Before crawling under the sheets, I'd lay the pistol on the nightstand next to a box of cartridges. At first, I was reluctant to surrender to sleep, and I'd lie awake staring out at the stars and drifting clouds, wondering what the night might bring. After a while, though, my preparations became routine, and I settled in each night bothered only by the worry that I might not wake up in time if someone came.

On my last day at the cabin, I'd been out in the woods collecting blackberries around the foot of the mountain all afternoon. The hollow had once been inhabited, and when the small meadows were abandoned, berry bushes had sprung up along their edges and spread over the years. Most of the fruit was inaccessible, tucked back into the middle of the patch, but the perimeter was long enough that I gathered a few quarts easily in plastic grocery bags we'd saved. I could have gathered more and tried canning them, but I was feeling lazy and put that off for later in the week. As it was, I made a small cobbler with Bisquick and powdered milk and had quite a feast for dessert that night, which I felt was fitting compensation for the scratches I'd accumulated during the picking. The berries I hadn't used, I left in the bags on the kitchen table to deal with the next day.

Settling into my chair at the desk later that evening, I placed my mug of tea within reach and opened my book. I was rereading Barbara Kingsolver's Prodigal Summer for the umpteenth time, and it seemed particularly fitting at the moment because, like the main character Lusa, I was marooned in the western mountains of Virginia. Sections of the book track the actions of a local coyote clan, and as I read them, I could easily picture the pack prowling the hills behind the cabin. I had just reached the part where the other main character, Deanna, finds a coyote den full of pups near Bitter Creek, when my attention was caught by a bit of light that appeared down in the woods. It wasn't so much a direct beam as a diffuse glow that hit the tops of the trees along the road and travelled slowly from right to left between the window frames.

Vehicle, I thought. I slapped my book shut, turned off the solar lamp, and ran down the stairs and into the pantry to lift the trapdoor and shut down the electricity. Then I ran back up the stairs and looked again. A pale halo of light had come to rest at the foot of the driveway, some three tenths of a mile away. Whoever it was had probably encountered the gate and was wondering what to do next. That would buy me a little time. Luckily, I was still dressed and had the gun strapped at my side. I picked up my mug and the cartridges from the nightstand and rushed back down the stairs. In the kitchen, I dumped the tea straight down the drain and stuck the mug back on the shelf. Looking around, I realized that the fresh-picked berries were a dead giveaway, so I grabbed the bags and threw the cartridges in one before heading out the back door. It would take up to ten minutes for someone to walk up the drive, and more than that for them to clear the driveway and drive up, so I had that much time to play with as I headed toward the woodpile where I'd hidden my backpack. After hoisting it onto my shoulders, I hesitated, wondering what to do with the berries, and ended up just bringing them along. The moon was about half full, and it wasn't difficult to make my way up the hill, using the barn as extra cover for the lower section. I set my feet deliberately as I climbed, though I had to fight down the sense of panic that pierced my gut. Within a few minutes, I was a couple hundred feet up, and I turned and sat on a tree root where I could see through the branches. To continue my climb after they reached the house might attract attention, so I decided to wait and watch until I knew what to do next.

I'd angled off to the west a little so that I was positioned to see the top of the driveway between the barn and the house, and I hadn't been waiting long when I saw a headlamp and two flashlights bobbing up the driveway. The evening hadn't had much chance to cool, and I was soaked with sweat. So were my visitors, apparently, because they paused at the top of the drive and the two on either side turned toward the one in the middle, wiping their foreheads and faces with their forearms, seeming to wait for their orders.

As the flashlights wavered, I tried to gather details. Three men, two of average size, with the third smaller, skinnier and maybe younger than the others, all wearing dark T-shirts and pants. The one in the middle had a full beard and seemed to be the leader by the way he cast his flashlight in a semi-circle across the house and the barn before lowering his head and beginning to speak. Of course, I couldn't hear anything, so I just continued to watch, hoping to read something from their body language. Each of the men wore a small back pack and held a rifle. The leader also wore a holstered gun at his right hip, which was revealed when he shifted his rifle under his left arm to gesture toward the house. The other larger man had a round face under a dark cap and the third had long, straight hair. He stood slightly away from the others, and there was a hesitancy to his posture that I noticed by the way that he didn't look directly toward the leader but toward at the ground off to his right. It crossed my mind that maybe he didn't want to be there.

They seemed to stand there for a long time, but probably less than a minute passed before baseball cap headed to the barn and the leader and the little man started toward the house. All three raised their rifle barrels to waist level as they came forward.

I lost sight of all three behind the buildings until the leader came around the side of the house and headed for the back door. He must have turned off his flashlight and stowed it somewhere because all I saw in his hands was his rifle. In the meantime, there was a knocking loud enough for me to hear from my perch and the smaller man yelled from the front porch, "Anybody home? Hey in there! It's your neighbor from down the road!"

Hmm, so they send the least threatening of them to make first contact, I thought.

In the meantime, the leader peered in the kitchen window and tried the door.

To that point, I had been watching as though this was all unfolding as a movie scene, but when the leader tried the kitchen door knob with one hand, keeping the other ready on his rifle, I started to shake. After a short pause, he smashed the door glass with the butt of the rifle and reached in to unlock the door. I imagined that if I had gone to answer the door, the leader would have come up behind me, and all escape would be cut off.

I thought about where I'd be if they had waited just another hour to arrive. Having settled into bed for the night, I wouldn't have known anyone was near until the knock and shout came from the front door. About now I'd be rushing into my clothes and heading for the window.

Off to the left, I saw the moon-faced man come out of the barn and head for the back door. His timing coincided roughly with the moment I would have been climbing out the window onto the roof of the back porch in plain sight. He walked to the back door and entered, and his gait was that of someone who was tired and maybe a little bored, like walking into strangers' houses was what he did every day.

After that they all turned on their lights, and I could see the bright dots moving around the kitchen and then one flashed around upstairs for a while. I was still damp from sweat and shivering as I sat and tried to decide what to do next. The intruders didn't seem to be in any particular hurry, and it angered me to picture them sauntering around as if they owned the place. But I knew that I should go while their attention was on the house.

I rose on stiff legs, still watching the house, and I saw the back door open, and the leader step out. He paused a couple feet outside the door and turned his head to examine the porch. Then he lifted his chin and surveyed the overgrown yard, pausing to look toward the barn. If he was looking for evidence of recent habitation, I was pretty sure I'd left no clues outside the house. Finally, he turned and went back in.

Whew, I thought, as I turned and angled my way toward the east-facing side of the hill. I walked slowly, choosing each step, thankful for the moonlight and mild temperatures. The only other aid I could have wished for was a strong breeze to create some background noise.

I walked for about forty minutes, crossing the creek where Peter and I first picnicked and heading along a line that would eventually intersect my usual route to the hut. I'd done this in the daytime, but I wasn't sure that I wouldn't overshoot the place where I needed to turn uphill, so after I'd put a couple of miles behind me, I found a good, flat place to stop. Though I was far from the cabin, I still hesitated to use a light, so I pulled out my tarp and sleeping bag by feel and spread them on the ground. I didn't expect to sleep much, and I didn't, instead lying on my back listening and looking at a patch of sky through the tree limbs. I sifted through what I had witnessed and speculated on what might have happened if I'd become trapped in the house. If the bearded man had stormed up the stairs to the bedroom, would I have had the resolve to shoot? What would the other two have done then? Tried to wait me out?

Looking back over what I've written, I see that time has allowed me to view these events with some detachment. In fact, as I lay there on the rough ground, I started at every sound, and when finally I dozed, I woke suddenly from a brief nightmare where the bearded man came crashing out of the brush toward me, rifle in hand, yelling, "Aha! I've got you now!"

After that, I scooted my sleeping bag over to a tree and sat with my back against it with the pistol in my lap and waited.

Part II

November 13

Today I was pretty productive. My eye felt better, and I had that energy that I always feel on the first good day after being laid up. After my water chores, I checked my traps. They were all empty and a couple of the snares had been brought down by the wind. As I reset them, I thought it would be nice to get another turkey and maybe try to smoke some of it. Next, I scouted for standing deadwood that was a little bigger than what I'd been cutting. Dead hemlocks were easy to find since so many had died in the wooly adelgid infestation of the 2000s, but though the wood wasn't as sappy as other evergreens, it usually burned so fast that it didn't produce coals that would burn all night. I located an oak and a couple maples of about the right size and started sawing sections out of one that was leaning into a neighboring tree.

As I worked, my mind was on the events of the night I left the cabin. In some ways, it was as though somewhere in the woods that night I'd crossed over an invisible barrier, a one-way door that said, "There's no going back." But that was silly. I could go back whenever I wanted to. So why hadn't I?

Though both homes offered shelter and warmth, the cabin had the advantages of running water, a washing machine, indoor plumbing and much more in the way of provisions, not to mention an actual bed. The hut was more primitive, but I didn't mind the chores or being a little dirtier. And it was almost comforting to have everything I needed concentrated in a small space. When I lived at the cabin, life had been almost too easy. I had food and all the creature comforts that Peter had been so careful to provide. And that, I have come to realize, was part of the problem. Peter made all the decisions for me, and the result was that I'd felt almost like a plant, rooted in place, waiting for him to tell me what to do next. But the idea that I'd so easily abandoned the place he'd prepared made me feel ungrateful.

It's different here in the woods. Life is harder, but I have decisions to make and to be responsible for. If I sit back on my laurels, I'll never make it through the winter. I know that everything Peter did was out of love, but the result was that at the cabin I'd felt like a "kept" woman, passively dependent on someone else for my comfort, waiting for my lover to come back. But in my case, that lover was never coming back. We'd never discussed exactly I was supposed to do with all my time at the cabin aside from keeping myself alive. I know what Peter would have said though, that survival was the main thing, and survival for what purpose was a philosophical question that was beside the point. Together, we could have figured it out, but alone, I'm not so sure.

I got several chunks of wood sawed, hauled them back to the hut, and started in on the second maple. I'd chosen trees that were scattered a few minutes' walk from the hut so as not to create a concentrated area of sawed-off trees that might attract attention. This one had fallen on top of an older log, so I had access to most of the trunk. It would take the better part of a day to get the best pieces. I started in on the job, working up a sweat and still thinking about the cabin and whether I should go and at least take a look. The thing was, even if the intruders had merely taken what they could find and left, there was always the chance that they or other scavengers would be back. Then I'd face the same choices: shoot, leave, or surrender. And that last option was unthinkable.

But it wouldn't hurt to look, a nagging voice started up in my head. This was new. I'd squelched the idea of going back many times with no second-guessing. But that was before Edie. It seemed that just that little contact with the outside world had put a chink in my armor. While I'd given up thinking about the people in my former life as a useless form of self-torture, I had to face the fact that Edie and her mom were out there right now, just a few miles away. Maybe it was time to stop hiding my head in the sand.

I had left the cabin in mid-July, and I'd gone to some lengths to try to make sure I could get out when need be. But now it was November, and there had already been a flurry and several frosts. Standing there in the woods with my arm getting sore and the sweat running down my face, it occurred to me that the cabin was not ready for winter. Sure, there was plenty of wood to burn for whoever might be there, but if it was empty, sooner or later the pipes would freeze. It had always been standard operating procedure for us to drain the lines and put anti-freeze in the drain traps, but of course, winter was the last thing on my mind the night I left. That thought threw a whole different perspective on the question. Now, I realized, if I didn't go back to winterize the cabin, I could lose the possibility of running water altogether.

Hmmm...That was a real kicker. I thought about it as I sawed and as I loaded wood into my backpack and made three trips to haul my afternoon's work back to the hut. Any way that I looked at it, it seemed I no longer had a choice. If I wanted to save the plumbing, I had to go. And while I was there, maybe I'd get the splitting axe.

November 14

Today I emerged from the hut to a cold, misty rain. I had already decided to take the day to prepare to go to the cabin. My plan was to spend one afternoon and evening just observing, stay the night in the woods near where I camped the night I left, and then approach on the second day, if all seemed abandoned. So today I went out and pulled down my snares. No point in catching something and leaving it to the other creatures. After my usual chores and a little more sawing, I retired early to pack. Dinner was a stew of dehydrated chicken, instant potatoes, and a few freeze-dried vegetables. I took care to make just enough for the evening.

In my pack I put one of my precious Mountain House meals, my Jetboil, and a small propane canister. Nuts and raisins would do for lunch and oatmeal for breakfast. As I packed, I thought about the food at the cabin. If I didn't move back, I could at least bring extra provisions back to the hut. I pictured myself browning granola on top of the woodstove with the extra oatmeal, nuts, and honey. You probably can't imagine salivating over eating granola with reconstituted powdered milk, but it sounded really good to me. And popping corn—we'd stashed several jars in the cellar. Pickles were heavy, but it wouldn't hurt to bring a jar. I realized that I was getting carried away, and that I didn't know whether any of this would be possible, but memories of food I'd forgotten about flooded my mind. Wait and see, I told myself, like a mother would tell a child. Just wait and see.

So, assuming that the weather clears overnight, tomorrow I will make the trek. I've packed my binoculars and the rest of my camping supplies, but I left a good amount of empty space for what I might carry back. As I settle into my sleeping bag, I feel quite excited. I hope that sleep comes fast.

November 15

I woke to scattered clouds and brisk temperatures, just a tad above freezing. But the day warmed quickly as I made my way south and then west along the mountainside. I'd given up on the easier route, which would have taken me downhill to the forest road, feeling that I'd be too exposed walking down the road. So, I basically retraced my steps of the night I left the cabin, just a little higher on the mountain. With the leaves down, it was going to be more difficult to hide, so I'd have to find a stand of pines or another rhododendron thicket. As I grew close to my earlier camping spot, I decided to leave my backpack and go on with just the binoculars, gun, water, a bag of nuts, and a headlamp, just in case. I was wearing my black rain jacket over a fleece, so I had plenty of pockets for everything, and if I stayed in the shadows, I would blend in nicely, or at least I hoped.

Even with all that has happened, there are times when I'm walking in the woods that I feel the same sense of peace I've had since I was a child exploring the mountains around Worcester. The amount of attention that it takes to put one foot in front of the other and actively observe my surroundings pulls my mind away from any worries that may be nagging at me. In spite of the high stakes, as I made my way toward the cabin, I again felt that peace. As I stepped along, I watched a pair of cardinals take flight in front of me and land in a bush, the male all bright and showy, the female seemingly okay with having a duller outfit. When I grew too close, they launched themselves out ahead of me again, as though leading the way, reminding me of the little animals that led Snow White to the dwarves' cottage. I guess that sounds silly, but it's really another of those lessons we tried to teach the girls—even when everything is falling apart, there's usually something you can appreciate, even if it's just a cardinal or a silly thought.

Soon I came to the creek that serves as a secondary water source for the cabin. Peter rigged a line to it that could be gravity-fed from a pool about a quarter mile uphill from the house, but we'd never submerged the line because we had plenty of power to run the well pumps. I followed the creek down to the pool and confirmed that the line was high and dry.

Rounding the hill, I stopped to scope out a good vantage point as soon as the cabin and barn came into sight. From this distance, nothing appeared changed, and as far as I could tell, the electricity was still off. A grove of young white pines caught my eye, just a little too far west to offer a good view of where the driveway came up between the house and barn, but it would have to do. When I settled in with the binoculars, I still had a good view of the back of the house and the entrance to the barn. I figured I was at least two hundred feet above the back yard and at a height where a person casually glancing out the back wouldn't look.

The yard was vacant except for a bit of trash up against the bottom of the porch. Unless one was parked directly in front of the cabin, there were no vehicles or signs of one. The window on the back door was still broken, and no one had tried to cover the gap. That was good news, too, since if someone were living there, they'd want to keep out the cold. The ladder was where I'd left it on the porch roof; apparently the town had no ladder shortage. I wondered what the intruders had thought when they saw it; surely, they'd at least looked out the dormer window.

I continued to inspect the house, but from the outside, it looked remarkably the same. I don't know what I expected…more broken windows? The doors hanging open? Graffiti? Perhaps the intruders had left it intact because they might want to use it later. But at the moment, it appeared empty.

That made me feel good, and I relaxed just a bit and thought about what to do next. It would be foolish to rush right in, but if no one showed up in an hour or so, I could do a little more exploring. I peered into the darkness of the barn, but I couldn't make out anything.

Lunchtime came and went, and I nibbled on some mixed nuts and began to feel pretty hopeful. But since I didn't know for sure whether someone was inside, I moved slowly back along the hill until the barn was between me and the house before I lowered myself down the slope. Here I encountered the first change since I'd left—someone had rolled the back door of the barn closed, so I couldn't tell whether the old tractor was still in place over the trapdoor to the root cellar. But it wasn't out front or anywhere outside, so I figured it was right where it belonged. Staying behind the cover of the barn, I went along to the brush pile where the truck was hidden. The tarp was intact and had weathered and accumulated enough dirt that a casual observer might think it had been there for years; indeed, it had gone from shiny brown to almost black.

As I entered the woods and headed down toward the forest road, I had plenty of reasons to feel good. Staying back in the scant cover of the trees, I approached the driveway. When it came into view, I was dismayed to find that the gate hung open. Coming closer, I saw that the boulders and saplings that had blocked the driveway had been hauled out of the way, so I was certain that, at some point, the intruders had brought a vehicle up to the house. Which meant they had taken stuff. Enough that they hadn't wanted to make trips down the driveway. This didn't really surprise me, since Edie's food had looked so familiar. It just got me to wondering if they'd found the cellar and how many times they'd come back. And where were they getting their gas? Siphoning it off of other people's cars? That sounded like something "Uncle Ray" would do.

There had always been a pair of ruts in the driveway near the gate that filled with rain water. Walking up the edge of the gravel, I inspected the ruts. I didn't think the rain from the day before had been strong enough to wash away any recent tracks, and I was heartened by the lack of tire treads. It was beginning to look like, just maybe, July's scavengers had gotten everything they thought they could use and moved on. Which didn't mean they wouldn't change their minds and come back, but it was something.

On the return trip to my lookout spot, I stayed close enough to the driveway to check the front of the house for vehicles and found none. Then I turned into the woods and circled back around to my hiding place. Sweeping the house with the binoculars, I saw nothing amiss.

It wasn't easy to just sit there, and I soon wished I'd brought along my sketch pad. The back view of the house had a peaceful, homey quality that I would have liked to try to capture, a kind of timelessness that recalled a world made up of solid people and predictable lives. Even the yawning blackness of the barn brought to mind a time of hot Sundays when the hay had been put up and the chores were done. But, as I didn't have so much as a pencil with me, I divided my attention between scanning the house, identifying bird calls, and reminiscing on the times Peter and I had spent reading in front of the wood stove in the living room or watching the stars through the dormer window.

Finally, when the sun settled toward the horizon and I started to get chilled from inactivity, I decided that I'd seen enough for the day and headed back to this campsite to ponder what I'd found. I am fairly convinced that no one has been around for a while, and I might safely venture into the house by midday tomorrow, winterize the pipes, grab some supplies, and head back to the hut. As I write, a pair of barred owls are calling back and forth with their distinctive "Woo-woo-woo-WOO, woo-woo-woo-WOO-ahhh" call, and it feels good to sleep outside for a change. I've gambled on the weather by not bringing a tent and just spreading my sleeping bag on a ground cloth. Tonight I'll wrap the ground cloth around me, burrito-style and pass the time counting stars until sleep takes me.

November 16

This morning I woke to a coating of dew and a cold nose. By eight or nine I was already situated in my hiding spot on the hill, this time with my pack so that I could fill it with supplies from the cellar. The back yard was still in shadow, but everything looked the same as it had the day before. I walked along the hillside contentedly with an insulated mug of mint tea, which I sat sipping as I surveyed the cabin. While the place had seemed foreign yesterday, today it felt more like home, my home, not enemy territory.

An hour or so passed, and I decided to check out the barn before venturing into the house. Still exercising an abundance of caution, I backtracked along the hill until I was directly behind the barn before descending. Bracing my feet, I pushed the door back along its rollers and slipped inside.

The morning sun was shining in the front, so it didn't take long for my eyes to adjust. In front of me, pretty much exactly where I'd left it, sat the tractor, and, as far as I could tell, it hadn't budged, which meant that the intruders hadn't found the root cellar. I remembered what Edie had said about maybe hiding in a barn, so I looked around for evidence of habitation. Nothing on the ground floor had been disturbed, so I slipped off my pack but not the pistol, and climbed the ladder to the loft. Standing at the front edge, I could see the back and east sides of the house, and I instinctively backed into the shadows, just in case. Some old hay bales were stacked three high against the back wall, but something seemed a little off about the way they were stacked. I walked around the side and saw an extra space of maybe fifteen inches between two rows of bales on the second level. It looked like just enough space for a small person to squeeze through. Like an entrance.

I didn't think anyone was in there, but I couldn't tell for sure, so I went back down the ladder and fetched my headlamp. If someone were there, they would have heard me roll open the door. But I hadn't detected a trace of movement, so it was just a precautionary measure when I pulled the pistol from its holster as I shined the light into the space, feeling like a cop in a crime show. Still, all I could see was a piece of cloth, so I stood and started pulling down haybales until I'd exposed a rectangular space about five feet long and three feet wide, lined with a gray comforter from my own linen closet and topped with a brown sleeping bag I'd never seen before. Not the one I'd given to Edie. Not Peter's.

So, someone had hidden out there, and I had no clue how long it had been since they'd left. It seemed odd that they would hide in the barn and not sleep in the house unless the person was hiding from someone in particular. I say person because the space seemed too small for more than one. Now that I thought about it, the loft was a pretty good lookout point for someone afraid of unwanted company. If someone came up to the house, they could always slip out the back, especially if it were dark. But why leave your sleeping bag if you weren't planning to return?

There was no way of knowing, so I abandoned my questions and restacked the hay bales. I'd already released a lot of dust, which had started to tickle my nose and throat and had me periodically sneezing into the crook of my arm and hoping that I was truly alone. Back outside, I shouldered my pack and stood at the edge of the woodpile to take a last, long look at the house before approaching.

When I mounted the steps to the back porch, I immediately noticed that the kettle grill that we kept in the corner was gone. Peering through the window over the kitchen sink, I could see some trash on the counter, a pot sitting on the woodstove, and some bowls and saucers pushed into a clump on the table. Everything looked dusty and abandoned, so I entered through the back door.

It appeared that whoever had been there had enjoyed a meal before leaving, and a smell like something long rotten hit me as I entered. Three bowls on the table were crusted with what looked like bean soup, as was a pot on the stove. The counter was littered with a cracker box, some jerky wrappers, and a couple empty cans of fruit cocktail. Mice had come to feast on the remains and left trails of droppings along the counter.

But the stench that was hitting me was too intense for mouse poop, and I followed my nose down the hall to the bathroom to find that a lack of running water hadn't stopped someone from using the toilet, which was about three quarters full of thick sludge. Jesus. If I wanted to winterize the trap below the toilet, I was going to have to get rid of a big mess.

Before starting that repulsive chore, I climbed the stairs to check out the bedroom. A quick look around revealed that pretty much everything that could be carried easily had been taken, including all the bed linens and clothes, writing supplies, notebooks and sketch pads. A large envelope of pictures I'd kept in my desk drawer was scattered across the mattress—my mom in a Hawaiian smock on her birthday a few years back, a picture of me with my graduate school mentor, and Peter and I feeding ostriches at the National Zoo. Seeing Peter's face so unexpectedly shocked me, and I started to gather the pictures to take with me, but then thought better of it. Best to leave things as undisturbed as possible.

Next, I headed for the cellar, noting that the pantry had been stripped totally bare. Raising the trapdoor and switching on my headlamp, I was relieved to see that all of the food stores below were intact. I'd need some water to clean out the toilet, so I made my way to the far corner where the solar boxes were located and threw the three switches that would get the power back on and the well pump running.

Back in the bathroom, I was happy to hear water trickling into the toilet tank as I started the repulsive task of bailing out the contents of the toilet bowl into a plastic bucket, using a small cooking pot. The manure had thickened and dried so that I had to add water to loosen it and stir and scrape to get it more liquefied. When the bowl was as nearly empty, I poured in a couple gallons of water and plunged it, hoping that my first flush wouldn't produce a clog. Of course, if an intruder came back, they'd know someone had been here to perform this chore, but if I wanted to get antifreeze into the trap below the toilet, I didn't have any choice. I held my hand over my nose as I pushed down the handle and was satisfied to see the familiar swirl of water go down. Flush by flush, I fed the rest of the waste back into the toilet and then rinsed the bucket and pot and left them in the shower.

After washing my hands, I drained the pipes, starting by shutting the main intake valve and then running the water out of all the faucets and flushing the toilet until it would no longer refill. Finally, I poured non-toxic antifreeze into all the drains and the toilet bowl, flushing some through the tank.

As I gathered up the empty antifreeze containers from the kitchen and my thoughts began to turn toward all the food I could gather from the cellar, I paused to look out the front window. I'm not sure which I became aware of first, the sound—a familiar low rumble—or the bobbing motion, just above the view line of the driveway, but as I watched, two heads came over the horizon, approaching fast on a motorcycle. With no time to weigh my options, I stepped back into the pantry, closed the door, and scrambled through the trapdoor into the cellar.

Damn! I thought. What are the odds someone would show up on this day? Caught off guard, I struggled to think clearly over the pounding of my heart. It was pitch dark, but I knew there was a headlamp on the hook next to the steps. With its light, I headed straight to the electric boxes and shut off the power. Then I crossed back to the stairs, switched off the headlamp, and strained my ears.

Muffled footsteps scraped on the hardwood. Voices, too far off to distinguish words. I lifted the trapdoor an inch. Now I could make out two voices, raised in disagreement.

"I'm telling you, this is a total waste of gas. Why would the brat come way out here when all the food is in town? Not to mention his little girlfriend. There's plenty of hiding places closer in."

That first voice was mid-range and a little whiny.

"Well, the night patrol's been on the lookout for two weeks, and they ain't seen him. And I'm not about to let that little runt get away with threatening me," a deeper, coarser voice replied.

"If you could keep it in your pants, we wouldn't be in this mess."

"Oh? Look who's playing Mr. Innocent! It's not like he doesn't have plenty of tales to tell on you."

"Maybe, but not them kind of tales."

"Why don't you shut your mouth and go search the barn? Sometimes, I think you're forgettin' who's in charge here."

A moment later the front door slammed, and I could hear the footsteps of the "boss" start down the hall. I lowered the trapdoor in case he was heading for the pantry, but instead the footsteps continued. Even with the door raised, I didn't hear anything else for a couple minutes, and I think he went upstairs. Then I heard the door to the downstairs bedroom open, and the footsteps came back a few moments later, paused at the bathroom doorway and went in.

Lowering the trapdoor again, I went through a mental checklist of what he was seeing. Pink liquid in the toilet and the empty pot and bucket in the wet tub. I raised the listening door again and heard the front door open.

"Nothing in the barn," the whiny voice called.

"Reese, get in here. Tell me what you think of this."

Footsteps sounded down the hall.

"Shit! Looks like somebody's been doing some housekeeping. What's that pink stuff?"

"I don't know. Deodorant? Antifreeze? Maybe Thomas is planning on moving in. He could've got water from the creek to flush the toilet. Could be he wants to clean the place up and bring Edie here. Stupid fool. This ain't near far enough to get her away from me."

At the sound of Edie's name, my heart tripped. Did that mean the gravelly-voiced boss was Uncle Ray? Then Reese was probably the other man I saw that night, and the smaller one would be Thomas. Remembering the hesitancy of the long-haired man, it all seemed to fit.

"This tub is still wet, and so is the sink. Are you sure there was no one hiding in the barn? He must've just been here."

"Yeah, and we must've just scared him off coming up the hill on that damned motorcycle. Not exactly a good way to surprise someone."

"I wanted to see if he'd been here, and it looks like he has, so as far as I'm concerned, this mission is a success. Plus, he knows we came looking for him, so chances are, he won't be back. But I'll send someone at night for a few days just to make sure. I've been through the whole house except the pantry. Go check it out while I take a piss. I'll meet you at the bike."

I ducked down and listened as footsteps creaked toward the kitchen, and I heard the door to the pantry open. I may have imagined it, but it seemed like I could hear Reese's raspy breathing as he looked around. But then all was quiet again until a second set of footsteps went by, paused for a moment, and then proceeded out the front door. The motorcycle rumbled to life, revved, and receded, but I stayed in my hiding spot for quite a while before climbing out. Thinking that they might park the bike and creep back up the hill, I stood out of sight by the front window and watched for several minutes. Then I was tempted just to leave, but I couldn't stand the thought of passing up the opportunity for more hot chocolate and oatmeal, not to mention chicken and tuna and more dehydrated vegetables. And I did get that jar of pickles, only I was so loaded down, I left the splitting axe.

Now that I've gone back once, I think it will be easier to return again. With the right amount of diligence, I can make periodic forays. And although being stuck in the root cellar was unnerving, I ended up with some important information: it was most likely Uncle Ray, Reese, and Thomas who drove me out in July. Somehow, knowing who my enemy is lessens my fear. Ray strikes me as a not-overly-intelligent bully who somehow manages to gain power over others. As demonstrated by Reese's criticism and Thomas's running away, his hold on them is at best tenuous. Sadly, I also now know who most likely got Edie pregnant. Does Thomas plan to rescue her somehow? If so, I hope he has a better plan than moving into the cabin. And if the two of them are close, Thomas most likely knows about me. That thought takes some digestion, since I can't think of any reason why Edie wouldn't have told him where I am. Of course, she may have told Ray, too, but somehow, I doubt it. Not if she has any thoughts of needing me again.

November 22

I have let several days go by without writing, days I have spent going about my usual chores and focusing just on the tasks in front of me. The day after I returned, I repositioned my traps and within a couple days, I snared two squirrels. As I was poking around some oaks, I came upon several growths of a fungus that Peter taught me are called "Chicken of the Woods." They're a kind of shelf fungus that's easy to recognize because their underbelly is vivid yellow and has spores rather than the ribbing of the mushrooms that are common in people's yards. We cooked some together at the cabin, so I was confident in gathering some samples. They're a bit tough by this time of year, so I trimmed some of the new growth around the edges, making a mental note to go mushroom gathering earlier next year. I added them to the stew I made with the squirrels and let it all cook for a long time. With all the flavors blending together, I didn't really get a strong mushroom flavor, but they added substance to the stew and made it more filling, even if they were a bit chewy.

The days have turned chilly, with highs somewhere in the forties, I'd guess. I've spent a couple of hours each day bringing in more wood, and in the early evenings I sit on the foot of my sleep platform and shell hickory nuts. It's a tedious chore, but good for mindless repetition. I put some of the nuts into the batch of granola I made yesterday, along with some raisins and dried cranberries I brought from the cabin. The sweet aroma of the oats, nuts, and honey roasting on top of the woodstove reminded me of the holidays and how, as a girl, I would help my mother bake cookies to give out as gifts. Oatmeal raisin was my favorite, so we'd always make plenty of those for ourselves. It was a pleasant thought until I started thinking about all of the traditions that children would miss this year.

I guess the thing I've been most actively doing since I got back is trying to ignore everything I learned on my trip. After the initial feeling of accomplishment wore off, I began to feel somewhat detached from what I had learned about Uncle Ray, Edie, and Thomas. In fact, I find myself missing the days before Edie came when I was totally isolated from the outside world. And, if you get right down to it, I'm also angry that Thomas might know where I am and show up any day looking for help. I know that I brought this on by helping Edie, and I would still do the same today, but the whole situation brings to mind that old saying, "No good deed goes unpunished." I can't solve the problem of Uncle Ray, and there are thousands of Uncle Rays out there, taking advantage of other peoples' desperation anyway they can. I'm angry, and I feel helpless, and I wonder a little bit whether Peter knew that this would happen, and that's why he planned it so that we would be separate from other people's pain.

November 24

I've been waking up early lately, when the narrow windows let in the merest gradient of light. Usually I make some coffee or tea and lounge on my sleep pad, just watching the light take hold and letting my mind relax. In these pre-dawn minutes, there is no pressing chore, no decision to make or problem with which to wrestle, and I can imagine for a while that I am safe and secure and that nothing of the outside world is real or matters terribly much.

Of course, I eventually get hungry, and I see that my water is low or my toilet bucket is full, and I force myself to address the needs of the moment, after which I am reminded of other chores that must be done and then I am up and dressed and dealing with them one by one on yet another solitary day.

This morning the sun was bright, and a thick frost covered the forest floor when I emerged from the hut with my toilet bucket. It was smelling more foul than usual, so I decided to take it down to the creek for an actual soapy wash and a good rinse. The snares needed checking, too, so I gathered up my water bottles, daypack, and toilet bucket, along with the gun, and set off down the slope, sliding along on the melting frost.

Since the weather has turned and food is becoming scarcer for all my wild neighbors, I've been checking my snares more frequently and earlier in the day. Deer still come regularly to the grove to eat nuts from the ground, and I've seen many a mound of bear scat there, too. My goal is to take my game before something else does. This morning I approached the area with my usual caution, checked a couple snares on the north side of the grove and made my way east to where a little deer path comes in from the northeast. It'd been so long since I'd caught anything big, I was quite surprised to see the doe lying in the leaves with her neck twisted and eyes staring sightlessly into the grass. Her coat was a winter gray and a little mangy, and she seemed on the skinny side for this time of year, making me wonder at her age. But food is food, and I dropped my pack to get out my buck knife and a plastic trash bag.

I intended to hack off the hindquarters and drag the rest farther into the woods to leave for the other animals because it's too difficult to get all the meat in one trip, and by the time I came back, I was likely to have company. As I raised my knife, I took a look around and caught sight of a dark shape through the trees a couple hundred feet to the south. It was one of the biggest black bears I've ever seen, an adult of at least two or three years with a coat so shiny, you'd think he'd just come from a salon. He was standing on his hind legs with his nose in the air, and I knew immediately that he must be picking up the scents of both me and the deer.

If I had found him at the doe, I would have respectfully backed off like I did with the coyotes. Challenging a full-grown bear was definitely not in my skill set. But at this distance, I wondered whether it might not be possible to scare him off. I set my knife back into my pack and shouldered it, just so I'd have it with me if this didn't go well. Then I stepped behind a tree and unholstered the gun from under my left arm. The bear continued to sniff the air, shaking his head slightly, while I lifted the gun, chambered a round, and decided where to aim. I didn't want to hurt him, but I wanted to hit close enough to make an impression, banking on the probability that he'd encountered hunters before. Finally, I settled my sights on the ground in front of him and squeezed the trigger.

As I've mentioned before, Peter and I did enough target shooting together for me to be somewhat comfortable with the 9mm; however, it had been a while since I'd fired it, and the crack of the shot and its kickback startled me more than I expected. Luckily, the bear seemed every bit as startled as me, and his head jerked up for an instant before he turned and lumbered off down the slope.

Wow, I thought, feeling pretty pleased with myself for salvaging my doe. I didn't want to become complacent, though, so I stayed vigilant as I pulled the knife back out, plunged it between the left hip and the femoral head, and worked it between the bones to sever the leg. The upper leg and hindquarters are prime areas; that's where the roasts and steaks come from, so my choice would yield the best cuts. It was a messy job, and my hands were soon sticky with blood and little wisps of fur. When I had the first leg off, I placed it hip end first into the garbage bag and started in on the other one. The length of the legs didn't fit into the bag, so when I pulled the top closed, a few inches of leg and the hooves stuck out. I shoved the bag into my backpack, hooves up, and zippered it as tightly as possible around the legs. Then I untied the noose from the tree and dragged the rest of the carcass about fifty feet farther into the woods. With so much meat to process, I wouldn't be back for a while, so I went back to the grove and made a complete circle, collecting my snares as I went.

I try not to butcher or cook too near to the hut, so I stopped near Edie's old campsite to skin the legs and slice the meat off the bones, making chunks about six inches long and an inch thick. This took some time, and I was getting pretty hungry by the time I abandoned the rest of the bones and headed toward the creek, where I was quite happy to get my hands clean, at least temporarily.

My satisfaction at bagging more meat and scaring away the bear lasted through the day. I used one big chunk to make a stew, adding some more of the mushrooms and some onion flakes and instant potatoes. As it simmered, I decided that I should take the rest of the meat up to my smoking cave and dry it out for storage. I was still feeling disconcerted about the possibility that Thomas might show up, and I'd been thinking about going off for a few days, anyway, so it felt like a good time to spend some time away.

Try to accomplish something every day. That was another one of the lessons we tried to impress upon the girls and perhaps the one that I'm proving the best at. If Peter were here, I'd be boasting of my daring and skill, and he would be teasing me about getting a big head or calling me Survival Girl or something. Our banter was always light-hearted and kind-spirited, and always made us stronger because it reinforced the feeling we each had of being totally understood and accepted. When I look back on how good we were for each other, I sometimes think that maybe a gift like that is never intended to last. I don't know; maybe that's just my characteristic pessimism breaking in, but I doubt I'll never have anything like that again. And I'm beginning to think that I'm okay with that.

November 25

I am writing tonight from inside my two-person, MSR tent, which has been a staple of my backpacking for years. I've hung a solar lamp from one of the overhead loops, and I'm sitting with my lower half in my sleeping bag on a nylon camping chair that uses my air mattress for cushioning. I'm wearing my down jacket, in addition to my fingerless gloves and a fleece-lined hat. I probably look like I'm freezing, but I'm really quite comfortable, if not a bit drowsy, from another productive day.

Last night I hung the rest of the venison from a tree, double-bagged to reduce the smell, and was happy to see that it passed the night undisturbed. After a breakfast of leftover stew, I gathered together the essentials for three nights at the cave, not that it will take that long to do the smoking, but so I'll have the option to hang around if I want to. The nearest water source from there is the same stream I use for the hut, just short of two miles upstream from my washing pool and maybe ten minutes east of the cave. The smoking will require at least a couple gallons, but I figured I'd save the weight and get all I needed when I got up there. The other major resource required is, of course, wood. I decided to take enough hardwood to get me started and then see what was available in the neighborhood, which meant bringing my saw. I put a few chunks of oak and hickory in my pack, along with the same basic supplies I always take, and strapped my tent along the bottom. When I was ready to go, I lowered the meat bag and attached it to the outside of the pack, so when I started up the hill, I felt a little bit like walking bear bait. But that was mostly my imagination, and, besides, I had the gun.

With the meat and the wood, my pack was on the heavy side, probably about thirty-five pounds. The sky was mostly cloudy and the air cold, but still, the climb soon had me sweating, and I slowed down to let myself cool a bit. I'd packed extra dry layers for this very reason, a good wool blend base layer and extra socks.

When I arrived at the cave, I saw that some of the brush I'd used before to hold in the smoke had blown off. I left it that way while I went for water and gathered kindling. I put the chunks of hardwood into a natural depression in the floor of the cave and wetted them down so they'd produce smoke when I finally got things going. The most time-consuming preparation was the stringing of the meat. The opening of the cave was about ten feet wide, and I anchored the ends of the rope in piles of rocks I'd brought up back in the summer. To keep the line from drooping too much in the middle, I wedged a five-foot sapling under it and pressed it against the ceiling. Getting all this accomplished without dragging the meat around on the floor of the cave was a little tricky, but by about noon I had everything ready on the inside and set about rebuilding the brush wall.

I was a little worried about being able to maintain a temperature of a round 200–220 degrees since the weather had cooled, so I built the wall a little closer in and laid some saplings vertically against the roof of the cave along the length to add more of a barrier. I didn't think I'd need any extra ventilation since my wall was so porous; I was aiming for just the right balance between air flow and heat retention.

By then it was mid-afternoon, and I decided that it was too late to actually start the fires, so I took down the string of meat and re-packed it in the trash bags and hung it well downwind of my campsite. Then I spent the rest of the afternoon gathering wood, stacking it outside the west end of the cave, and dousing it with water, so I'd be ready for a full day and evening of smoking in the morning.

My tent is set up off of the east end of the cave, downhill about twenty feet, on a little knob. Dinner was another Mountain House meal, this time sweet and sour pork with delectable little pineapple chunks and white rice. Dessert was hot chocolate, which I brought into my tent and sat sipping in my chair as the sun went down. I kept the rainfly open so I could watch the clouds morph into purple and orange mounds behind the bare trees. When the light show was over, a pack of coyotes started yelping off to the west, calling their den mates home. From somewhere down below me, a strangled bark sounded, and I thought of the feral dog I'd seen, not too far from here, just a couple weeks ago. I wondered how it was fitting in with its new family. But then a chill breeze wafted in, and I stopped musing to zip the rainfly against the cold.

I started solo backpacking in college, not too long after I joined the TRAILS outdoor program at George Washington University. TRAILS stands for Teaching Recreation and Adventure Incorporating Leadership and Service, and it was the link that led me to a career where I could combine my love of hiking with serving at-risk youth. But, although I enjoyed the camping that I did with the group, I got a bigger sense of accomplishment from slogging along the Appalachian Trail on my own and spending quiet evenings sipping coffee outside my tent as the sky dimmed. People always asked me if I was scared to be out there alone, to which I replied that getting off the subway at the Foggy Bottom-GWU metro station after dark was probably more dangerous and definitely scarier.

In a commercial smoker, you can smoke meat for as little as twelve hours, but since I'm unsure of how well I can regulate the temperature in the cave with this cool weather, I plan on getting an early start in the morning and possibly continuing through a good portion of the night. With my sketch pad, chair, and Kindle, I should pass the day comfortably enough, and I can sit in the tent or make another fire if it gets chilly. Everything in the tent is arranged the way I've always done it, my backpack behind my head, and my headlamp, Kindle, and water bottle within easy reach. The only difference is the gun on the tent floor beside my head. The coyotes have finished their concert for the night, and all is quiet except for a faint stirring of the wind.

November 30

I haven't written for several days and with good reason. I have had another accident, much worse than the incident with my eye. Four days ago, I rose at first light and started the smoking fires as planned. A light wind was blowing from the west, and after a couple hours, I decided that the cave wasn't staying quite hot enough. My solution was to take my nylon ground cloth and use it as a tarp to help keep the heat in the cave. I tied the corners to the saplings that I had laid over the brush wall. The ground cloth measures about five by seven feet, and by positioning it on the east end of the wall, I hoped that it would keep some of the smoke and heat from blowing out of the cave. This seemed to work pretty well. When I needed to enter the cave to tend the fires, I released the upper corners to cool it off while I worked.

The day passed pretty quickly. Save for a trip to the creek, I sketched, read, gathered wood, and tended the meat until well after dark. Finally, in what I judged were the wee hours of the morning, I stoked the fires one last time and headed for the tent.

I don't know what woke me, whether it was the roar of the wind or the crash as a strong gust lifted the ground cloth, saplings and all, and sent it careening like a flying raft off the ledge and toward the tent. I scrambled out just in time to see the jumble of nylon and wood hit the ground a few feet from where I stood, as almost simultaneously, the next gust blew out the rest of the brush wall and sent embers raining like fireworks down the slope.

There's no rational explanation for what I did next, whether I thought I was protecting the ground cloth or the forest or just following some instinct that wants a fire out. But as the coals landed around me, I tried to stomp them out, forgetting entirely that I was in my stocking feet, and then, within seconds, I realized that little embers were landing all over me and burning through my long johns, and I finally had the sense to hit the ground and roll away.

I writhed around for a minute or so on the damp earth under the leaves before I was pretty sure that all the sparks on my clothes were out, but I didn't realize that my socks were still burning; there were sticks and debris poking me all over, which disguised the searing pain in my feet. At that point, I sat up and shoved them under the leaves, piling more debris on top and pressing it all down hard as the full knowledge of what I'd done to myself set in.

Then I closed my eyes and rocked back and forth, chanting, "Oh God, oh God, oh God…" until I remembered that there was no one to help me but me. When I opened my eyes and looked back toward the tent, I could see that the rest of the embers were burning themselves out on the tarp and the rainfly. Occasionally, a fresh gust of wind sent a few more sparks flying, which extinguished themselves in mid-air or quickly burned out when they reached the ground.

How could this happen to me? I thought, though the answer was right in front of me. "Basic lack of foresight." That's what we counselors would say to each other with a knowing nod, when we were talking about someone else's screw-up. As though we'd never do something so stupid. Not us.

The burning sensation in my feet was so intense that I was afraid to stand, so I scooted backward the twenty feet or so to the tent on my heels, hands, and butt. I stopped with my rear in the tent and my legs sticking out and reached for my water bottle and flashlight. Pulling on the headlamp, I tried to brace myself for what I was going to see. The bottoms of both socks were burned through in different patterns, mostly along and inside my arches. Unfortunately, I was wearing two layers of socks, a nylon inner sock under a wool outer layer. From what I could see, the inner socks had melted rather than burning, and they were stuck to the burned skin underneath.

Burn treatment 101. Water, water, and more water. But all I had within reach was the bottle in my hand. In my Camelback bladder up in the cave there were about three liters more left from soaking the wood. I unscrewed the lid from the water bottle and doused both of my feet. I suspected that my arches must be burned pretty badly because the worst pain was coming from around the edges and also from along a swath of my inner right ankle and calf. The embers that burned into my long johns had also left little pinpricks of pain that I hardly noticed compared to my feet.

I sat there for another minute, dreading what had to be done and taking turns dribbling water back and forth on each foot, though I knew it wasn't nearly enough. The wind gusted now and again, streaming through my long johns so that by the time I had mustered enough nerve to tackle the first set of socks, I was starting to shiver. I started on the right, grasping the tops of both layers together and ripping downward as fast as I could.

"Ahhhh!" I screamed as the melted liner pulled away from the charred skin below. I dropped the socks, trying not to notice the debris attached, and tackled the left foot without pause.

"Argh!" The second set wasn't quite as bad, or maybe that pain just blended in with all the rest.

Sitting with my knees out to the sides and the bottoms of my feet just an inch or so apart, I drizzled the rest of the water over them, hoping that the cool air would compensate for the lack of volume. I cursed myself for not having more water at the tent, and I looked up the slope to the cave, wondering if there were any chance of my getting up there. I knew I should. My heels seemed to have been spared, so I could do it, I thought, if I scooted up backward like I'd gotten back to the tent. Or I could crawl into my tent, which had survived with a dozen or so burn holes in the rainfly, take a bunch of pain relievers and a couple Benadryl, and wait for morning.

I was shivering and losing heat from the burns and the holes in my clothes. But I couldn't unknow what I knew should be done, so I reached into the tent for my down jacket, slipped it on over my scorched shirt, and started scooting.

The rest of the night was one burst of pain after another. I scooted up to the cave with tears streaming down my face and poured most of the rest of the water over my feet, saving just a couple cups for the morning. I heaped ashes over the rest of the embers and hoped they'd stay put. By the time I dragged the bladder back to the tent, my heart was racing, I was shivering again, and I thought that I might be going into shock. Eventually, I knew, I would have to clean the burns and remove all the debris and dead tissue. But it was too soon for that. What I needed most at that point was to get warm and stay hydrated. So, I took double doses of ibuprofen and acetaminophen along with two

Benadryl, drank about ten big gulps of water, and wrapped myself in my sleeping bag. The weight of the bag was too much for the burns on my feet, so I let them stick out of the bottom, covered loosely with a spare shirt, and tried to breathe slow and deep. As I warmed, the Benadryl kicked in, and after a while, I dozed.

The next day was a blur of pain. The weather stayed cold and overcast, and I tried to sleep, dosing on pain meds and Benadryl and drinking water between bouts of tortured sleep. Every couple of hours, I woke to intense pain and a sense of doom that I could only remedy by rolling over and trying to just forget, forget, forget what a horrible predicament I'd brought upon myself.

Finally, in the late afternoon, I woke feeling more lucid and having to pee. I rose to my knees, pulled down my long johns, and managed to pee into the wide-mouthed water bottle I'd emptied the night before. Then I reached for the water bladder and was dismayed to find that I was down to a few swallows. I collapsed back onto my sleeping bag, aware that the pain was as bad as ever, and that I didn't even want to look and see how badly I was screwed. I knew that the places I could feel were probably deep second-degree burns that would blister and weep and hurt for days or even weeks. They'd have to be cleaned out once a day, and the process would be excruciating. On top of that, they'd probably get infected, and then I'd be in deep shit. The insides of my arches were burnt too, and that was what really scared me because they didn't hurt as much, which meant they were burned more deeply, maybe through all the layers of skin.

What happens if you have third-degree burns and you can't get a skin graft, I wondered.

In spite of myself, I dozed again, but when I woke this time, it was as though I'd heard a voice, insistent, right at my ear hissing, *Water. You need to get water. You have to. Get up. Now!*

I sat up, startled fully awake. It was Peter's voice but with a tone he'd never used with me before. *But it hurts*, I wanted to tell him. *Can't I just sleep until the pain goes away?*

But he didn't answer. Because he knew I already knew what he'd say.

Deciding that I needed to get to the creek was one thing, but figuring out how was a whole other story, and I wished Peter had had the grace to stick around and talk me through it. But he was gone again, and I was on my own. I couldn't walk, so I'd have to crawl or scoot over the downed trees and rocks, around the bushes, and across uneven terrain with hidden sticks and stones. The more I thought about it, the more it seemed it could take forever. And how would I protect my feet along the way?

It took over an hour to come up with some sort of plan and execute it, just to get ready to leave. Though it may have been futile at that point, I took a tube of antibiotic ointment and squeezed it onto the bottoms of my feet. To do this, I had to look at them and see the bulging blisters and the charred centers of my arches, and I cried and bit my lower lip and just tried to focus and do the next thing, which was to cut an ace bandage in half and wrap each foot, the most excruciating thing I have ever done to myself. By the time I was finished, the pain was almost unbearable, and I had to lie back and catch my breath, all the while telling myself that I didn't have any choice, and I had to keep going. I pulled my pants on over my long johns, which required putting my feet through the pant legs, another excruciating process. Then I cut the garbage bags I'd been using for the meat and wrapped both feet in plastic, securing them by wrapping adhesive tape around the top of the plastic and my pant legs. I didn't think that I could make it to the creek and back all at once, so I put my sleeping bag and the burned tarp into my backpack, along with the water bladder, the Jetboil, some hot chocolate and soup mix, and the meds, thinking I could roll up in the tarp and stay the night. My food was still hanging in the tree down the hill, but I thought that the soup and chocolate would tide me over until I made it back, not that I had any appetite anyway.

Dusk had settled over the mountain by the time I buckled the backpack over my hips and pulled on my gloves. I crawled along gingerly into the beam of my headlamp, wincing, not just from the burns, but from debris that hid under the leaves and bit into my knees. At first, I tried to keep my feet up, but that just seemed to make the pain worse, so I let them trail lightly along the ground. To distract myself, I tried to recall all the stories I'd ever heard or read about people who survived horrible accidents in the wild against crazy odds, like a guy who fell into a crevasse while ice climbing and was given up for dead by his partner, but who managed to climb out with a broken leg and crawled for two days to make it back to camp. A teenage girl who walked for days out of a South American rain forest when the plane she was in crashed. Or the hiker who cut off his own arm after it was pinned under a boulder. In all of the stories there was one common thread, a person who doggedly did what needed to be done in the moment, even though things seemed hopeless. You can be that person, I told myself.

November 30, continued

I made it to the stream and then back to the tent the next morning. At that point I had plenty of water but only another day's worth of pain killers. On top of that, I knew it was time to debride my burns and see what was actually left of my feet, a task which would require anti-bacterial soap and plenty of sterile water, not to mention sterile gauze and antibiotic ointment. After a short rest, I decided which supplies I could realistically haul back to the cabin. Retrieving my food bag was the most painful because I had to use my heels to raise myself to a near-standing position with my butt against the tree trunk in order to reach the rope. I debated just leaving the smoked venison, which had miraculously gone unmolested overnight. But I couldn't bear to waste it all, so I scooted up and pulled off about five pounds of meat strips and stuffed them, unwrapped, into my food bag.

As I sat at the edge of the cave with my legs splayed in front of me, sliding meat along the rope, a movement in the brush below the cave caught my eye. *This would be a hell of a time for a bear to show up,* I thought, but what I saw next was a black nose on the end of a sharp, tawny snout and two pointed ears that I immediately recognized as belonging to the dog I'd seen feasting with the coyote pups. Without a trace of fear, she trotted out of the bushes and sat down quietly just a stone's throw away, staring straight at me.

There was nothing threatening or even feral in the way she sat. If anything, she seemed to be saying that the whole wild act was just for survival, and she wouldn't mind being friendly if I would just share a bit of my meat.

My first thought was to ignore her. I'd be leaving quite a bit of meat, anyway, which she and her new family could gorge on all evening. But my second thought was that perhaps it wouldn't hurt to have just one creature in the woods that thought of me fondly, so I took the next chunk of meat and flung it in her direction. It thudded about ten feet in front of her, and, to my amazement, instead of pouncing on it immediately, she sat for a few moments, still watching me, before she rose and approached the food, grasped it matter-of-factly in her teeth, and turned to trot off. Her demeanor was so deliberate that it left me with the distinct feeling that she somehow knew all along that I was going to share, and all she had to do was to wait patiently for me to fulfill my role.

"Hummph," I said as I closed up the food bag.

I took two bladders full of water and left the tent. The last thing I did before starting my long crawl was to cut the burned tarp into strips and wrap them around my knees, which were already bruised and sore from the crawl to the stream.

A walk that I could normally do in an hour took about four on my hands and knees, feeling my way along and resting when the pain got bad. On the steep downhill slopes, I scooted feet first, though I'd occasionally bang the bottoms of my feet on rocks and branches, which produced excruciating pain and a fair amount of cursing. When the hut finally came into view, I cried again, from the relief of being back to a place that felt solid and safe. But before I let myself go in, I kneeled at the end of my woodpile and threw wood toward the door until I thought I had enough to last at least two or three days. All I remember after that was crawling in, starting a fire, and collapsing on my sleeping bag in front of the woodstove.

December 1

When I awoke the day before yesterday, I was so weak I could barely rise to my knees to use the potty bucket. I hadn't eaten since before the fire except for a single mug of hot chocolate that I drank at the stream. After a while, I pulled the last of the pain meds from my backpack, which was still lying beside me on the floor, and took them with a few long pulls of water from the bladder. There were so many things I knew I should be doing: eating, boiling water for the debriding process, locating more pain meds, antibiotics, and salve. But a mantle of pain still dulled my mind, and I wished I could lose myself in a deep sleep until I could wake up feeling like myself again. *But that will never happen if you don't get moving,* I told myself. As a compromise, I reached into the food bag for some of the smoked meat and lay there, chewing with slow deliberation until I'd downed several bites.

I eventually crawled out from under the sleeping bag and threw some more wood into the woodstove, opening all of the vents to get it going hot. After that, every task was a logistical challenge. From my knees, I pulled a camp chair near to the stove, hoisted myself into it using my arms and heels, and from there managed to empty the rest of the water from one bladder into two pots on the stovetop. Then I was back on the floor, crawling and scooting to gather a clean towel and all the other supplies I would need to operate. The scariest challenge was getting the pot of water off of the woodstove after it began to boil. I could reach with a potholder from a kneeling position, but I didn't feel at all steady as I lowered the pan and dumped it into the Dutch oven, the only container besides the potty bucket that was large enough to stick a foot in.

While the water cooled, I hoisted myself back into the chair, rolled up my pant legs, and started to unwrap my left foot, which I thought was the least severely burned. The last few layers of bandage were stuck together with the fluid that had seeped from the wounds, and I started to tug at it with the idea that I could somehow salvage the bandage, but that set off a wave of pain that was so intense that I had to take a break. After a few minutes, I cut the bandage down the front of my foot and braced myself to pull it off but decided at the last minute to wait until the water was cool. That way, after I pulled off the bandage, I could stick my foot right into the water and maybe that would reduce the pain. It was worth a try, I thought.

So that's what I did, gritting my teeth and letting out a loud groan as I wrenched the fabric from my foot and stuck it into the water. I don't know whether the trick really worked or just had some kind of placebo effect, but within a couple minutes I could release my iron grip on the chair arms and calm myself with more deep breathing. I'd squirted antibacterial soap into the water, and I thought that maybe all the dead skin would turn white and maybe slough off a little and I'd have less rubbing and cutting to do.

I gave the foot a good fifteen minutes or so to soak and munched on some granola from my food bag in the meantime. From above, I could see that the outer edge of my foot was swollen and a little red; this was the part that was barely burned at all but was probably swelling from the burns underneath. I could feel the water on most of the bottom, save for a couple areas of my inner arch, so I was encouraged that I might only have some deep second-degree burns, which were painful and would scar, but would probably heal over. When I laid my ankle over my knee, I saw that this seemed to be true except for a dime-sized section just under the ball of my big toe. What I basically saw there was a blackish hole, and I couldn't see how deep it really went. All the other burned areas were deep red and weeping except for a blister about as long as my thumb and a few smaller ones nearer the outer edge. Using scissors, I cut off everything that seemed to be dead and hanging. Then I took a large syringe and squirted the whole area with sterile water as forcefully as I could. This brought tears to my eyes, but wasn't nearly as bad as pulling off the bandage. I probably should have been more aggressive, but I really couldn't bring myself to actually rub at the wounds the way I knew I should. Finally, I squeezed on some antibiotic ointment and laid on some large gauze pads, bandaging the area moist-to-dry, the way they'd always taught us in the WFR training.

The right foot went about the same except that I got brave enough to look at it before it went into the water and saw that the kidney-shaped blackened area on it was about the size of two silver dollars, making me wonder again exactly how it would heal without a skin graft. "Evacuate all patients with a third-degree burn," the line from my first aid book taunted me again. *If only,* I thought. *If only.*

I rested again after the trauma of cleaning and bandaging my feet and then set about rearranging things so that I could reach what I needed without getting up. First, I pulled my sleep pad, heavy sleeping bag, and pillow onto the floor in front of the woodstove. Then I rigged up my camping chair with my inflatable sleep pad so I'd have a chair close to the ground. Everything else—food, water, meds, this notebook, and my Kindle—I set within easy reach of the bedding and chair.

My last chore was to get out of my dirty, stinking clothes. The jeans were a muddy mess, and I'd worn holes in both knees on the trip to the creek and back. Underneath, my long john bottoms were pocked with scorch marks, and the mud and dirt that had come through my jeans had made holes in those knees, too. If it were only a matter of going online to replace them, I would have tossed them both, but as long as there was a way they might be patched, I had to save them. I'd left the holey long john top in the tent and put on my spare shirt before starting back, but it smelled like it had been forgotten in someone's gym locker for a week or two. I wadded them all up together and pushed them under the bed platform to deal with at some yet-to-be-imagined time.

At that point, the pain had subsided to a constant searing ache that seemed to pulsate around the bottoms of my feet. It was always there, but could almost be forgotten for a few seconds at a time. Any sudden movement or pressure, though, whipped it into a frenzy that brought me to tears. But if I stayed mostly still with my feet slightly elevated, the pain was just bearable. My biggest worries were infection and the depth of the burns on my right foot. I'd started oral antibiotics, but I wasn't sure they'd do the trick like the intravenous antibiotics that burn patients receive in the hospital. I settled into my chair with my heels propped on my pillow and tried to relax. Like the song said, what would be, would be.

December 2

I've been home for almost three whole days, and except for a couple trips to the creek for more water, I've spent the time tending my feet, writing, and sleeping. I dug a potty hole near my water path so I can use it on my way to the creek. I must look odd, setting the bucket a couple feet in front of me, crawling up to it, and then setting it out in front again. After I empty it, I leave it by the hole while I go for water and pick it up on my way back. Even with two Camelbacks and a couple water bottles, I use so much water cleaning the burns that this will be an every-other-day ordeal for the foreseeable future. At least it tires me out so that I can sleep, which I do for a couple hours at a time all day long. Those hours are my only real reprieve from the pain, and yet they are not peaceful hours, since I am dogged by feverish dreams in which Peter appears to reproach me for my carelessness.

Today I tried to lower the amount of pain medication I'm taking. I'd been downing almost twice the usual doses of both acetaminophen and ibuprofen, a combination that the WFR training claims is almost as good as opioids. But by midday, the pain seemed to be worse, and I felt a little feverish, so I reverted to the higher dose. In a day or two, I'll try again. I have a good supply, but if I start to run out, I'll have to make a trip to the cabin. I thought about doing some exercises with my toes and rotating my ankles to help my feet retain their range of motion as they heal. But then I thought that I might inadvertently open up the wounds and invite more infection, so I decided against it. It's hard to know what to do when even your wilderness first aid manual assumes that you can get to a doctor eventually. The deep burns on my right foot look about the same except that the charred parts are coming off bit by bit. Underneath is raw flesh that I don't know what to do with. So, I just continue my routine of wash, irrigate, medicate, and wrap, hoping for the best.

December 3

Today I will talk about something, anything, other than my burns, which infuriate me to no end because the pain still prevents me from ever being totally comfortable, and I am getting impatient with this whole God-awfully slow process and not knowing how it will all turn out.

Early this morning, I dreamt about Peter again. In the beginning, we were in a four-poster bed in a fancy hotel with old-fashioned, brocaded curtains and red velvet-covered furniture. I can't say that it was like The Greenbrier or The Homestead, two of the fancier historic hotels near the Virginia-West Virginia line, since I have never been to either, but it was like I've always pictured them—places where you can imagine that you are living in a different, more genteel time. We were there for a special occasion, maybe an anniversary, and I was crouched on top of him, my crotch nuzzling his limp penis, tummy to tummy and breasts to chest, and we were drowsing the way we often did after sex. One of my hands rested on his chest, and he smelled the way he smelled before the cancer, and the world was the way it always should be.

Then the scene changed, and Peter lay in a hospital bed in an otherwise empty room, with a single, tall window opposite the bed. It was early evening, and the light coming through the window was gloomy and gray. I tried to snuggle in beside him on my side, but it hurt for me to touch him, so he edged away from me with a little smile, and just offered me his left hand, which I sandwiched with my own between my thighs. He opened his mouth to say something, but a voice in my head interrupted and said, "That's not Peter. Peter is dead."

The dream reminded me of the voice that I heard up in the woods when I ran out of water. I don't believe in God, and I don't believe in an afterlife either, so I have no explanation for why I sometimes feel Peter's presence so strongly. Perhaps it's wishful thinking or delusion, but I want to think that it's something more, something almost physical about the connection between us that was so strong that it will take a long time to dissipate. I don't know; I'm sure this sounds a little crazy, and I guess it doesn't really matter. But if Peter could do anything to help me, I know he would.

December 3, p.m.

This morning I put down my writing to tend to my toilet bucket, and when I dragged it outside the frost was already dripping off of the leaves of the rhododendrons, so I decided to get my water run out of the way. I've been dismayed at how much my injuries have increased my water usage—water to cool, water to drink, water to soak my feet, water to sterilize bandages. I can't reuse the gauze, so now I am cutting up Peter's old T-shirts. I rinse them at the creek, and by the time I'm done, my hands are red and numb, and I'm ready for the sweaty, uphill climb. The weight of the water alone is over twenty pounds, and I imagine that I must look like some unnatural creature as I scoot myself backward up the slope, resting and cursing occasionally along the way.

Today, as I reached the top of the slope, I hit my left foot on a stick that poked into the space between my sandal and foot. For a minute or two, it was as though someone had held a match to my burn, throwing the nerves into a wild frenzy. I was thankful that my foot was so thickly bandaged or I would have thrust it into the cool earth (and all of its resident germs) for relief. As it was, I just sat and fumed at how hard this whole survival thing was becoming, which was dangerous territory, and I knew it.

When I got over my tantrum, I continued my crawl, soon coming over a slight rise and in view of the hut. Even in my current condition, I paused to look around, but I am so used to seeing nothing amiss, it took me a few seconds to register the presence of a visitor. Sitting between the roots of a large tulip poplar about thirty feet from my thicket was my pointy-eared friend, staring straight at me as though to say, "It's about time you showed up."

"Humph," I said, quite loudly. "If you're looking for another handout, forget it. I need everything I've got."

She stood and wagged her tail before trotting off.

I suppose it isn't so surprising that this dog is initiating contact. Someone must have cared for it before the blackout, and after all, I did feed her. I remember reading somewhere that anthropologists now believe that dogs made the first overtures in the human-canid relationship, sensing that by making eye contact and ingratiating themselves, they could get a few extra meals and maybe even decrease the likelihood of their becoming dinner. Yet, the experience has left me with an irrational sense of being chosen. Looking at it objectively, she (I think I'll call her Daisy) has shown that she can survive independently of humans, so I'm at no real disadvantage in becoming closer. And if she provides a little distraction to my days, why not?

December 4

I woke early this morning to the slap of branches on the west window and a draft swirling across the floor. The weather warmed so much yesterday that I left two of the vents slightly open and forgot to shut them when I loaded the stove for the night. After crawling around to close them, I went to the door and opened it a crack. A frigid blast pushed in, and I saw that a trace of snow had settled against the door, which convinced me to spend the day inside and make my water last for another day.

I've started a project to help me while away the hours, a story map of sorts depicting my life since the blackout. Like this journal, I believe that it may help me step back from my experience and render it more objectively than I can manage through words. It will be a multi-paneled work, perhaps using nine or more pages from my sketchbook, so that each important place can be drawn at a decent scale. This morning I started with the cabin and was soon stymied by the question of which view to draw, as seen from the driveway or from the back. I finally decided that there was no reason not to include both, but I started from the rear, being eager, for some reason, to draw the porch roof with the ladder, lying at a slant awaiting my escape, and the broken window in the door.

A number of my students at the wilderness school and a few of our friends suffered from PTSD, so I am well enough versed in the particulars to realize that I may be experiencing it in some mild form, and that this journal and my drawings may be attempts to integrate the loss of Peter and the world I knew into the world that I must face today. I don't know whether there is value in recognizing this or not. I mostly feel that I am grabbing at straws to find a way to move forward. But if that is so, so be it.

It's a little ironic that if I had been immune to mistakes caused by the "basic lack of foresight" mentioned earlier, Peter and I would never have met. It was April, and I'd been working for the wilderness school for almost a year and still lived in the apartment in Georgetown that I'd rented since the beginning of grad school. It looked out over a yard with lots of trees and birdfeeders, and I enjoyed the views from the big windows so much, I didn't bother to move when I graduated, though I could have afforded something bigger. I was near the end of a break, and the weather had been warm, so I decided to head to Rock Creek Park for a run. A cold front was predicted to move in after lunch, and with it scattered showers, but when I hopped on the subway in running shorts and a nylon shirt, I expected to be home before the weather turned.

About a mile into my run, just as I passed the tennis courts, clouds overtook the sky, and the wind picked up. But I chose to run on because I'd hit my stride and was moving so effortlessly. Another half mile and the first tiny drops dampened the sidewalk, so I gave it up and turned around at Dumbarton Oaks. But a few moments later the clouds opened, and I was running in a full, driving rain, with the temperature dropping fast.

By the time I got to the street, I was just about shaking with cold. I could have ducked straight into the subway, but there was a Panera at the intersection, and I thought I might warm up with some soup before heading home. I ducked in, thinking I'd head straight for the ladies' room to dry my face and squeeze some water from my ponytail before ordering. When I stepped through the door, I glanced around to see if the fireplace was on and saw him. He was sitting in a booth along the wall opposite another man, cradling a hot drink. His hair was a shade redder than my own, with a cowlick that stood up in the front and a two-day beard that drew my attention to his square jaw. As I moved toward the restroom, he looked up, his gaze so direct that I blushed and looked quickly away.

I exited the ladies' room trailing a bit less water, ordered the black bean soup, and chose a seat with my back to the gas logs. Although I could just see him out of the corner of my eye, I gazed toward the window and ate my soup as though engrossed in the streams of people heading in and out of the subway tunnel, clasping various items over their heads to deflect the rain. I like to think that I had forgotten he was even there when he stood up, grabbed his jacket in one hand, and approached my table. He was wearing jeans and a gray, cargo-style shirt that made his eyes some indeterminate color between slate and deep blue.

"May I join you for a minute?" he asked.

I looked up and nodded, and he placed his jacket over the back of the opposite chair and sat down, crossing his legs straight out in front of him and looking back and forth between me and the rainy street.

"I'm Peter Scott."

"Aurora Mills," I said, using my middle name instead of my last, which is what I often did when approached by strangers.

"The weather changed pretty fast out there. I see you got caught out."

"I got a couple miles in, so it wasn't a total loss." I let myself smile a little.

"Hypothermia can set in fast if you're not prepared, though."

He sounded concerned but his remark teetered too close to condescension for me not to react.

"I lead backpack trips for a living. But thanks for the heads-up."

"Oh, sorry." He frowned. "That didn't come out right. I really was just wondering…I don't know how far you have to go, but I'd be happy to loan you my rain jacket."

His tone was so boyish and humble that I had to hold back a laugh.

"Really, that's very kind, but I work out of town a lot, and I have no idea when I could get it back to you. I'm sure I'll be fine."

It occurred to me then that he might just get up and walk away, and I didn't want that, so I asked with a smile, "Do you go around offering your coat to every damsel in distress?"

"No, no, of course not!" He blushed, and I had to admit, the effect was pretty cute. "I just noticed how cold you looked when you walked in. And also how you looked around before you went to the ladies' room."

"How I looked around?"

"Yeah. Most people don't, you know. Listen, how about this? I'll give you my phone number, and if you want to call me when you get back in town, we can arrange for you to return the jacket. If you don't want to, just keep it."

He pulled a pen and a receipt from his breast pocket and scrawled his number on the back. Then he slid the paper across the table and stood.

"Are you sure?" I asked. "That's a really nice jacket." It had a soft outer shell and an Eddie Bauer insignia near the collar, and it looked brand new.

"You just look like an interesting person. And I don't want you to be cold," he said as he turned for the door.

As soon as he was out of sight, I grabbed the jacket and pulled it on because I was still chilled. It smelled like pine needles.

After I got home, I ran a hot bath and thought about his eyes and how it seemed that they didn't miss anything and weren't afraid of what they saw. Later, I called the number on the receipt and arranged to meet for lunch the next day. When I hung up, I turned the paper over to see what he had bought. The receipt was from the Eddie Bauer down the block from the sandwich shop. I guess he'd been surprised by the rain, too.

When Peter appeared in my life, I wasn't looking for a relationship. Most of the men I had dated were either looking for a sex kitten who liked to party or a companion who could be there for them every day. I didn't fit into either category, nor did I want to. Somehow, Peter seemed genuinely interested in knowing who I was and always seemed thankful just to be a part of my life. I even wondered for a while whether he was just faking it, and I was being played. But there were no warning signs, and through humility and constancy, he won my trust, and I had to admit that life was much better with him than without. Then I worried about becoming dependent and therefore, weak. But since he had to go to work when I was on break, I still had space for solitary hikes and the occasional overnighter. We married a year later.

December 6

The wind that started when I last wrote continued into mid-day yesterday, driving showers of snow that battered the trees and lay a scant coating over the forest floor. I finally ventured out in the afternoon to do my chores, freezing my hands on the crawl to and from the creek, the sun a weak disc behind thin clouds. The rest of the day I spent drawing, laying out an overall plan on one sheet and gridding it into nine rectangles which will each make up a single panel in the finished map. Then I started on the section where I first saw Daisy tearing into the deer carcass with her coyote brothers and sisters. Drawing the coyotes posed quite a challenge, and I used up two pages in my sketchbook before I got them nearly right. Violence in nature is necessary, but it is hard to depict without inserting human values. The pups and Daisy were cuddly characters performing a task that would seem to most people vicious and cruel. My goal was to portray them without interpretation: as animals who merely needed to eat. Perhaps that is why I enjoyed drawing the coyote mother the most, sitting pridefully by as the youngsters gorged.

The pain in my feet has lessened, so I have been a little more aggressive with my scrubbing efforts. The left foot appears to be healing and the skin underneath is toughening, save for the area around the deeper burn in the middle. Even that area seems to be shrinking, though, so I am optimistic that the left foot will recover totally. The right foot, however, is another matter. Since the first and second degree burns cover so much more territory on that foot, the new skin has been tightening as it heals and occasionally cracking open, with each occurrence creating an opportunity for infection. In addition, I'm not seeing much change in the deep burn area just below the balls of the toes. Every day after the soaking, I dab at the hole with antiseptic soap and water and trim off any dead skin. But the hole looks as big and deep today as it did on the day after the burn. Soon I'll finish the second bottle of antibiotics, but I need them for a long while yet. There are more stashed at the cabin, which means I'll have to make the trip before I can properly walk. It would make sense to stay there where I would have running water, better bandages, and more food. But I'm stalled by the knowledge that Ray and his goons are most certainly keeping an eye on the place.

If I did go back and Ray and company returned, I could try to scare them off, but I'd certainly be outnumbered. What chance would I have if attacked from more than one direction? I could barricade myself upstairs, but Ray and his gang could just wait me out. I've even thought of hiding in the cellar, nailing the trap door shut, and going in and out through one of the windows. But do I really want to live like that? And what would happen if someone moved in above me? Then again, maybe Ray and Thomas have settled their score, and Ray has lost interest in the place. Really, unless he knows I have more supplies, why would he want to fool with me? But I have no way of knowing, and all of my conjectures are just my mind chasing its tail. What I do know, though, is that in a week or so, I will have to make the trip.

December 7

This morning I woke in a dark place, and I wonder whether looking back may be doing me more harm than good. Thinking about the cabin and what I've given up there has made me feel trapped in a way I didn't before. I know that I should be thankful for having food and shelter while others are suffering far more than I. But today reality has come seeping in, and I think of my mother and Aunt JoAnn, most likely dead. Linda and the baby—hungry, cold, or also dead. In all likelihood, I will never see anyone that I knew before the blackout again.

I stayed in my sleeping bag most of the morning, crawling out just to pee and throw some wood into the stove. In the afternoon, I forced myself to go for water, but I did not soak my feet or change the bandages when I returned. I do not even have the energy to be angry, but I am achingly tired, and I feel that my life now is mostly pretending. Pretending that I will be okay, pretending that I am strong enough to do this, pretending that I have a reason to go on. I wonder how long it would take to die of sepsis if I stop taking care of my burns. There will be some pain, a high fever, and I'll eventually become disoriented. I won't know where I am or how I got here. And then I will lose consciousness altogether. Not a bad way to go, comparatively speaking.

Somewhere in the far reaches of my mind, I can still hear Peter urging me on, but his voice has become as thin as a wisp of smoke in the distance.

December 8

Last night I rolled and tossed in my sleeping bag, torturing myself with memories of Peter and the world that I hadn't realized I loved so much until it was gone. After a few hours, I reached for the Benadryl bottle and downed three, an all-time high. Soon, I passed into a deep, coma-like sleep. I woke groggy as the sun stormed the eastern window. In my depressive stupor, I had neglected to close the blackout curtains behind the bed. After peeing and stoking the stove, I squirmed back into my sleeping bag and sat up against the foot of the bed platform to think about what to do with myself and the day.

First, I tried to decide what to eat, but there was nothing that I wanted enough to be worth the effort, so instead I sat and made a mental list of all of the things I knew I should be doing: Number 1, eat and stay hydrated; Number 2, take care of the burns; Number 3, stay warm. The devil was in the details, though. Eating and staying hydrated required constant trips to the stream, and, as my food ran low, a trip to the cabin or at least to the meat that I had buried. Taking care of the burns required more water and thus more frequent water trips and would also soon necessitate a trip to the cabin for antibiotics and salve. Staying warm required using up wood that was now difficult to replace due to my injuries. The woodstove needed a good cleaning, too, as ashes were beginning to spill out whenever I opened the door.

After all of this analysis, I still sat, knowing that my main problem was not what to do but why. Which brought me to item Number 4: find a reason to do all of the above. I leaned my head back on the sleeping platform, closed my eyes, and thought about Peter. Peter pouring water into the French press in our kitchen in Arlington. Peter, covered in grime as he rolled himself out from under the truck in the garage. Peter toweling himself off after a dip in the little pool here at the creek with that playful smile that I found so enticing. The last time we'd been at the hut together was two years ago and just a few weeks before his diagnosis, when he'd hauled up the thick sleep pads for the bed. He had insisted on making two trips himself, one with each pad, while I carried the food and a few other supplies for the weekend. We'd put his nagging back aches down to two years of home improvements; it was the increasingly painful stomach aches that finally sent us to the doctor, and that only after he'd already lost ten pounds that he didn't have to spare.

Even if his voice had stopped whispering in my ear to urge me on, I still knew what he would say to me if he could. I'd tried so hard not to disappoint him, but I felt like I'd hit a wall, and there was nothing his memory could do to make my survival seem worthwhile. I thought while I sat there that perhaps it was my burned feet that had brought on this sense of hopelessness. If I could just go for a hike, take my sketchbook up to the lookout, or set some snares, I might regain some of the inner strength that I used to think I had. But there I was, once again, unable to follow the advice that I'd doled out for years to the girls in my charge.

As the wood in the stove began to blaze, the hut warmed quickly, and my feet began to sweat and itch under their layers of bandages. Physical discomfort is perhaps the greatest motivator, and it wasn't long before I found myself dumping water into the pot on the stove and unwrapping my feet. As I went through the motions of soaking, cleaning, and bandaging, a feeling of resignation swept through me. It reminded me of the sensation I'd felt when I had my gall bladder removed in high school, as the anesthesia hit my bloodstream, and a wave of numbness spread over me. In that moment it no longer mattered whether I was strong or weak, or whether I disappointed Peter or even myself. Whatever standards I'd been holding for myself were disintegrating around me, and I realized that how I felt about any of it was of absolutely no importance. I thought back to my list of "shoulds," and all the judgements they implied, and I decided that I was done with that word. Henceforth, I would do exactly what I felt like doing. I would drink when I was thirsty, eat when I was hungry, and do only what I really felt like doing. Maybe I'd be dead in a week and maybe my life would be nearly the same. But everything I'd do, I'd do for me. And only if I really wanted to.

As though to thumb my nose at fate, for breakfast I cooked up a double batch of oatmeal, sprinkling it liberally with dried cranberries and pairing it with a large mug of cocoa. When I was done washing out my bowl, I prepared to take the toilet bucket out, but instead of donning my rain pants and wrapping my knees, I rummaged under the sleep platform until I found the box with Peter's rain boots. His feet were only a couple sizes larger than mine, so I had to strip down the layers of bandage a bit to squeeze my feet in. This produced some stinging and pressure, but nothing unbearable. I'd been putting this off because trying to walk too soon could open the wounds and increase my chances for infection. Next, I hoisted myself backward onto the bed, pushing a little with my heels. So far, so good. I sat on the edge for a moment or two, stalled with anticipation, and then slowly transferred my weight to the outsides of my feet and heels. The stinging reminded me of that "little pinch" the dentist describes as he pushes the Novocaine needle into your gums. My legs were unsteady as they took my full weight, but there I was, standing for the first time in two weeks. I hobbled back and forth across the open space in front of the woodstove until I started to get the hang of this new way of distributing my weight before I picked up the potty bucket with its lid tightly attached and launched myself out the door.

When I returned from my potty dump, I felt almost manic in comparison to my recent mood. Although I knew that this, too, would pass, I decided to make the most of it and replenish my water supply. Of course, I wasn't so deluded that I thought I could walk down and up the steep slope from the creek, but just the idea that I could walk any of it was world changing. Once I had all the containers in my backpack and my knees wrapped, I got down the hiking poles that Peter left hanging from a nail on the wall and adjusted them for my height. I'd always despised the things, choosing to have all of my weight over my feet, but now I was glad that he had insisted on bringing them. Walking on my heels and the outsides of my feet, and letting the poles take some of the weight, I made it more than halfway down the hill before I felt a kind of tearing sensation in my right foot and sat down to scoot the rest of the way.

By the time I got back to the hut, my feet were buzzing with a kind of staticky pain, similar to the pins and needles effect when your foot falls asleep, only a bit worse. I downed my antibiotics and some ibuprofen but did not unwrap the bandages. Instead, I rummaged through the books and games until I found an old literature anthology and spent most of the rest of the day propped up in bed, rereading short stories and deciphering poems that I hadn't looked at for years.

December 10

My improved energy carried over to today, and since the weather was mild when I emerged with my potty bucket, I decided to try my endurance by digging up some of the buried meat. If I'd done a decent job with my smoking,

I thought that now that the weather had cooled, some of it would keep in plastic containers under the floorboards. It would become much harder to retrieve if the ground froze, so I planned to bring back several pounds. The nearest burial site was about a half mile away, in the general direction of the viewpoint, and the terrain was not too steep, so I anticipated being able to walk most of it.

I started out in a knit cap, sunglasses, and gloves, but I soon was stripping off the hat and gloves and unzipping my down coat. The balancing required by my new gait had me sweating, and the temperature was well above freezing. Within a few minutes I tripped and landed on my hands and knees in the damp leaves, but it was a slow fall. I resolved to take it more slowly as I rolled onto my butt and struggled up. Even so, it wasn't long before I stood in the clearing, matching my map to the landmarks around me.

The first site was between the roots of an oak on the southern end of the clearing. I took the trowel from my pack, laid the pack on the ground, and sat on it with my legs splayed as I stabbed at the earth with the trowel. Soon the green edge of the nylon tarp appeared, and within a few minutes I lifted the package from the hole. It had survived the months totally intact, and when I unwrapped it, the meat inside, about three pounds, looked clean. I rewrapped it and crawled to the next site, dragging my pack and hiking poles along the ground.

The second site was near the base of a downed poplar sapling. I wasn't sure exactly how close to the root ball I'd dug, so it took some time before I hit an edge of the second package, a little farther out from the tree than I remembered. By then I'd dug a trench about two feet long, fifteen inches wide, and eight inches deep, and I was exhausted. Again, I unwrapped the layers of tarp to find the meat as pristine as the day I'd set it in the ground. This was meat from the wild pig, and I decided to try some before I headed back.

I tore an edge off of one of the jerky-like strips and smelled it. It smelled smoky and greasy but not like any particular type of meat, which made me think of the "mystery meat" we used to get in our soup in my grade school cafeteria. I pushed that image from my head, popped a bite in my mouth, and was happy to find that it tasted better than it smelled and was slightly reminiscent of sausage, though it could have used more salt.

I was sitting against the tree trunk, chewing and noticing how the tree shadows striped the ground even though the clouds seemed to be thickening to the west, when I heard a rustle in the brush. I stopped chewing and stared toward the sound, which was gentle and low, not big enough for a bear or anything of great size. As always, I had the pistol strapped inside my jacket, so I reached in and pulled it out, just to be on the safe side, and I pulled back the hammer and levelled it at the sound. But by the time I'd armed myself, I recognized the skinny muzzle and pointed ears that appeared out of the brush about twenty feet from where I sat.

"Daisy," I said.

She met my eyes, sat down, and waited as though directed, mouth open, panting lightly.

I released the hammer of the gun and slid it back into its holster.

"Looking for a snack, are you?" I asked, and I saw her tail wave back and forth behind her. "And what exactly can you give me in return?"

At that she stood and wagged more profusely, as though to assure me that she would be friendly and forever grateful if I'd just hand over some jerky.

"Well, you'll have to come and get it," I told her as I pulled a little chunk from the strip in my hands and held it out.

Though her backside trembled with excitement, she approached cautiously and sat when she came within reach of my hand.

"Okay," I said, and she reached her for the meat and gently pulled it from my hand. "Good girl. Someone really trained you well."

I raised my hand slowly toward her head and she lifted her nose to sniff it before letting me stroke her. She sat quietly as I rubbed her behind the ears and never broke eye contact. Then I tore off another chunk of meat, which she took with the same gentle restraint. Drawing the line at three bites, I rewrapped the meat, shoving it and the trowel into my backpack and preparing to hoist myself off the ground.

"You can do as you please," I said, "but it's time for me to go home."

Now perched on the fallen trunk, I shrugged into the pack and picked up the hiking poles. When I stumbled off through the woods, I didn't look back.

Back at the hut I wanted to start a stew with some of the pork, but the Dutch oven was also my soaking pot, so I decided to take care of my feet first, wash the pot, and then start my stew. I was dismayed to find that the layers of bandage closest to my foot were moist and sticky. I wasn't surprised, though. I'd reconciled myself to that possibility when I started walking. If my feet got infected, so be it. At least I'd have a bit of freedom on my way out. After bandaging my feet, I washed the Dutch oven carefully, even using a splash of bleach, before I started my stew. By then it was mid-afternoon, and I was exhausted, so I put off washing the bandages in the smaller pot and crawled into bed for a nap. I'd stoked the fire, and the hut was hot, so I stretched out with just a light sheet over me and fell into a sound sleep.

December 11

Sometime during the night it began to snow. When I pulled back the curtain on the west-facing windows, swoops of white had softened the corners and large white flakes swirled among the trees and lined the branches of the rhododendrons. I shoved my feet into Peter's crocs and went out for wood, dragging a day's supply to the door on a tarp, which slid easily over two inches or so of wet snow.

Back in Arlington, those rare snowy weekends when Peter and I were both home were occasions for decadence, which for us meant a festival of carbs. Peter would whip up some pancake variation, full of nuts or cranberries or blueberries, and we'd slather them with real maple syrup, all the while sipping mimosas and pressed coffee. We'd eat at a table in front of the French doors in the bedroom so we could watch the snow settling on the balcony and the railing and the yard below. Later we'd walk the neighborhood, so strange and hushed under its new blanket, and often end up at the little store down the street, buying beer and chips to continue the feast. Then we'd snuggle on the couch in front of the gas logs and watch movies or make love.

At the wilderness school, we always had a student or two from a warmer climate, and the other girls would demonstrate the wonders of snow angels and how to make a proper snowman. If the accumulation was sufficient, we'd break out the snow shoes or cross-country skis, and everyone would get a dose of exercise. The day would end in the dining tent with popcorn and hot chocolate in front of the fireplace. Although some of our girls were accustomed to ski vacations at the best resorts in the U.S. and even abroad, others had never seen the inside of any kind of resort and perhaps had never seen a fireplace outside of the mall or the nearest Cracker Barrel. But the snow somehow managed to smooth over those differences, at least for a day.

Today I had no company, but I did have a bit of cornmeal left, so I made myself a large corncake and ate it dripping with some of the honey I'd brought from the cabin. I sat in bed to eat to get a better view of the snow. I'd looked for dog tracks around the hut, but all I saw were littles traces in the snow left by squirrels and chipmunks.

The snow continued throughout the day. In the mid-afternoon, I opened the door to push a five-inch drift away from the threshold with a broom. Though my feet still stung when I walked, getting around was getting easier as my muscles adjusted to the job of balancing my weight differently. I'd been planning a trip to the cabin as soon as I thought my feet and legs could stand it, but if it snowed much more or stayed cold for a while, it would make for a difficult trip. I would just have to wait and see. My last bottle of antibiotics was down to a couple days' supply, and I'd just started on the last tube of ointment.

For dinner, I ate more stew, transferred what was left to the smaller pot, and heated water in the Dutch oven to clean it and soak my feet. Keeping the fire hot made the hut almost unbearable, so I opened all the vents to cool it down. Standing by one of the upper vents, I was sure I could hear the snow whispering in the woods around me. Then, drifting on the breeze with the snow, came the yipping of the coyote clan from somewhere to the west. Along with the sharp calls came that same gargled yelp, the sound that didn't quite belong. They kept at it for maybe five minutes, locating each other and making sure that everyone was accounted for. For a moment I had the urge to go to the door and add my own voice to the mix, and I wondered how convincing my coyote voice would be. Silly, I know. But I was tempted.

December 13

I didn't write yesterday because I was exhausted from gathering water and besides, I had company. When I woke, I found that the snow had stopped overnight; a good eight inches greeted me when I opened the door to set out the potty bucket. The temperature had dropped, the sky remained a steely gray, and a brisk breeze knocked clumps of snow from the branches. Though the day eventually brightened a bit, the wind kept up, and I decided to forego my trip to the creek and gather snow instead. This turned out to be a labor-intensive process. My smaller pot was still full of stew, and the Dutch oven too unwieldly to tote out and in, so I started by tossing a strange variety of containers out the door, including a couple of one pound coffee cans I'd emptied, the extra bucket Edie had used for a toilet (since cleaned and sanitized), my two Camelbacks, the larger Jetboil pot, and a few odd plastic containers that had held various foods that I'd eaten. It takes a lot of snow to make a little water, so I figured I'd fill them all, set them near the stove, and consolidate them in fewer containers as they melted. Then I'd go out and refill those containers and repeat as needed.

I thought that I'd prepared myself well for the cold in Peter's rain boots and a pair of his wool socks. My legs were covered with wool long john bottoms and rain pants, and on my top half I had a base layer, a medium-weight fleece and a down jacket. I'd pulled a fleece-lined cap down over my ears and donned a pair of ski gloves. But when I stepped into the snow, the wind coming around the edge of the hut hit my face like an arctic slap. I immediately yanked up my hood, but there was no tying it with my thickly gloved hands, so I retreated into the hut to reconsider my wardrobe.

When I reemerged, I'd added another layer pretty much everywhere, a scarf covered my lower face, and my hood was securely tied. I gathered up my containers, put most of them in my backpack, and dragged a foam pad to sit on. A snowdrift had formed on the lee side of the hut, and there I plopped myself to dig, filling each container with my trowel and pounding the snow down with my fist. Soon my feet felt like ice, and I was forced to stop. I had filled about half of my containers. I repeated this process two more times throughout the day, and it seemed that each time, the air was colder, my feet chilled faster, and the wind had grown more teeth. Through it all, I netted about three gallons of water.

As I headed back in from my last foray, Daisy came trotting down the slope above the hut as though returning from a carefree jaunt, and I was surprised as she came right up to me with no hesitation at all. I set down a bucket of snow and petted her awkwardly with my thickly gloved hand.

"Hey, girl. Did you come to check on me or for a handout?" I asked her.

When I opened the door, she paused for just a second and then followed me inside. Foot by foot, she made a round of the interior, sniffing here and there until she'd satisfied her curiosity. Then she nosed her way back over to where I stood stripping off my layers and hanging them by the door.

"Okay. You can come in for a while, and we'll just see how it goes," I said. Growing up, I'd never been allowed pets, but I figured that a foam sleep pad would make a decent dog bed, so I laid one on the far side of the woodstove and proceeded to arrange my snow containers on the side by the door to melt.

Daisy nosed around a bit more and then settled herself on the pad with her head up, watching me.

"Good girl," I told her.

I'd long since closed all of the vents except for a tiny sliver of one of the upper ones, and the hut had remained plenty warm, but I felt chilled from my last trip, so I made a cup of hot tea with a generous addition of Tang and sat in my camp chair with my feet propped in front of the stove. From this position, all I could see was a few branches and a bit of gray sky, which heightened my sense of being closed in. I tried to shrug off the feeling and gathered my sketch materials to work on my picture map. My latest addition was a drawing of Edie's tent and clearing, which I'd sketched with the two of us sitting in the camp chairs in front of the fire ring and the flames reaching high. As I worked and stumbled about to make more tea, Daisy lay, inert, on the sleep pad by the stove, as though she'd always been there.

At suppertime, I cooked some rice to extend the stew, and I fed Daisy a cup of stew over a cup of rice, which she downed in less than a minute. Then she sat and watched me as I ate my own portion. I told her no and she went to her pad, lying with her head on her paws but still attentive to my every swallow. Only after I swallowed my last bite did she stretch out on her side and close her eyes. After a while I crawled over to her and spent a few minutes running my hand down the back of her head and her side, thinking how nice it felt just to stroke another living being. She opened her eyes and lifted her head in acknowledgement before she relaxed and went back to sleep.

I turned to a fresh page in my sketchbook and did a quick drawing of her, stretched out with her sharp muzzle pointed toward me and her legs splayed as though in mid-trot. After a while, I got drowsy, and when I roused myself to close the curtains and load the woodstove for the night, Daisy went to the door and looked back at me expectantly. It was likely to be the coldest night since the blackout, and I noted Daisy's short coat as I let her out. Then I pictured her nestled among her thick-haired coyote family and figured she'd be okay. If she scratched, I'd let her in, but I wasn't going to beg.

Today was pretty much a repeat of yesterday, windy and brutally cold, but Daisy did not reappear. After my third snow trip, I tended to my feet and decided I had enough water to clean up a little. I'd let my hair grow for several weeks, so I took out my mirror and tried to trim it and then washed my scalp with a damp cloth as a substitute for real shampoo. Then I bathed my other vital parts and settled in for dinner feeling a trace more human. I had just a few of the meals that Peter had prepared left, and I splurged and pulled out a pouch of white bean chicken chili. I was unusually hungry and ate the whole thing, even though it should have been enough for at least two meals.

After dinner I settled myself on the sleep platform and took out this notebook to write, but I couldn't focus. Since I'd decided to give up on worrying about disappointing Peter, he'd retreated to the outer edge of my consciousness where I could almost ignore him. But that stance was beginning to get old, too. Since Peter's death, my life had become a series of paradoxes. I had to survive without him without wanting to, and I had to push him away while at the same time wanting him close. In the months immediately following his death, while I was still working through all of the paperwork and legal aspects of losing a spouse, I quickly became frustrated with my new identity as Peter's widow. In these supposedly enlightened times, nothing was more reductive than being defined by my loss. This was compounded by the expectation that I be gracious when I just wanted to scream at someone: the insurance people, his boss, and pretty much anyone who seemed to accept so easily that he was gone.

Finally, I dug into the envelope of photos under the sleep platform that I'd been avoiding for months. I flipped through them until I came to the one that was stuck in my mind. It was taken on the day that Peter's friend Charles took us out on the Potomac in his little inflatable outboard boat. Charles had handed the helm over to Peter, and he was sitting sideways on the pilot seat, the wind whiffling his cowlick, navigating with that intense expression of concentration that I knew so well, but when he saw me looking at him through the camera lens, he broke into his most boyish, look-ma-no-hands grin. It was as carefree a day as we could imagine and well beyond my imagination now. As I looked at the joy in his face, a joy that I was part of, I wondered how I could ever have thought that he would be disappointed in me. I stared at the picture for a long time. Then I reached for my sketchbook.

December 17

As I sit on the sleep platform to write tonight, Daisy is curled on her pad, and she seems to be happy to stay the night for the first time. I haven't written for several days, mostly because nothing of note has happened other than Daisy showing up about every other afternoon and inviting herself to dinner. I've continued to stretch the meals with rice or instant potatoes, so Daisy and I are both getting more carbs than usual, but I have been looking at my food stores and noting how they've dwindled, particularly the oatmeal and rice. Of more dire concern, though, is the fact that I've run out of both oral antibiotics and ointment. The open wounds on my feet still weep, and the ointment takes the place of actual skin to create a germ barrier. At the same time the oral antibiotics have taken care of any bacteria that crosses in. Without both of them, I am defenseless.

That said, the idea of dragging myself back to the cabin for supplies has seemed impossible during this cold snap. I've hiked in icy conditions without crampons before, and it is arduous work with two good feet. To make the attempt on unsteady feet is just too risky; I'd be coated with sweat, and if I injured myself, I'd quickly become hypothermic. But the weather started warming yesterday, and in less than two days, the snow cover has diminished to mere inches on the south-facing slopes.

Another challenge of making the trek is my lack of the right footwear. I've used wool socks to cushion the soles and fill in the extra space in Peter's boots, but rubber boots are rubber boots, and they aren't made to insulate. If I can find a pair of his hiking boots at the cabin, I may be able to wear them back, but I still have to get there first. I would still be waffling about going back if I had any choice at all, but I don't, so assuming the weather is good, I will leave by noon tomorrow.

As I look at Daisy snoozing by the woodstove, I'm surprised at how calming it is to have her here. My father always claimed to be allergic to pets, though Aunt JoAnn's cats never seemed to bother him. His no pet rule was so sacrosanct that I gave up asking. Mom would have stepped in if there had been a chance of swaying him, and when she didn't even try, I knew it was useless.

I don't mean to paint my father in a negative light; he was good and faithful at the obligations he claimed. It's just that he delineated those obligations so unwaveringly. He was a 50s dad in the 90s, just like on the old sitcoms, minus the cheerful smile. He took care of the major breadwinning, chauffeuring, and outside chores and pretty much left everything else to my mother. They met when they were both attending Clark University in Worcester. He was studying math and ended up as an actuary for an insurance company. Mom was studying English and was happy to land a job at the city library. The way she described it, they were both serious students and a little wary of the party scene, which explains how they happened to meet in the campus library on a Saturday night. I picture them as two socially awkward nerds who took refuge in the fact that they weren't totally alone. The marriage, I think, happened because it just seemed the next logical step, and it gave them a blueprint for how to become adults after college.

When I was six or seven, Mom tried to encourage a stronger bond between Dad and me. Saturday was cleaning day for Mom and fishing day for Dad, and she decided that he should take me with him a couple times a month so she could clean "in peace," which was odd because I always stayed well out of her way to avoid being assigned extra chores.

That first Saturday was in early May, and my father took me up to the Wachusett Reservoir toward Clinton. We dragged folding chairs and fishing gear along the edge of a peninsula and set them up at the foot of the trees. The new leaves were just out, and I remember how wonderful it was to be there on such a warm, sunny day, even though we were on the eastern side of the lake and our chairs were in the cool shade. There was a pretty steep drop off there, and Dad was adamant about my not going into the water, not even to my knees. He said that the fish would be about ten to twenty feet down, and at that part of the lake that was only a few feet from the shore. Once he had everything arranged how he wanted it, he poured himself a cup of coffee from the thermos he'd brought and handed me a juice box.

When it came to the actual fishing, though, we didn't last too long together. I watched carefully, standing off to one side, as he demonstrated his cast. He was an average-looking man, with shiny black hair, a slightly thick nose, and a bit of a paunch. He'd never been athletic, but standing there on the bank of the reservoir in his short-brimmed fishing hat and Orvis vest with all the little pockets, he was graceful in a way I'd never seen before.

"Hold the rod out like this, and then bring it back around just so, and then fling it and press this here, like you're going to throw the rod into the water, but don't let go."

I can still hear his voice. It had a little edge to it that told me that he had low expectations for my success, and he was right. When he finally gave me a turn, the timing escaped me and a little length of line whipped crazily around the end of the rod.

"That's okay," he said as he took it from me. "We'll work on it a little bit every time."

The whole fishing thing seemed pretty boring at that point, so I asked him if I could go play in the woods. He said that was fine and I could follow the trail to the end of the peninsula and back, but not to follow the trail around to the other side because it was too steep and too far. He gave me a whistle on a bright orange string and said to blow it as loud as I could if I needed him. It didn't occur to me until several trips later that this was what he had in mind when he agreed to our outings: five or ten minutes doing his best to instruct me and then a couple hours of peace as I amused myself exploring.

I skipped along the path holding the whistle in my teeth, sending out a little toot now and then and feeling very grown up to be allowed to wander on my own. When I looked back, I could see my father's hat through the trees for a while, but then he was out of sight, and I was really alone. In a short time, I came to the point. The shoreline there was strewn with boulders, and I immediately began to jump around on the rocks until I reached the largest one, which was about as big as my desk at school and sat right at the water's edge. Between it and the next rock was a little strip of dirty sand, maybe a couple of feet wide, and I could see that the water stayed shallow for a bit, so I thought it would be okay to wade in just up to my ankles. I sat down on the rock to pull off my tennis shoes and socks. I had set them behind me and started to slide a foot or so down the rock onto the sand when the head of a snake rose up out of the water within a foot of where I was about to land. It had large, black splotches and a big head, and it seemed to be coming straight for me. I let out a little scream and scrambled back on top of the rock and then jumped along the rocks in my bare feet until I was almost back to the trail. Then I put the whistle in my mouth and blew three times as hard as I could.

I don't think it took my father more than two minutes to come pounding up the path.

"What? What?" he shouted as he ran up.

"A snake! It was going to bite me!"

"Where?"

"Over by the water." I pointed, and he saw my shoes on the rock and then looked at my feet.

"What are you doing with your shoes off? Didn't I tell you not to go in the water?" His shirt was soaked and his shirttail was out. He wiped his forehead on his sleeve.

"I was just going to get my feet a little wet. I was hot. But then this big snake came swimming up."

"Show me."

I took him over to my rock, but of course, the snake was gone.

He looked at me and frowned and when he did, his eyebrows almost met in the middle.

"Okay, listen," he said. "Number One: most snakes don't bite. Number Two: poisonous snakes are very rare in Massachusetts."

"Are you sure? You're not just saying that so I won't be scared, right?"

"I'm sure. Number Three: if you see a wild animal or a snake or something, just leave it alone and it won't bother you. If you think it's acting funny, just back off slowly. It could have rabies. And, please, don't blow that whistle if you aren't really in trouble 'cause if you scare me like that again, you can just stay home and help your mother."

I looked down at the ground and tried not to cry, which was hard because he made me feel so stupid. But it had been fun to walk along the path by myself, and I didn't want him to leave me home, so I said, "I'm sorry. I'll try not to ruin your fishing trips."

"Apology accepted. You can stay here for a while longer if you want to, but put your shoes back on. No wading means no wading."

He turned and set off across the rocks, and I picked up my shoes and found a different rock to sit on in case the snake was still around.

After Dad left my mother, and I was still at GWU, I asked her over the phone whether she was angry at him for leaving just when she began to get sick. She said, no, she knew he would be leaving as soon as I grew up. I was shocked.

"Why?" I asked.

"Aurora, we were already having problems when I got pregnant. I was in perimenopause, and you were a big surprise. But his sense of duty wouldn't let him abandon us. That and the expense of supporting two households. Your scholarships made college much more affordable than we'd planned, so he didn't have to wait until you actually graduated."

"So, for all those years he didn't really want to be there?" I asked.

"Well, you can look at it that way," she said, "but he also didn't want to be someplace else very much, either. You know, even though we'd never planned to have children, I adored you the moment I saw you. You weren't just a baby;

you were this amazing little being. I think everything turned out fine. Don't you?"

She was very calm and matter of fact about the whole situation, but by the time I hung up the phone, I was seething. My father had stuck around for twenty years because it was less expensive than leaving. And, if it hadn't been for me, my parents would have split years before, and both might have been happier. My only solace came from the knowledge that, whether they planned me or not, at least one of them loved me.

December 18

I did not leave for the cabin this morning. An hour or so before dawn, I was awakened by a curious sound which I soon realized was the rattle of ice pellets against the windows. It sounded like someone was outside throwing gravel at the hut. I hobbled over to the door and Daisy joined me. I could make out a few skinny branches and oval leaves, shellacked with ice and dripping onto the black ground. Daisy gave a dismissive sniff and returned to her place by the woodstove. I was wide awake by then, so I stoked the fire, made some tea, and sat on the sleep platform listening to nature's assault and watching the dark gloom fade to gray.

When I finally got up, I decided to at least accomplish something, so I made a plan to clean out the woodstove. I didn't have a metal bucket, so it took me a while to figure out what to do with the hot coals. My potty bucket was about a third full, so I decided to dump the coals there. I put on ski gloves and scooped the coal and ash into the bucket with my trowel, slapping the lid on each time to contain the smoke. The resulting stench was almost unbearable. When I'd freed up most of the space in the woodstove, the bucket was just a few inches shy of full, and the mixture looked like ash stew. Yuck, yuck, yuck.

After the usual production of readying myself to go out, I grabbed a walking stick and the bucket and headed through the door, leaving it open a crack to dispel the noxious smell. Daisy had long since departed, so I faced the icy world alone. The rain had ended, and the ground was littered with leaves and twigs. Icy leaves crunched under my feet with each step, but the boots had enough of a heel to bite into the debris, so walking on the level ground was fairly easy, even with my odd gait. I took the bucket to my latest potty hole and dumped it in. The ashy sludge stuck to the sides, and I wished I had something to wipe it out with, but I hadn't thought to bring a rag. The thought of getting the muck on my gloves was pretty repulsive anyway, so I just scraped it as best I could with a pine branch.

Since I was already dressed, I stopped at the hut to pick up my water containers and headed toward the creek. Here the walking was much more treacherous, and I still felt that stinging, tearing sensation in my right foot whenever I dug it into the slope for traction. The cold had already crept through the boots, and the descent was more painful than usual. As I jolted along, the wind gusted, and all around me bits of ice and small twigs came raining down, pelting my shoulders and falling down my neck. The leaves of the rhododendrons were curled into fat straws, and the thinner branches all sagged toward the ground.

I slipped several times trudging back up the hill with my pack heavy pack. The edge of my foot kept sliding, and I had to resort to my old method of scooting. Had I attempted my cabin trip, I would have had to give up at the first steep knob. But still, it was frustrating to be so limited in my movements, and I arrived at the hut sweaty and discouraged. I hadn't eaten much, but I was too tired to decide what to eat and bored with all of my choices, so I just got the wood stove going and crawled back into bed.

Sometime in the early afternoon, the clouds thinned and the sun burst through, causing me to wake again to tubes of ice raining down on the hut. This time I was hot and groggy and thirsty, and I downed about a third of the water bottle I had sitting above my head. Looking around the hut, I felt almost drugged. The bright light illuminated all of my familiar things: the coats hanging near the door, the camp stool in front of the stove, my backpack leaning against the right wall. Everything seemed familiar and strange at the same time, as if I'd gone so far away in my dreams that I'd lost some connection with it all. It occurred to me that I was very hungry, but also that my foot was aching and that maybe if I didn't move, the pain would go away. But that was just wishful thinking. Even so, I sat there for a long time before reluctantly swinging my feet over the side of the platform and pushing myself to a stand.

I made my way unsteadily to the shelf that held the ibuprofen, took three and made myself a cup of strong coffee before settling down in the chair to wait for the pain to fade. Surrounded by all of the accruements of my present life: my sketchbook and journal, buckets and pots, food containers and water bottles, I felt strangely ambivalent. I picked up the sketchbook and leafed through the pages until I came to the panels of my story map. What was I thinking when I began that project? The drawings seemed suddenly cartoonish and silly. What did they really mean, these vain representations? And why did I ever think that my story was important? It seemed funny in a bizarre sort of way that I at one time had enjoyed a happy life in the make-believe world that existed before the blackout. I remembered how strong I felt then, and how proud I was of that strength. I had work that I liked and that helped people. I had a talent for drawing that I thought made me at least interesting, if not special. And I had Peter who saw me just the way I saw myself and validated all of it with his love and attention. If it was all real, how could it disappear so quickly? I no longer felt strong or purposeful, special or loved. As easily as some enemy had brought the country to its knees, I could see how I, too, have fallen so that I barely recognize myself. I am reduced to an assortment of physical needs and have no energy to think about or deal with anything else.

As the coffee and pain killers took effect, I was able to turn my attention from my dark thoughts to tomorrow's challenges. My backpack was already packed, but I went through it anyway, adding an extra package of ramen and more hot chocolate. I made sure that I had three nylon tarps for making a shelter and added an extra water bottle. By the time I soaked my feet in the morning, the day should be warm enough to melt the leftover ice. In my condition, the trip would take at least three hours. I'd set up camp in the mid-afternoon behind the cover of the last hill and take a look at the cabin just before dusk. If someone was staying there, they'd probably be in by dark. But even if the cabin appeared deserted, I would sleep behind the hill and wait for daylight before going in.

I whiled away the rest of the afternoon and evening sipping rehydrated chicken soup, doing Sudokus, and dosing myself with pain killers. When I crawled into bed to write, it was barely dark, but I am already drowsy, in spite of my long nap. Strangely, I am neither worried or excited or even very curious about what tomorrow's journey may bring. It is just another chore that I must accomplish to survive.

December?

After writing the other night, I fell asleep quickly but woke after a few hours, soaked in sweat and with my right foot throbbing. I took some more ibuprofen and added two Tylenol and a Benadryl to the mix, hoping to salvage some more rest before the trip, but knowing that my foot had become infected in spite of my efforts kept me tossing and turning. When dawn finally came, I was exhausted but also anxious to examine my foot, so I stoked the wood stove and readied the water. Soon I had the bandage off and was tugging at the strips of T-shirt underneath. The wound had wept quite a bit, and without any salve to keep the area moist, the bandages were stuck fast. I clenched my teeth and pulled. The bandages came away, along with some new and dead skin and some grayish looking crud. The pain was bad, and I had to wipe my eyes to clear my vision. The center of the hole didn't look much different, just dark and gaping, as always. But the area immediately around it had faded from deep pink to an almost white and produced sparks of pain when I prodded it with my finger. I looked for the telltale streaks of red out further that would signal serious infection, but the healthy area of new skin was still a deep enough pink to camouflage any streaks if they were there.

As I finished my cleaning routine, I racked my brain for some moist substance that I could use in place of the salve. I first thought of honey, but I was afraid that it wouldn't stay moist enough. If I had some vegetable oil, I could have sterilized it and soaked the first layer of bandages in it, but that was a luxury item I didn't have. After some more consideration, I decided that the honey probably couldn't make things any worse, so I dribbled some over my feet before rebandaging them. I made the bandages thick and extended them from my heels to my toes for extra warmth and pulled Peter's socks back on. My foot still throbbed, and I knew that the trip would probably be slower and more painful than I had originally imagined, but the fact remained that I had no choice.

When I emerged from the hut, the sun was up and strong and most of the ice had melted. I set my potty bucket outside the door and pulled it shut, wondering how long I would be away. With so many unknowns, there was no point in speculating. While putting weight on my right foot made me wince with each step, the left felt almost normal as I started off, hobbling along with the help of Peter's hiking poles, my backpack at about half its usual weight, and the pistol strapped in place.

I made the trip in fits and starts, scooting on the steeper hills and resting often. The temperature was above freezing, but I was moving so slowly that after the first sweaty climb, my damp clothes had me shivering. By the time I reached my camping spot, the shadows stretched toward the east, and I calculated that I had just two hours or so before dark. I changed into a dry shirt, found a couple of trees about six feet apart, and began constructing a shelter. Had I been healthy, I would have settled for a lean-to, but instead I strung a rope between the trees and made a make-shift tent by overlapping two tarps over it. The third tarp I would use as a ground cloth. My tent ran north and south, and I heaped dry leaves against the western wall to keep out the wind. I left my sleeping bag, pad, and a solar lamp inside and shouldered my pack once more.

It felt like déjà vu as I settled myself into the same stand of pines where I'd hidden on my last trip. Below me the cabin and barn looked mostly the same except that someone had put a piece of cardboard over the broken window in the back door, and the barn door that faced the house was closed. So, someone had been there, but there was no way of telling when. It made sense that Ray had been back or sent some of his henchmen, and they'd probably stayed in the cabin. I peered through my binoculars to look for movement behind the windows. But the inside of the house was dim, and I couldn't see much. I thought I'd watch until I could just make my way back along the side of the hill without my headlamp. I sat on my backpack and ate hickory nuts as the sun sank toward the treetops, but the stillness was so pervasive that the sound of my own chewing seemed raucous and out of place. I was getting stiff and my feet were cold. I examined the chimney. No smoke, no tremulous waves of heat. The tip of the sun reached the trees. The shadow of the house reached the barn, and the shadow of the barn extended far into the woods on the other side. I was exhausted. I scanned the house one last time. No movement and not the slightest flicker of light. I stood and hefted my pack.

The walk back woke me up a bit, and I thought that if I waited until full dark, I ought to be able to make a fire without being seen. Before I made my dinner, I snapped dead branches off of some pines and downed trees for kindling. I cleared a space on the ground and set my fire near a fallen tree downwind of the shelter. The wind was calm, and by the time I had everything ready and my cooking supplies laid out, I was ravenous and the first stars had appeared. I lit the fire, using some pine cones to get it going. I hadn't sat in front of a fire for a very long time, and I'd forgotten how sedating it could be to watch the flames licking hungrily around the sticks. With so much pine, there was a lot of crackling and snapping, and sparks flew up sporadically and twirled out of sight. My ramen, when I ate it, was tastier than anything I'd eaten in days, and for a few minutes it felt like I was back in my old life, out for an overnighter without a care. Even the pain in my foot had subsided a bit. I sat on the log and fed the fire well into the evening, letting my mind be consumed by that one task, until I ran out of sticks and reluctantly swept some damp earth over the coals. After a final dose of pain killers and a Benadryl, I burrowed down into my sleeping bag and listened to the faint rustlings of the leaves until I slept.

Once again, however, I woke well before dawn, sweating and needing to pee. I pulled on my fleece and headlamp and stumbled out into the night. Clouds were massing in the sky, obstructing the moon, and I clicked the headlamp onto its lowest setting, just so I could make my way to the nearest tree. I didn't have the balance to pee at a squat, so I backed up against the tree trunk before pulling down my pants, and even then, I lost my balance and sent a trickle of urine down my leg. I cursed a little and pined for the days of disposable wipes as I straightened. That was when I saw the eyes, two of them, glowing, a couple feet off the ground next to the shelter. I froze and raised my hand to my headlamp. I didn't have the gun, or even a hiking pole. I clicked the lamp to its highest power and the rest of my visitor came into view.

"Daisy," I said, and she approached me with her head down, tail wagging.

I had been glad that she wasn't around when I left the hut because I thought having her trailing along might give me away. But now that she was there, there wasn't much I could do about it. I petted her for a few seconds and crawled back into the shelter. She paused before following me in, as though to ask permission, and then trotted in and curled up on the sleeping bag.

"Oh no," I told her, edging her off with my legs.

She resettled herself against my side as though it were a regular thing.

The bathroom trip had chilled me, and the pain in my foot had taken on a sharper, almost jolting rhythm. I downed some more ibuprofen but spent the rest of the night rolling back and forth, alternately sweating and shivering, and enjoying just a few short breaks in between when I spooned with Daisy and hoped that I wasn't so far gone that a new course of antibiotics wouldn't help.

The sky that morning was a mottled gray as I took down the shelter. I felt woozy from all the repeated stooping and standing required to take down the tarps and repack everything. There didn't seem to be any point in fixing breakfast; I had no appetite and just wanted to get the trip over with, but I gave Daisy some chunks of smoked venison. Although I'd appreciated her company, I wasn't sure what to do with her. If someone were around the cabin, she might give us away by barking. So, before I started out, I made a rope leash and tied her to a sapling, promising to be back soon. She barked briefly as I left but quieted as soon as I was out of view.

I paused at the top of the hill to look down on the cabin through the bare trees and all appeared unchanged—dark windows, cold chimney, general look of desertion. I cut across the flank of the hill and headed for the back door.

I hesitated as I put my hand on the doorknob. Whoever had patched the window had done so quite neatly, taping the cardboard with strips of silver duct tape that ran dead straight up the sides and along the top, the kind of person who wrapped Christmas presents with surgical precision. Probably not one of Ray's boys. Encouraged, I pushed on the door.

A loud clatter of metal sounded from the other side, and I stepped back and dropped to a crouch below the window. What the fuck? I thought. It must be some sort of booby trap. I pulled out the gun and cocked the hammer. My foot screamed with pain and I had to go down on my knees, not a good position from which to flee, but if someone came out, fleeing wasn't going to be an option, anyway. I waited for a minute or two. Nothing. I pictured a dark figure standing in the kitchen, just daring me to show myself.

After a few more minutes, I stuck the pistol back in its holster and crawled backward to the edge of the porch. As long as I stayed low and walked up against the house, I thought maybe I could get around front and look in one of the windows. I backed my way under the railing and crouch-hobbled around the corner, past the blackened windows of the cellar, and around to the front. The porch was empty, and I crawled onto it and past the door, where I stopped under the living room window. I didn't pause before lifting my head to look in. Just one quick glance through the gap in the curtains then down. In that first glance, all I saw was the familiar form of the woodstove. I raised my head and looked again. The wall, the woodstove, the kitchen doorway. No figure. No movement.

Retrieving the gun one more time, I rose and approached the door. I turned the knob with my free hand and pushed slowly. Before there was a gap of even an inch, the door hit something. I looked in and saw the edge of a two-by-six about three feet off the floor. I widened the gap by another inch. Now I could see that the board was weighted down to the back of the armchair with several thick books. Another trap, or, perhaps more accurately, alarm. Someone had rigged the doors so that they could hear someone coming. But if both doors were rigged did that mean they were still inside? Or had they left through a window?

Not wanting to create more noise, I stepped off the porch and went back around to the back. The kitchen door stood slightly ajar, just as I'd left it. I pushed it open. The board that I'd hit was hanging off the counter at an angle, still anchored by a heavy pot. On the floor behind the door lay an antique iron and several pot lids. The thud and clatter they'd produced would be enough to wake anyone in the house. But all was silent now, not with the silence of waiting, just an emptiness that felt relaxed and normal. The trash on the counter was gone, and someone had piled the empty soup bowls in the sink. I remembered the feeling of violation I'd felt when I saw the trash before. This felt different. Nevertheless, I tiptoed as best I could through the house a room at a time with the gun raised. Living room, pantry, bathroom, bedroom, closets—all empty. I pulled myself up the stairs and peered around the half wall that separated the stairwell from the second floor. No one.

Finally able to relax somewhat, I looked around the bedroom, my bedroom. The pictures I'd found scattered across the bed on my last visit were gone and the envelope was on my desk. I picked it up and felt the weight of the pictures inside. It was an oddly considerate thing for a trespasser to do, putting away my pictures like that. I placed the envelope back on the desk.

Even without any bedclothes, the mattress looked inviting, and I wished that I could lay down my pack and collapse onto the bed. Sunlight was falling through the south-facing dormer window in front of me, and the dust motes drifting through the beams seemed to beckon me to stay. But whoever had been using the cabin could be back any time. The smart thing to do was to get what I needed and leave.

Down in the pantry, I tugged on the carpet and lifted the door, mentally reviewing what I needed: meds, salve, bandages, a pair of Peter's hiking boots, and whatever food I still had room for. I started down the wooden stairs, leaning heavily on the rail. My foot was pulsing with pain, even though I had already taken a large dose of pain meds. I clicked on my headlamp about halfway down and was halted by what I saw: two rumpled sleeping bags in the middle of the floor, each with a real pillow. A Jetboil, probably mine, sitting on one of the lower shelves next to a couple gallon jugs of water. A trash bag hanging from one of the supports. A couple of headlamps, a thick candle, and books on the lowest shelf, along with the Scrabble game. And directly under the window, the stepstool from the kitchen. Although Peter had painted the window black, there was a blanket nailed to the window frame, for extra light blockage, I assumed. Someone, or ones, had made themselves a pretty cozy hideout right in the middle of all my supplies.

I nudged aside a sleeping bag to examine the books. They were all from our shelves: Deep Survival, a book about Laura Ingalls Wilder, and Peter's copy of Cormac McCarthy's The Road. In our cabin, they'd never run out of reading material.

There was no way to know who had been staying there, but I couldn't imagine that it was anyone other than Edie and Thomas. They both knew about the cabin, and it would explain the respect evidenced by the gathering my pictures and the taping of the window. And I knew that Edie was a reader. I looked more closely at the shelves. There were gaps where rice, oatmeal, and other foods were missing, but it wasn't the total theft I'd expect from Ray's gang. I went to the area under the steps where we stored medical supplies. Again, there were perhaps a couple bottles of Tylenol missing, and maybe some Band-Aids. I opened the little medicine container where we'd put the antibiotics. Five bottles. One missing, if I remembered correctly. I took all five and rummaged around for some ace bandages and rolls of gauze, taking all I could find. All the painkillers, too, and some eye drops, toothpaste, and antibacterial soap. The space left in my pack I filled with more rice, oatmeal, coffee, and honey. I noticed then that a few cans of chicken and tuna were gone. I took what was left and topped my pack off with two Mountain House meals. My pack was now very heavy and bulging.

The last item I needed was a pair of Peter's boots. We'd stashed some clothes down in the cellar, too, in boxes under the east window. I limped over and opened the first. It was empty except for a few pairs of shorts. The second still held some rain gear, and I grabbed a new pair of rain pants. The third held running shoes, sandals, one pair of hiking boots in my size, and one in Peter's, nice brown and black Keens. I took Peter's back over to the steps and tried them on. They fit perfectly over my bandages with just a bit of extra room at the toe. They'd probably been too small for Thomas.

Looking around, I wished there were some way I could let Edie know that I'd been there. A note wouldn't work; if it wasn't Edie, I didn't want someone else to know who I was. I sat on the bottom stair and thought for a minute. If only I had the Maya Angelou book with me. Leaving that on one of the sleeping bags would be the perfect sign.

I hauled my pack to the first floor and set it by the back door. Then I went up to my bedroom and looked around. I spotted one of my Wilderness First Aid manuals on the shelf and remembered Edie's question, "Are you a nurse or something?" Back in the cellar, I neatly folded the sleeping bags and laid the manual on top of one. If I was right, and it was Edie, she would know it was me. If it was someone else, they would know they'd been discovered, and that was all.

I wasn't interested in climbing out any windows if I didn't have to. So, I pushed the iron and pot lids out of the way and went out the back. When I reached Daisy, she was lying in a weak patch of sunlight. She stood and stretched as I approached, waited patiently for me to release her, and fell into step behind me as I started home.

December?

I still haven't figured out how many days I spent sleeping and generally unconscious after my return. I am starting to move around a little, but I don't want to try to use my foot again yet, though I suppose I will have to empty my pee bucket sometime soon. Yesterday I limped to the door to let Daisy out, and she has not returned, as though she understands that I am not capable of providing much for her now.

When I sleep, it is as though I am sinking deep into a dark, formless void, where I float and swim without ever getting anywhere. My dreams, when I have them, have been about travelling—the settings change, and I am trying to get somewhere, usually on two-lane rural roads where the high weeds form canyons, and I can never see beyond the next bend. In one dream, Peter and I are travelling across the country by stealing horses or trading the ones we have for fresh mounts. The countryside is flat grassland that stretches on forever, so that, again, we never seem to reach our destination, though the names of the towns change. Peter is kind, but distant, preoccupied with our journey. Even so, it is a comfort to be with him.

My memory of the trip back to the hut ends an hour or two after I started. I think that until then I'd been running on pure adrenalin because as soon as I started to drag myself over the first hill, I became overwhelmingly tired. I thought I'd perk up as I started down into the hollow, but the effort of keeping the weight off of my right foot was putting a lot of strain on my knee and turning my thigh muscles into jelly. As I reached the bottom of the slope, my left leg gave way, and I sat down hard, with my foot under my butt, overextending my thigh muscle as I landed. I straightened the leg, but the burning in the muscle continued, so I just sat there in the leaves for a few minutes, hoping that it would recover after some rest. After a while, I pulled both feet up against my butt and used the hiking poles to bring myself to a squat. From there I managed to stand, but I swayed under the weight of the pack. It was too much. Before me was another steep hill, and I thought that if I could make it over that second hill, then I could come up with a plan for getting at least the meds and bandages home. I'd have to abandon the rest of the pack, but maybe I could get back to it in a day or two.

It took about twenty minutes to get to the top of that hill, scooting backward and dragging the backpack a couple feet at a time. When I reached the top, I laid back in the leaves to rest. I'd climbed out of the shelter of the hollow, and a brisk breeze soon found its way through my fleece. I fumbled with the drawstring of my pack, knowing that my raincoat was buried beneath my new supplies, but I finally found it and pulled it out. Then I stuffed everything back except for the meds, bandages, and honey, which I repacked into the detachable compartment on top. This I unbuckled and strapped around my waist. Then I dragged the rest of the pack down the other side of the hill, looking for a good branch to hang it from because it bothered me to think that animals would get my food. I was lucky to find a tall pine that had fallen against another tree, and I got a carabiner and rope over its trunk at a height of about twenty feet. I leaned back against another tree to steady myself, heaved the backpack into the air, and tied off the rope.

Though my load was lighter with just the pouch tied around my waist, the going was still tough. I made it down the rest of the hill and turned north up the hollow with my foot screaming with pain and my left leg burning, too. I was soaked with sweat, but at least the raincoat was keeping the wind off of me. Another quarter mile and I collapsed in a clearing for another rest. I remember swallowing a couple mouthfuls of water and sipping honey straight from the jar.

That's all I remember, although Edie says that as she and Thomas dragged me the rest of the way to the hut, I kept mumbling, "My foot, my foot." Daisy walked along with them and whenever they stopped, she'd go a few yards farther, showing them the way. But that was redundant because they'd already found the hut one day when Edie was showing Thomas her camp site. They crossed the stream that day to see whether I was okay, but when they found the hut and saw smoke rising from my chimney, they figured I was warm and safe.

"You could have come knocking," I told her.

"When you were taking care of me, you never talked about where you were camped or took me there. I figured you wanted to be alone. It's part of why I went back."

Her words hurt, but she was right. By the time I'd really considered taking her in, she was gone.

After they'd gotten me onto the platform in the hut, they unwrapped my feet. You didn't have to be a doctor to know that the right foot was in trouble, Edie told me. They sterilized some water and used the antiseptic soap to clean both feet, slavered them with salve, and rebandaged them. Just looking at the items I'd taken from the cabin told them what to do.

"Thomas scrubbed your foot hard," Edie said, "but you barely groaned. You were really feverish and dehydrated. So I did what you did for me, with the Gatorade, Tang, and antibiotics, and I woke you up every couple of hours and made you drink."

She told me all this on the morning that I first became fully conscious. The fever had broken the night before, and I could sit up and actually eat something. She sat on the edge of the platform while I tried out some instant mashed potatoes with canned chicken between questions.

"Why did you bring me here instead of back to the cabin? When you saw the pictures, you must have known it was mine," I asked.

"We don't think of the cabin as safe. When it's really cold, we start a fire in the woodstove after dark and sleep in the pantry. With the doors booby-trapped, we figure we can get into the cellar before anyone finds us. We keep a window in the downstairs bedroom open at night, so they'll think we went out that way. But usually we just sleep down there. It's not really warm. You wouldn't have been comfortable there. Besides, if you wanted to be there, you'd have stayed."

I next asked how she'd found the cellar. She looked away as she answered.

"My mom is an LPN, and she used to help old people with their housekeeping and medications. She brought me to the Bensons' with her a couple times to help. I remembered that they had a cellar because Mrs. Benson sent me down there to look for some canning jars she wanted to give my mother. I was really confused when I saw the pantry last month, but then I tripped over the rug, and it didn't move, so I tried to pick it up, and I found the trap door."

She looked down and picked at the skin around her thumb.

"My mom stole some of their painkillers. And when they died, Uncle Ray took the rest. Mrs. Benson died just a few months after Mr. Benson, and Ray found the body. He told the sheriff that Mom worked for the Bensons, and he'd come out to check on her for Mom. She didn't hear too well, so she wouldn't pick up her phone. He said it looked like she died in her sleep." She looked at me and said, "I think maybe he killed her."

"Did you think that right away?" I asked.

"I wondered. Then when all this happened and he started to go around checking on all the old people and finding them dead, I think I knew. I know he was getting pills somewhere and giving some to my mom. She thinks he's her savior."

I set my bowl down and patted the edge of the bed beside me.

"Edie, come closer," I said.

She stood, a skinny waif of a girl with a long pony tail and oversized sweatshirt. She stepped closer and sat.

I took her hand in both of mine.

"Edie, was Ray the father of the baby?" I asked.

She looked straight into my eyes and said, "I don't know. He found out I was having sex with Thomas. It had happened maybe twice. When he came into my room the first time, he said that if I was going to whore around, he might as well get some, too."

Tears began to slide down her cheeks.

"I tried to tell my mother that he wasn't what he seemed, and she got really mad and said that he was the only reason we were alive, and I should be grateful. She loves me, I know she does. But she really believes that."

In spite of my job, I'm not really good at true confessions. At the school we usually found out the really bad stuff from the students' records. But it didn't feel totally unnatural when I reached out my arms and pulled Edie close.

She sniffled against my chest for a minute or so before she sat back up and said, "I didn't want to tell you before. I was afraid you'd be disgusted."

A litany of clichés streamed through my mind: it wasn't your fault, you didn't deserve it, it's all in the past…Finally, I rubbed her upper arm with the back of my hand and said the only thing I thought could possibly be of comfort.

"He's not going to get away with this. I promise."

December?

For the first couple of days that I was conscious, Edie and Thomas checked on me once a day, soaking my feet and replenishing my water supplies. After I finished writing the other day, they showed up and emptied the pee bucket. Thomas fetched the backpack right after they brought me home, so I have all of the food I packed, and I can always ask them to bring me more. The one question that I forgot to ask that first day, how they happened to find me, has been answered. They'd seen the water tank in the barn and followed the pipe up to the stream, trying to figure out a way to fill the tank. They were loaded down with water bottles when they saw me head over the first hill with Daisy tagging along. They took their water to the kitchen and set out after me. They were just going to make sure that I made it alright because they had noticed that I was limping. About halfway to where I collapsed, Daisy came trotting back toward them. Edie said she was sure they'd have found me anyway, but Daisy led them right there.

I am amazed at how good it feels to have someone looking out for me. When we soak my foot, Thomas is more aggressive and meticulous at cutting away the dead flesh than I ever was. Luckily, his long, straight hair makes a curtain in front of my feet, but I close my eyes and grit my teeth anyway, and it's a blessing not to have to look. His uncle was a vet in the next town, and Thomas had often tagged along with him on farm calls, which explains his general lack of queasiness. They apologized for staying at my place and eating my food, which was when I told them about the root cellar and the trap door under the tractor. It's okay, I told them. I would have done the same.

"And I'm sorry that I was with Ray the night he first went to your place," Thomas told me. "It started out like we were helping people by going out and finding food. Then it turned into something else, but Ray wasn't going to let anyone quit. By that time pretty much all the guys had done something they didn't want to get out, so he used what he knew to keep people quiet. When we went to your place, he had just begun to force people to give us stuff, mostly the folks who were farthest from town. That was when I started trying to leave.

Then Edie ran away, and I left to try to find her, and since then I've been running from Ray."

He'd kept an eye out on the town, and when Edie showed up again, they'd run off together.

When they left yesterday, I told them that I thought I'd be okay for a day or two. But they insisted they'd be back today with something good to eat, so since breakfast I've just been reading and relaxing and enjoying the odd feeling of having something to look forward to.

December...

Somewhere around noon, I heard the thudding of Edie and Thomas knocking the dirt off their boots before they gave a quick knock on the door and came in. They each wore a backpack and carried an armload of wood. Daisy rose from her spot by the woodstove to greet them with a few sniffs and then settled back in her spot.

"We'd better open some vents, 'cause there's gonna be a lot of cooking going on," Edie said as she emptied her pack.

Thomas nodded at me and smiled as he bent to load the woodstove.

"Surgery first, though."

I sat and watched as they took over the hut. For want of a table, Edie cleared the bottom corner of the sleep platform and laid out a mixing bowl, a pizza pan, peanut butter, a can of lard, a bottle of oil, a container of beautiful white sugar, and a plastic bag of something I later realized was powdered milk.

"It's amazing what you've got in that root cellar," she said.

The final item she pulled from her pack was a can of cocoa.

"Okay, where's your oatmeal?" she asked.

"You're making preacher cookies!" I exclaimed. "Wow!"

"Yup. I found some butter-flavored lard that I hope will work instead of the real thing."

They'd also brought a couple of extra pots, and Edie soon had the cocoa mixture on the stove beside the Dutch oven where Thomas was heating the water for my foot. Knowing what was coming, I went ahead and took my max dosage of ibuprofen and Tylenol.

Thomas helped me onto a camp chair and unwrapped my foot. Before "operating" he always poured some of the heated water into a clean bucket and washed his hands with antibiotic soap. Then he'd put the soiled bandages into the bucket to soak. For a kid his age, which I estimated to be around seventeen, he had an unusual calmness about him. With that kind of composure, he'd make a great medic, I thought.

After my foot had soaked for fifteen minutes or so, Thomas lifted it out of the water and set it on a clean cloth across his knees. He was sitting on the same camp stool I'd taken to Edie's tent way back when.

"Do you mind if I try something?" he asked.

"Like what?" I answered.

"I found some clove oil at your house. My uncle used to use it to numb the skin of an animal before he gave it a shot or had to clean a wound. I wonder if it might help when I clean the burn areas. Too much will actually burn, but just enough can have a numbing effect. It's a natural antiseptic, so it should help with the infection, too."

"Sure, go for it. If it makes things worse, I'll be sure to scream."

He'd already opened the vial and placed it on top of the new bandages he'd set out. I'd heard of using clove oil for toothaches, but this was new.

He dribbled several drops of the oil onto a clean piece of gauze and gently dabbed at my foot. The pressure hurt, but there was no stinging or other discomfort. He waited a minute or so and then began to snip at the pieces of dead skin and flesh with a pair of nail scissors. In the meantime, my "better" left foot was soaking.

"Here," Edie said, handing me the bowl with the remains of the cookie mix. "Maybe this will take your mind off the pain."

I scraped the bowl with my finger and licked off the warm chocolate mixture as I watched her empty Thomas's backpack. After she'd spooned out the cookies, she'd put them outside since the bed platform was really the only large, flat surface in the hut. Peter had always planned to make a table that would fold up flush with the wall, but the cancer had stopped him with a few projects left on his list.

Among the items Edie spread on the platform were bags of dehydrated turkey stew, more instant mashed potatoes, bags of dried cranberries, onions, and mushrooms, a large jar of green beans, and a bottle of red wine.

"I hope you all brought a corkscrew for that," I commented.

"Thomas has one on his army knife," she replied.

"Okay. I'll just shut up now," I promised.

As I spoke, she pulled out a couple more items: some red and green candles and a couple of quart canning jars.

"Well, don't you think we should splurge a little on Christmas?" She continued to talk as I sat, dumbfounded. "I figured you must have lost track of the date. If we melt some wax in the bottom of these jars and stick the candles inside, they should be pretty stable, right? We can close the curtains and eat by candlelight."

Thomas had started to bandage my foot by then, and I realized that the clove oil had helped a lot. But there were tears in my eyes anyway.

December 26

Edie cooked extra mushrooms and onions in with the stew and made a kind of compote with the cranberries, throwing in a bit of Tang for extra flavor. It tasted like cranberry orange relish without the peels. We pulled camp chairs and the stool up to the corner of the bed platform and set the candles in the middle. After dinner, we played Scrabble, and I tried not to win by too much. Then I finished off what was left of the wine before we switched over to coffee and ate most of the preacher cookies. It felt a bit like game night at the outdoor school but with alcohol and no particular responsibilities on my part. In other words, the most fun I'd had in a really long time. I invited them to stay, but they wanted to get back.

Over a last cup of coffee, we discussed the water situation at the cabin. If they turned on the electricity and ran the water, they would have to keep the woodstoves going so that the pipes wouldn't freeze. Then if Ray came back, it would be obvious that someone was living there. They'd already managed to fill the tank in the barn, so they could get water directly from there, but even if they only used the kitchen sink, those pipes could still freeze if they didn't keep the woodstove going.

I asked them if they thought he'd been to the cabin lately.

"I don't think so," Thomas said. "They had a lot of gas for a while because they managed to break into the tanks at the gas station out on Rte. 42. But then they didn't seal them up right, and a bunch of rain got in. I go out and watch the town sometimes to make sure that Edie's mom is okay. From one of the barns where I hide, I can see them going in and out of the garage they use as their base."

I asked him where his parents were and he said that he honestly didn't know. He lived with them near Lexington until he was seven or so and they split up. His dad stayed and his mother brought him back to Wagner to live with his grandmother and then took off about a year later. The grandmother died of a stroke when he was fifteen.

"The neighbors agreed to keep an eye on me, and the sheriff said he would consider me an emancipated minor as long as I checked in with him a couple times a week and stayed in school. I could have gone to my uncle's, but he hasn't been well, either."

"How did you eat?" I asked.

"I had a part-time job at the feed store that paid the electric bill, and I did a lot of odd jobs for people, and they would give me food. Some folks I did stuff for pretty regular, so I usually had enough to eat, and Grandma's house was paid off," he explained.

His words made me wonder why I continue to be amazed at how some people could get by with so little, even before the blackout. It made me ashamed for not doing more—then and now.

I asked them what they thought would happen if they turned on the electricity during the day and stayed in the house like they belonged there. What would they do if Ray showed up?

"I don't know. I guess it would depend a lot on how many people he brought with him. All I've got is the Winchester rifle that I've had since I was around thirteen. I couldn't take on a whole posse," Thomas told me.

"Can you shoot?" I asked Edie.

"Not really," she replied. "Thomas has been showing me how, but we don't want to waste bullets or attract attention by actually firing."

"Well, I suppose you could hide in the cellar like you have been. You had a pretty good system with the booby traps."

After a bit more discussion, I told them how to turn on the electricity during the day so that they could have running water. There was enough antifreeze left to winterize the pipes a few more times, and even if they left for a few days, there would have to be a pretty extreme cold snap to freeze the pipes. If all went well, they could keep the woodstoves going most of the time.

"It looks like you could use some more firewood yourself," Thomas commented as they got ready to go.

"Yeah, unfortunately my saw is up near the cave, along with my best tent," I answered.

"The next time we're here, I'll go get them," Thomas promised. "And one of us will be back to check on you at least every third day."

After a round of "thank yous," they shouldered their packs and left. Daisy walked out behind them, and I let her, wondering how far she'd tag along, but in less than hour, she scratched at the door. Before I settled back down in my camp chair, I pulled her pad over next to me. She stretched out on her side with her back to my thigh, and I spent a few minutes stroking her and making sure she knew how much I appreciated her company. If there was one mistake I was never going to make again, it was to take any relationship for granted.

December 27

When I went out this morning, the air was surprisingly warm and had that damp, earthy smell that I always associate with a good spring thaw. Energized by the warmth, I dragged a camp chair into a patch of sunshine and settled myself with my sketchbook and a mug of tea. My left foot was feeling better all the time, and I seemed to have made it through the infection in the other, so I had a lot to feel good about.

Instead of working on the story map, I started a drawing of our Christmas dinner, including the wine bottle, the candles in their canning jars, and the plate of preacher cookies, sitting off to one side. I'd never drawn Thomas before, but I'd had plenty of time to observe his features as he worked on my feet. He had a hawkish curve to his nose, thin lips, and high cheekbones that gave him a bit of a Native American look, an impression strengthened by his straight, shoulder-length hair. In the picture he is sitting back in his chair with a little closed-lipped smile, looking toward the space that will eventually become Edie.

As I sketched, I thought about the Ray problem. From what I could tell, he was still able to retain a group of subordinates that could outnumber anyone who tried to stand up to him, and he had an arsenal of guns and ammunition they'd collected from people's houses. It would be interesting to know how closely they kept track of the guns, and whether they'd miss two or three if they disappeared. Stealing guns from Ray would be pretty risky, but it was hard to imagine how to launch a defense without more firepower. If I went back to the cabin, we would have three guns between us. We would be three armed people against how many?

The fact wasn't lost on me that I was now contemplating stealing (though the guns didn't belong to Ray any more than they did me) and taking up arms to defend Edie and Thomas. But, absent the usual methods of recourse, what choice was there? That got me thinking about the sheriff and the other people in town. They couldn't all be in cahoots with Ray. Could there be some chance of getting help there?

I thought and drew for a long time until my muscles began to get stiff and hunger had me thinking about lunch. I'd had to shift my chair several times to stay in the sun, so I must have been out for a good while. But the sunlight had crept off into the woods, so I figured it was time to go in. I limped back to the hut with the sketch pad and mug and returned for the chair. As I turned once again toward the door, Daisy came trotting out of the brush with something gray in her mouth. She headed straight for the hut, so I followed behind, curious to see what she'd found. At the door she sat and waited, and I could make out a furry head and long ears dangling from her jaw. It was a rabbit, and a decent-sized one, too.

"Wow! Daisy! You brought dinner! You are such a good girl!"

I let the chair drop and petted her enthusiastically because in my mind there was no praise too great for this offering of food. I grasped the rabbit by the ears and said, "Give," and wasn't a bit surprised when Daisy opened her mouth quite readily.

"Daisy, you are so wonderful," I continued my praise and went straight to the jerky jar when I got inside. She sat, smiling, as I tore off a chunk and held it out.

Enough mushrooms and onions were left from what Edie brought to put into a rabbit stew, so tonight I had an awesome feast for the second time in three days, and there is enough left to feed Thomas and Edie if they come tomorrow, which they should. Looking back over my time since the accident, it seems that my life has swung like a pendulum between pain, despair, and amazing good fortune. I wonder what would have happened if Edie hadn't left her bandana on the bush by the stream. Or if I had put my tent somewhere other than downwind of the smoking cave. Or if I had never seen Ray and Reese and Thomas coming up the driveway that night. Of course, such speculation is pointless, but in my case, I think that perhaps I am actually learning something from all of this. Something that hearkens back to that lecture that I so often repeated to the girls at the wilderness school. Stop judging everything that happens to you as good or bad. It is all going to lead you somewhere, and your story isn't over yet.

December 31

I've skipped another few days of writing, one day having been pretty much like the other, but as I sit on the bed platform this evening, I am aware that it is the last day of the year, and it feels appropriate to acknowledge it. Peter and I never made a big deal over New Year's Eve. Usually we'd go out for a late dinner and then watch a movie in bed like we did on any number of Friday or Saturday nights. But the last New Year's Eve before Peter got sick stands out in my mind. It was the year that Charles's wife left him, and he was still out of sorts over it, so we invited him to stay over. Erica had been much more social than Charles, and for years he'd allowed her to drag him to parties and rock concerts, though he was never at ease in crowds. Finally, he'd drawn the line when cocaine was showing up more and more often at people's houses, since he could lose his NSA security clearance if he was connected in any way to an illegal drug. After that he'd stayed home while Erica partied, and they drifted further and further apart.

In spite of the cold, Peter had roasted Cornish game hens on the gas grill, and we ate in front of the fireplace with plenty of white wine, and Charles had seemed finally to relax and laugh a little. We watched an old sci-fi movie and toasted in the New Year before Charles headed for the guest room.

Up in our room, Peter and I made love very quietly and talked about how lost Charles seemed, even though Erica had been mostly absent from his life for a long time before she actually left.

"You know what makes me feel good?" Peter asked.

"Uh, yeah, but didn't I just…?" I teased.

"Ha-ha," he answered. "But really, I love the fact that I know that you don't need me, but you want me anyway."

"True," I admitted. "If only you weren't so damned charming, I'd still be a happy spinster, doing my part for feminism."

"Ah well, their loss is my gain," he replied, snuggling his face between my breasts.

I will always treasure those words, but I am thankful that I can now finally think about them without hurting.

A light snow was spiraling down this afternoon when I went for water. Daisy followed along, and I made faster progress since Thomas brought me some crutches he found in the root cellar. I can't use them on the steeper part of the hill, but they help on the level areas, and I can get a rhythm going in my stride that feels almost natural. He also brought back everything I left at the cave and moved the wood pile so that I can reach it more easily. Edie took my dirty clothes and left some clean ones, so most of the time I feel almost civilized.

I don't think this snow will amount to much, but if it does, I have plenty of water and food to last for a couple days. I'm not soaking my feet as often anymore; I've moved on to just a good scrubbing once a day with sterilized, soapy water and the usual layers of ointment and bandages. New skin has grown over the partial thickness burns, and even the hole in my right foot is shrinking.

Now that my injuries are healing, my mind turns more frequently toward the town and what is happening there. On their last visit, I asked Edie and Thomas for more details about how the townspeople are managing. Apparently, although he has given Ray and his group unrestrained freedom, the sheriff has done a lot to ensure that supplies and food are distributed fairly. Every old cart that's been rotting in someone's barn has been retooled, and horses are being used to deliver necessities like food, milk, water, and firewood. The older population has been concentrated into houses in town that have woodstoves to make it easier to care for them. Every seed that could be rustled up was planted in the spring, and the community canned much of the resulting produce. Some of the houses still have hand pumps in the yard for their wells, and in the weeks immediately following the blackout, a line was run from a nearby creek into town. A dozen or so outhouses were built, mostly from reusing the wood from old sheds and barns. And most everyone who had something that the town could use gave it up in the interest of getting back something they needed. As a result, the elementary school is now a working farm with a milking parlor, chicken house, pigsty, community kitchen, and food processing area. Some of the classrooms are being used to house the single deputies and livestock caretakers, which means there are always plenty of folks around to keep an eye on things. Before she left, Edie spent most of her time helping her mother take care of the elderly. The worst part, Edie said, was the stench of unwashed flesh and potty buckets, the emptying of which fell mostly to her.

I asked Edie whether she thought her mother was doing alright. She said she didn't know; all the painkillers must have run out and that would be hard on her. Ray yelled at her and bullied her a little, but he hadn't ever seriously hurt her, as far as she knew.

"But I'd sure like to have her with me, if we could get her to leave," she said. "Ray doesn't do a thing for free."

As I mull this over, my desire to go to town and see the situation for myself grows, but the logistics of the journey escape me. The round trip walk from the cabin would be close to ten miles—not something I'm up for yet. I could get the truck going, but I rather Ray not know of its existence. We did have a couple of bikes in a stall in the barn…I hadn't thought to check on them while I was there. But, transportation issues aside, I would want to talk to the sheriff if I went, and he might feel that I'm obliged to turn over some of my supplies to the town, something I'm not prepared to do, at least not yet.

When I let Daisy in a few minutes ago, the snow had drifted about two inches deep against the door. She knocked a bunch of it onto the floor as she trotted in and headed for her pad, where she now lies, licking the melting snow off her paws. She seems as content as can be, though sometimes she noses along the edge of the bed at night before she finally settles in. I'm not sure whether she is checking on me or looking for an invite, but if she were to make her intentions more obvious, I could go along with that.

January 3

The snow of New Year's Eve melted off quickly, and this morning feels absolutely spring-like, so I decided to make a trek up to my lookout spot. I packed just the very basics: my sketch pad; water; some snacks; a first aid kit with fire starters; a small, light tarp; a headlamp; and, of course, the pistol. You may wonder at the tarp and fire starters, but after my last accident I am careful to always be prepared for an unexpected night in the woods. At the last minute, I added a pair of binoculars, thinking there might be some birds flitting around on such a nice day. With the small, folding camp stool strapped to the outside of my pack, I called Daisy, and we started over the mountainside by mid-morning. Though I had to raise the crutches high to avoid limbs and rocks, I still made good progress, except on the steeper slopes. Wearing Peter's boots keeps my feet dry and comfortable, so I found myself actually enjoying the new normal that I've settled into.

By the time I reached the overlook, I had stripped off my down jacket, but the breeze was brisk, so I put it back on before settling on the stool, which I placed up against a tree for back support. Daisy had taken off after a squirrel, and I expected that she'd roam for a bit before returning, though I'd noticed that she'd never been gone for more than a few hours since the day that Edie and Thomas brought me home.

At the north end of the overlook stood a gnarled oak with a small hollow at its base. It reminded me of a tree in the small patch of woods behind our house where I used to play. I would spend hours pretending that the hollow was the doorway of a gnome's house, making a little stone walkway to it and sticking twigs in the dirt to stand as trees and shrubs. In the spring I added flowers, mostly dandelions, and one Christmas I pinned holly around the "door." Taking out my sketchbook, I spent at least an hour drawing the tree and recreating my magical gnome house.

After a while, Daisy reappeared and reminded me that it was lunch time, so I took out some jerky and nuts and shared a bit with her as we sat and basked in the sun. Daisy got restless when I put away the food and took off again, so I decided to take out the binoculars and see what I might find on the opposite hillside. Scanning a section of woods at a time, I mostly found squirrels and their nests until my eye caught a movement on the trunk of a dead hemlock. Skittering up and down the trunk, not far off the ground, was a little bird with blackish wings, a dusky-orange breast, and a black stripe through its eye. It was facing toward the ground, and I figured it might be some kind of nuthatch looking for insects. I watched it for a few minutes and then picked up my sketch pad and added it to my gnome house picture, placing it on the tree trunk above the doorway. I was intent on my drawing, trying to get the angle of the short, narrow beak just right, when Daisy came trotting out of the woods again and sat down near the edge of the clearing. She looked at me for a moment and then turned her head back toward the woods. I followed her gaze and was amazed to see the four coyote cubs step cautiously up to the edge of the clearing. They sat tentatively and looked from Daisy to me as though waiting for directions. They'd grown taller and heftier since I'd seen them back in November, and their coats had become sleeker, losing all trace of their former fluffiness. I sat still, trying to watch without exuding the merest trace of a threat. If anything, I was a bit downwind of them, but I could see their noses stretching forward, straining to catch my scent.

It seemed like a moment frozen in time, and I wondered how this encounter would end. Daisy obviously wanted her two families formally introduced, but what now? My question was soon answered as there was another movement in the brush and the mama coyote's head appeared behind the cubs. Ignoring me, she nudged the closest cub and they all stood and wheeled around, disappearing into the woods so completely that I almost doubted the whole exchange. Daisy watched them leave with her head down and then trotted over to me.

"Good girl," I told her. "You wanted me to meet your family, eh? They were very nice to help take care of you. Tell them I said 'thank you' the next time you see them." I scratched her behind the ears and kissed her forehead. "It's you and me now, though. Okay?"

After that I put my sketchbook away and as I started to pack up, I noticed a strong smell of smoke. When I looked toward the west, a wide plume of gray was rising into the sky, maybe three or four miles off. I thought a bit and decided that it was coming from a spot slightly north of Wagner. There was no way to tell how large the fire was from that distance, but it got me thinking about the town again. I'd told Edie and Thomas on their last visit that I thought I could manage pretty well if they wanted to slack off for a bit, but I suddenly had the urge to talk to them about the possibility of my visiting the town. Thomas has slipped in and out several times, not to mention that he knows the sheriff, so maybe he would have some good advice.

If I want to talk to them soon, I'll have to go back to the cabin. And maybe this time I will stay for a few days and have that hot bath I've been craving. It's comforting to think of the cabin as a haven again and not as potential enemy territory. Maybe I should enjoy it while it lasts.

January 6

Tonight I write from my bed in the cabin with the light of my bedside lamp. I did not turn off the electricity as was my former habit, but have merely drawn the blackout curtains across both dormer windows. I arrived just a bit after midday, got the electricity going, and after giving the water a while to heat, finally got that bath.

Edie and Thomas are not here. After I let myself in the back door, I went straight down into the cellar where I found a note that read, "We have gone to Wagner to talk to my mom. Plan to spend at least one night." But the note wasn't dated, so I couldn't tell how long they'd been gone. When I went back upstairs, I raked the ashes in the living room woodstove and found them cold. The kitchen cookstove still had a few golf ball-sized embers, though, so I figured they hadn't been gone more than a day or so.

After loading up the kitchen stove, I tooled around the house, just taking stock and getting used to being here. The pans and boards Edie and Thomas had been using for noisemakers were stacked neatly near the doors, and the bowls and dishes were all put away in the cupboards. There were towels hanging in the bathroom and fresh water in the toilet bowl, and in general, the house had a nice, lived-in feel to it. I brought up some bouillon, dried vegetables, wild rice, and canned chicken and started a pot of soup on the cookstove. They'd apparently brought a good-sized load of food over from the root cellar—a good move since moving the tractor back and forth over the entrance is such a chore.

By the time I got out of my bath, the soup was simmering and sending off a wonderful smell. Daisy had been outside exploring most of the afternoon. When I called her in through the back door, she sniffed around the kitchen, paused to take in the aroma of the soup, and then retreated to the living room, where she jumped onto the chair by the door and curled up immediately. After my bath, I dressed from head to foot in clean clothes that Edie had left folded on top of the dryer. We'd agreed to use the laundry soap very sparingly, but the trace of detergent and, more obviously, the lack of other smells on the clothes was heavenly. As Daisy napped, I fixed a cup of tea and surveyed the bookshelf, finally choosing a book of Flannery O'Conner short stories before settling onto the sofa. But for some reason, I still felt restless, wondering how things were going with Edie and Thomas in town and when they would return. I was thinking about how nice it would be to sit around after dinner and play cards or board games when it occurred to me that having some music would be fun, too. I'd brought my solar charger and cell phone, but neither was charged, so I went and got them out of my backpack and plugged them in on the kitchen counter.

That was when Daisy jumped off the chair and stood growling at the door, and I heard the drone of a motor drawing near. My first thought was that it was

Ray again, and I cursed the odd force I seemed to possess that kept drawing him here. My gun was still in the bathroom, and by the time I ran to get it, I could see through the window in the door that the motorcycle had stopped at the edge of the lawn, and the rider was hopping off.

Something casual in his movements stood out to me as he pulled the helmet from his head and sat it on the seat, revealing his round face and bushy beard. It was Ray, for sure. He was wearing tan boots and trousers, a tight cap, and several layers of jackets. Though I couldn't see a gun anywhere, I assumed that there must be one hidden underneath all those layers. He rubbed his sleeve over his moustache before stripping off his gloves and barely glanced at the house, as though he was certain that he was totally alone.

And then Daisy barked with a low, guttural force I had never heard from her before.

The look of surprise on Ray's face was almost comical as he jerked his head up to look at the house. Since he didn't have a weapon ready, I figured that was my chance, so I opened the door and let Daisy rush out. Leaning against the door jamb, I lifted the pistol in front of me with both hands.

"Stay exactly where you are," I called over Daisy's barking.

She'd stopped about ten feet in front of him, prancing from side to side.

Ray raised his hands in front of his chest and yelled, "Call off your dog!"

"In a minute, maybe. Who are you and what do you want?"

"I'm from town," he yelled.

"Daisy, sit!" I commanded, and she sat between him and the porch steps and stopped barking.

"Are you the lady of the house?" he asked.

"Hah!" I laughed. "If you're asking whether I own this place, the answer is yes. What do you want?"

"I'm just looking for a couple of runaways, teenagers that ran off from the town."

"Huh. Can't say that I've seen any. So, now that you've got your answer, get off of my property. You're trespassing." I gestured with the pistol toward his motorcycle.

"Are you sure?" he persisted, which pissed me off because it showed that he was not sufficiently deterred.

"Get off my yard. Now," I answered, and then I very deliberately aimed the gun at the ground near his feet. I squeezed the trigger, and the blast of the pistol seemed to shatter the air around us. He took a quick step backward.

"Jesus, lady, I'm going."

"Faster," I ordered.

I watched him carefully as he turned and pulled on his helmet and gloves, alert for any movement that would signal that he was going for a gun. When he mounted and started the bike, he was still facing me, and I trained my sights right at his chest to be sure he'd gotten the message.

Tracing a careful U-turn at the top of the driveway, he took off down the hill as though he thought I might send another bullet his way. I lowered the gun and listened until the buzz of the motorcycle was lost in the distance. Daisy rose as soon as he disappeared and stood on the porch facing me as if to ask whether her performance was acceptable.

"Good girl," I said, stooping to rub her head.

Back inside, I ladled some soup into a bowl for her and added a bit of cold water to cool it before setting it on the floor. I wasn't ready to eat yet, but I wanted her reward to be quick. Then I sat back on the couch with a fresh cup of tea to ponder what had just happened.

For some reason, I was sure that Ray hadn't expected to find Edie and Thomas at the house, perhaps because he knew they were in town somewhere. Then why had he come? To look for evidence that they were staying here? To leave them a threatening note or mess up their stuff? To see if anyone had joined them? That was an interesting thought. Perhaps there had been other defectors. Or maybe he was planning to ambush them when they returned.

He'd come by himself, also interesting. Was he having trouble getting cooperation from his crew? That would be good news; we'd outnumber him if he came back alone.

Sipping my tea, I was surprised to find that I was more angry than scared. I would have thought I'd feel shaky, like when you have a really close call on the highway and you can't believe you're alive and not dying upside down in a ditch. Ray was a bully and a coward, but even so, his ego was probably suffering a decisive blow from being faced down by a woman. But perhaps I'd rattled him enough that it would take time for him to recover, time enough for us to come up with a plan.

Before I came to bed, I reassembled the booby traps in the kitchen and living room and opened the downstairs bedroom doors to make it easier to hear if someone breaks through a window. Although the upstairs is plenty hot, I haven't undressed, planning to sleep on top of the covers with my gun nearby. Daisy is curled at the foot of the bed, and my boots and jacket are by the chair, but I did not pack my backpack for flight or hide it outside. If I leave this house tonight, I'm not going far, and whoever chases me out will find out that they've asked for more than they planned to handle. After I turn out my headlamp, I will open the curtains and take one last look around the yard. And while I may not sleep soundly, I will enjoy a measure of peace from the fact that I am now determined that Ray will never have the upper hand again.

January 7

Although I can't say that I slept well last night, I did sleep, and whenever I woke, the house was unnaturally quiet. Daisy, on the other hand, slept without stirring, save for once when she wriggled her way up from the foot of the bed to press up against me. The house had cooled considerably by then, and I made a mental note to find a light blanket today that I can cover her with at night.

It was just light this morning when we descended the stairs. After stoking the kitchen stove, I went into the bathroom to pee and brush my teeth, marveling at how strange it was to be in a house with running water.

For most of the morning, I hobbled around outside, continuing to take stock. In the barn, I managed to get myself up the ladder to the loft. The sleeping bag I'd found on my earlier visit was still squirreled away behind the hay bales. I'll have to remember to ask Thomas about it. Back down on the main level, I poked my head into the chicken room. It was such a shame to have all those ready-made coops and no chickens. Maybe we could rig up some traps and get some turkeys. I could clip their wings and we could make a turkey yard. A check of the wood pile showed that we still had plenty of wood to make it through the winter. Thomas had disconnected and drained the line to the water tank, and there were no signs of disturbance around the truck.

Around noon I heated up the soup and took a bowl out on the front porch. The sun had been shining brightly all morning, and the thermometer that Peter hung on the post read forty-six degrees, which probably seems a bit chilly for eating out, but I was finding being inside claustrophobic. Without a constant view of the yard, I felt that Ray and his friends could sneak up any minute.

From the porch, I could watch in three directions at once. Peter had talked about putting in security cameras, but that was another item on the list that we'd never gotten around to. As I sat there wondering if we could get a couple from somewhere in town, Daisy jumped up and began wagging her tail, and soon Edie and Thomas walked up the driveway.

"I thought you might come by," Edie said as she climbed the stairs to the porch. "Did you get my note?"

I said I had and offered them some soup, so we went in and sat at the kitchen table. I held back on telling them about Ray's visit, wanting first to hear what had happened in Wagner.

"My mom seemed okay, maybe a little skinnier than I remembered," Edie started. "She was shelling dried corn on the back porch when we walked up yesterday morning. I thought she was a bit startled to see us. Don't you think so, Tommy?"

Thomas nodded and said, "I'd seen her just a couple weeks before. She shouldn't have been too surprised."

They'd all gone inside to talk so that no one would see them, and they'd tried to talk to her about Ray.

"I even told her that he'd run you out of your own house back in July by showing up with his buddies and a bunch of guns in the middle of the night. She said, of course he had a gun, it's a dangerous world now. She still doesn't want to believe that he's not one of the good guys."

"That's not too surprising," I said. "It's something like Stockholm syndrome. She's so dependent on him, she has to give him the benefit of the doubt."

Edie went on to say that while they were talking, they heard someone coming up the front steps. It was Reese with a jar of milk and a bag of food. Thomas had jumped out the back door, but Edie just sat there.

"I could tell he was stunned to see me. So I said, 'What's so strange about me visiting my mom?' He just stuck the food on the counter and took off, probably to tell Ray, and we left right after that."

"But we hid in a barn last night, in case he had people watching the woods and the roads. Then we made a pretty wide circle before we headed back here," Thomas added.

"Well, he's got his mind made up that you've been staying here," I said, and then I told them about my own encounter. Afterward, we speculated some more on Ray's motives, and I told them how I wanted to go to town and talk to the sheriff. "What do you think?" I asked.

Thomas said that Sheriff Shaheen always been a pretty low-key, behind-the-scenes kind of guy before the blackout—divorced, no children, and the job was pretty much his whole life. He was using the principal's office as his own, so he could keep an eye on the farm and because it had better light than the police station.

"Why don't you think he's done anything about Ray?" I asked.

"I think he wants to, but what can he? There's no real jail in Wagner, and no courts working. Ray would have to do something pretty bad in front of a bunch of people for him to be able to do anything."

By then they'd finished their soup and volunteered to clean up. Thomas and I made plans to go through the root cellar together later, and I retired upstairs to try to think through what they'd told me. I sat on the bed with a notebook in front of me, thinking I would write out some notes to clear my mind, but the next thing I knew, Edie was peering around the landing asking if I still wanted to go the root cellar. She said I'd slept for over two hours.

When I got to the barn, Thomas had already moved the tractor. I tossed him a solar lamp, and we descended the stairs. The new entrance came down along the wall opposite the original door. Under the stairs, Peter had stored an assortment of tools including two scythes, some saws and axes, rakes, and a variety of shovels. The outer room contained mostly canned and dried foods, a large store of ammunition and batteries, clothes, and camping gear. I felt Peter's presence strongly in the care that he had used to prepare and organize so much stuff, but I pushed the feelings away and tried to focus on the task at hand, which wasn't so much an exact inventory as just a reminder of what was there. I scrounged around gathering baking supplies, a few bottles of wine, some pasta, and canned meats. Thomas and I had both brought backpacks down with us, and by the time we'd gone through all three rooms, they were full and heavy. As I dragged my pack toward the steps, I had an idea, and I asked Thomas whether he knew what kind of gun Sheriff Shaheen used.

"I don't know what the department uses, but I'm pretty sure I've seen him with a 9mm," Thomas said.

That thought led to another, and soon I was rummaging around the electronics boxes, trying to remember just what Peter and I had decided about communications. Finally, back behind the batteries, I found what I was looking for, a box containing six sets of four walkie-talkies each. I checked the packaging to figure out which batteries they used and threw in a few dozen, plus a couple of chargers. Thomas had already hauled the backpacks up the stairs and met me halfway down to take the box.

"Nice," he said. "We can really use these around here."

"And I bet the sheriff could use a few, too," I answered. "If I'm going to visit, I might as well go bearing gifts. He won't be able to recharge the batteries, but maybe we can work out some sort of deal."

Back in the house, we opened up one set of walkie talkies and then spent an hour or so calling each other from different locations around the property. More for fun than camouflage, we each chose an alias: Edie was Lambchops, Thomas was Hatchet, and I chose Scout. Daisy didn't understand what was going on, but she seemed to enjoy following us around and running back and forth. Finally, as the afternoon light dwindled, I called them into the kitchen. While I worked on a pasta sauce, we established some guidelines for using the radios and worked out an emergency code word in case one of us was in a position where we couldn't speak freely. After some discussion, we came up with uncomfortable, thinking it could easily be worked into lots of contexts, such as, "I'm so uncomfortable sitting here, would you please let me move around?" Or "I think I twisted my ankle; it's really uncomfortable." It still felt like we were play acting, but we also knew that Ray could come back any time, and we needed some sort of plan for that contingency.

We played Rummy for a while after supper, and I played a mix of rock oldies from my downloaded music, keeping the volume low so as not to drown out any unusual noises. Daisy again helped herself to the chair by the door, which was now her seat of honor for having warned me of Ray's approach. With the curtains drawn and the only light coming from the solar lamp, I felt almost as imprisoned as I'd felt at times in the hut. But it also felt good to be with Edie and Thomas, and the mood was light as we sang along to Lynyrd Skynyrd and pretended to care who won the game. When we turned in, I convinced them to sleep in the back bedroom. Thomas has his rifle, and I have my pistol. We set up the noise traps and parted ways at the foot of the stairs.

January 11

A slow-moving front has kept us in for the past few days with alternating drizzle and sleet, making me wonder how the early settlers ever made it through the boredom of winter. But I guess they had more chores than we do to keep them busy, like milking cows, churning butter, mending harnesses, sewing, and hunting. If it weren't for church and sewing bees, though, I think the women would probably have all gone crazy with "cabin fever," which I read someplace was a real thing. As for us, there weren't too many inside chores that needed doing. Thomas dragged some wood into the barn and spent a couple hours each day splitting it. Then he found the bicycles and lubed them up. I cleaned my camping equipment and dried it out so that it wouldn't get dry rot. Edie helped me reorganize the cellar this morning, but by early afternoon, I couldn't stay in any more, and I asked her if she'd like to take a walk up the forest road. Thomas stayed to keep an eye on the place, and Edie and I bundled up in layers and rain jackets and set off down the driveway with Daisy. I had my gun, and we all had our walkie-talkies, just in case.

As I probably mentioned before, the forest road climbs gradually and dead ends a couple of miles past the cabin. If we walked it to the end and back, we'd get a decent workout, particularly in my case since my injury has kept me from much exercising. I told Edie to set the pace and I would keep up as best I could on my crutches. But when she got out in front of me by twenty yards or so, she slowed to my pace, which was good because I was coated in sweat already and a bit shocked to realize how out of shape I'd become. I continued to push myself a bit faster than was comfortable, though, and vowed to make the hike a part of my daily routine.

As we climbed the road, we noticed all kinds of tracks in the mud: deer, coyote, turkey, and near where the creek met the road, some large tracks without claws that I took to be bobcat.

"How do you know all this?" Edie asked, and it occurred to me that I still hadn't told her much about myself.

I started with the TRAILS program at George Washington and how it had led to my job at the Mountain Shepherd Wilderness School. She said she figured I was some sort of teacher, but hadn't realized how the whole outdoors and medical training figured in.

"Did your husband work there, too?" she asked, and then added, "If that was your husband in those pictures, I mean."

"No, he worked for the National Security Agency," I answered and then tried to explain that the NSA was like a bunch of spies who sat around in buildings and did electronic surveillance and code-breaking. "It was his idea to buy the cabin and put in the solar panels," I told her.

"Like he knew what was going to happen," she commented.

"Yeah. Sort of," I said.

"And he died?"

I felt guilty at making her prompt me like that, but it was still a hard topic to bring up.

"Yes. He died of pancreatic cancer. About seven months before the blackout."

"Oh. Sorry," she said. "Do you have anyone else?"

So then I told her about my mother and Aunt JoAnn, and how I had no way of knowing what had happened to them. By then, we were approaching the turnaround at the end of the road, which was crisscrossed with other tracks that we examined and tried to identify, plus some coyote scat. I thought that our conversation was over when we started back down, but suddenly Edie said, "I don't know what I would do if something happened to my mom. It's like I can't totally leave while she's still in town, but I can't go back, either."

"Maybe you need to tell her," I said.

"Tell her? About...?"

"Yes. Maybe then she would leave with you, and we could bring her home."

As we walked the rain picked up, and we fell into a pensive silence, each absorbed in our own thoughts. Daisy, soaked and subdued by the rain, trudged along behind, and I imagined that we probably looked quite the sad little parade, splashing along with our heads down, rain dripping onto our legs and into our boots, eyes fixed on the ground in front of us.

January 13

Today the clouds were finally absent, though the temperature has dropped, and I fear we are in for a cold snap. While winter temperatures in Virginia are usually above freezing during the day, at least once every winter the jet stream dips and sends the mercury plummeting toward zero overnight, with daytime temps that barely rise out of the teens. After the second day of rain, we had limited our electricity use to just the water pump and hot water heater in order to preserve the solar power. We hadn't been using the refrigerator much, anyway. With no dairy products, mayonnaise, or meat there wasn't much need.

We've frozen containers of ice on the back porch overnight, and if we want to keep something cold, we put it in the freezer with the ice chunks and use it like an ice chest. In warmer weather, I think we'll just turn on the fridge enough to freeze more ice. We limit the laundry to no more than a load every third day or so, and we forgo that if it's been overcast for more than a twenty-four hours.

I'm writing today from the loveseat in the living room with the sun finally back on duty and flooding in through the front window. Thomas and Edie are up in the woods with his Winchester and my rifle, working on Edie's shooting skills. The noise of sporadic gunfire and the expenditure of a hundred rounds of ammunition will be worth it to ensure that we can all use each of the guns. My plan is to have them practice at different times for at least four days, and if Ray is within earshot, all the better; he will know that we are not mere sitting ducks. Unfortunately, I don't have a lot of ammo that is suitable for Thomas's gun, so they are mostly using my AR-15. Maybe the sheriff will be able to help in that regard, too.

I think more and more about our trip to town. This morning I did my third walk to the end of the forest road, and I am putting more weight on the outside of the right foot with hardly any discomfort. In a week or so, I think that I'll be able to make the trip, and with three of us, we can easily carry some camping gear so that we don't have to come all the way back if I get too tired. Thomas and Edie can go talk to Edie's mother while I try my luck with Sheriff Shaheen, and, hopefully, my offer of walkie-talkies and battery charging will buy us some good will. Ray will undoubtedly find out about my conversation with the sheriff, which could make it riskier for him to harm us. At least, I hope so.

I am not lounging in the living room just for comfort. We've been trying to arrange ways to surveil the area around the house on a routine basis. As we do our various chores, each person is responsible for keeping an eye out in one direction or another. Unfortunately, the west side of the house has the fewest windows, and with Edie and Thomas gone, every few minutes I must get up and look out the window at the end of the hall and then go into the kitchen to stare out the back door. When I settle back onto the loveseat, I have good views out the front and east windows. It's not a very full-proof arrangement, but if Ray and his crew were to approach slowly enough, I might see them.

Another advantage to being obvious about having weapons is that, in a pinch, we can use them for hunting. I'm still hesitant to use up a great number of bullets that way, but it's good to have the option. Thomas has never used snares before, but one afternoon in the woods is all it should take to teach him, and then we can stop using up so much of our stores of protein.

During the days of rain, I watched our moods deteriorate. Edie snapped at Thomas about leaving a mess in the bathroom, and he spent the afternoon in the barn, sulking. I realized then that we needed a greater sense of order and purpose. After dinner last night, I instituted a new routine, and we wrote out two lists: one of regular chores and another of more sporadic projects that needed doing. After we agreed on the daily stuff, we also determined that every night we would discuss the next day's goals and assignments. At breakfast we would make changes to allow for the weather and other factors. Everyone would have some free time during the day to do as they pleased, and we would all be responsible for airing our grudges before they got out of hand. I stressed that the schedule was mostly so that we had a sense of purpose and cohesion, not a tool of control, and we could scrap it any time it didn't seem to be working. They were both agreeable to that, and I think it will be interesting to see how it works.

All of this organizing and planning have made me feel a bit like I'm back at the wilderness school, and I've assumed the care of Edie and Thomas as though it were a job. I have mixed feelings about this, and I even wonder if they have moments when they wish I'd just stayed up in the woods, although they've never shown anything but gratitude. If we manage to convince Edie's mother to come back with us, I'll have yet another dependent. Another mouth to feed, but also more help. Looking even further ahead, I wonder what will happen if the Ray problem is somehow solved. Will they all just go back to town? Will I want them to?

January 16

Again, I haven't written for a couple of days. The arms training has been going well, and yesterday Thomas and Edie spent about an hour with the 9mm in the afternoon. In the morning we retrieved the truck battery and coil wire from the root cellar so that we could find out whether the truck would run. First, we had to pull off all of the brush I had piled over it—a scratchy and awkward job. The tarp underneath was black with dirt but had held up well. After we got it off, I raised the hood and showed Thomas and Edie how to insert the coil wire. Finally, Thomas heaved the battery into place, a chore I was glad not to have to do myself. Once we had the cables attached, I turned to them and asked, "So who would like to do the honors?"

Thomas turned toward Edie, who promptly said, "Don't look at me. I don't even know how to drive."

Thomas grinned like he'd just won a trophy, and I tossed him the keys. He'd noticed the truck before but hadn't felt that he had the right to investigate, so the reality that I had an antique Ford F-250 had only just hit him. He jumped in and turned the key.

The engine rumbled to life, such a strange sound after all this time.

We let it run for a few minutes, and then I gestured to him to pull it forward about a foot, just to have it resting on a different section of tire. Then I did a cutting motion across my neck. He switched off the engine and just sat for a moment, looking around the interior. Before he got out, he ran a hand along the dashboard, almost as though he were petting Daisy.

As we were heaping brush back over the tarp, Thomas asked me whether I thought we might actually use it sometime.

"Sooner than you may think," I answered.

But as satisfying as it was to get the truck going, that wasn't the high point of the day.

At about mid-afternoon Thomas and Edie headed up the slope with the 9mm. Daisy set off with them, but I imagined that the gunfire would send her back before too long. Peter had left earplugs with the ammunition in the cellar, so Edie and Thomas were better equipped for the noise than Daisy. They'd waited for the warmest part of the day since the temperature was still below freezing. At least the wind was calm, though, and they seemed to be enjoying their firearms jaunts.

After loading the woodstove, I went upstairs to put away some clothes and stare out the front dormer for a while. I'd already done my walk up the hill and back, and I was a little drowsy from the heat coming up the stairs. But I hadn't done the lunch dishes yet, and it was my turn, and I'd also been thinking about doing some extra cleaning in the kitchen, so instead of lying down, I headed back downstairs, pausing to look out the west-facing window for a minute on my way. One of the nice things about winter is that you can see so far into the woods and get a feel for the lay of the land. This was the time of the year when everything was at its grayest, the dark trunks barely standing out against the dull brush and only the occasional pine or rhododendron interrupting that sameness.

Before getting started in the kitchen, I surveyed the hill behind the house. From the back door, the porch roof obscured the top half of the hill, so I stepped out into the chill air to take a quick look. I could see the stand of pines where I'd twice hidden to watch the house. But, save for a bird flitting here and there through the bushes, all was still. I soon stepped back into the warmth of the kitchen and ran some water, glorious hot water, for the dishes. In the distance, I could hear the slow, steady report of the 9mm.

By the time the gunshots ceased, I had the kitchen floor swept and mostly mopped. If you've ever used a woodstove, you know that a fine layer of ash eventually accumulates on every surface and takes a lot of effort to get up. But I've always subscribed to the "good enough is good enough" philosophy of cleaning; after all, it wasn't like anything was going to stay clean for more than an instant. I was giving the sponge mop what I hoped was one last rinse when the walkie-talkie I had clipped to the waistband of my pants crackled to life.

"Scout, Scout. This is Hatchet. We are approaching the house from the north and observe a person walking up the driveway. A large person, walking very slowly. Do you copy?"

I grabbed the receiver and answered.

"Scout here. Message received. I will arm myself and get ready to intercept. How soon will you be close enough to cover me?"

"We'll be there in two minutes," he answered.

"Where's Daisy?" I asked.

"Don't know. Last seen as we started shooting."

"Okay. Be sure that you can hear me, maybe around the edge of the barn," I instructed.

"Roger."

The AR-15 was leaning against the corner behind the door. Through the window I could see that whoever was coming hadn't yet crested the top of the driveway. I slipped into my coat and grabbed the rifle, all the while keeping an eye out the window. Soon a hood-covered head appeared. Thomas was right, this was a large dude. Under the hood I could make out a black knit cap, a pair of black sunglasses, and a thick, dark beard. His stride was slow and measured, as though he was conserving every bit of energy. By the time his shoulders came over the rise, I was sure that it wasn't Ray, or Reese, or anyone I could think of. He was wearing a large backpack, but his mitten-clad hands appeared empty.

The figure was about twenty yards away when I opened the door and stepped out onto the porch.

"That's close enough," I yelled. "Who are you, and what do you want?"

At my words, the figure stopped and held up his hands.

"It's okay," he yelled back. "Aurora, it's okay! It's just me!"

As I struggled to recognize his voice, a voice that sounded both familiar and other-worldly at the same time, he cautiously reached up to pull off his hood and cap. And that was when Daisy came around the side of the house at a dead run.

"Daisy!" I screamed. "Stop! It's just, it's…CHARLES!"

I laid the rifle on the top step and grabbed my walkie-talkie, forgetting that Thomas and Edie had probably heard everything.

"All clear, all clear," I yelled. Then I dropped the walkie-talkie, too, and lunged toward Charles.

We wrapped each other in a big bear hug that didn't end until with both lost our balance and pulled apart to keep from toppling over.

"I can't believe it's you!" I said.

Thomas and Edie walked up and I introduced them, my tone full of amazement.

"This is my friend, Charles! He worked with Peter in D.C!"

I had to wipe my eyes as they shook hands. I'd spent nine months since the blackout getting used to the idea that I might never see anyone from my old life again, and it felt as though Charles had suddenly risen from the dead.

Daisy approached and started sniffing at Charles's pant legs and hands.

"You got a dog?" Charles said.

"Yeah, though I'm not sure who adopted who," I answered.

I ushered everyone inside and got some water heating for coffee and soup. As Charles peeled off his layers, I could see that his belt was cinched tightly to hold up pants that were now at least a couple sizes too big. The double chin that I remembered was gone, and his eyes protruded from deep sockets. I went back to the kitchen and got a large glass of water, which he drank straight down.

"Wow," he said, "I was starting to think that I wouldn't make it." He rested his head on the back of the couch and closed his eyes.

"Just relax," I told him. "I'll bring you some soup and coffee in a minute, but I think you should just chill for a while. We can talk later."

I went into the kitchen where Thomas and Edie were sitting at the table. The water was starting to bubble, and I poured some into the French press and added a package of ramen to the soup in the pot.

"He looks really beat," Thomas said.

"Yeah. When I first got here, I kept expecting him to show up. He helped Peter with a lot of the work on the house and the hut. But after a while I figured he must have found somewhere else to go. He's divorced, and his folks live in Hawaii," I told them.

I took a mug of coffee into the living room, but Charles was dead out, snoring with his head hanging to one side. I put the coffee on the end table and kneeled to unlace his boots. He barely stirred as I pulled them off. When Ray had ransacked the house, he'd taken all the bedclothes and pillows, but he'd left the little decorative ones that matched the furniture, so I made sure there was a pillow at the end of the couch and covered Charles with his jacket.

Back in the kitchen, I filled Thomas and Edie in on more of our history with Charles. Thomas was curious about the whole spying angle and wondered what would have happened at the NSA when the blackout hit.

"I guess we'll just have to wait to find out. If he can tell us," I said.

Charles slept all afternoon, eventually slumping over onto his side and curling into a fetal position. When he awoke, the living room was darkening, and Edie and Thomas were busy in the kitchen starting dinner. I'd been rereading Surfacing by Margaret Atwood on my Kindle and just watching Charles sleep.

For dinner, Edie combined two dehydrated stroganoff meals and extended them with extra gravy and noodles. There were stewed apples for a side, and as a special treat, orange Jell-O with dried cranberries. I still had a thousand questions I wanted to ask Charles, but I waited until we were sipping whiskey-spiked coffee after dessert before I started.

"So, Charles," I said, "Where the hell have you been?"

January 17

That first night, Charles gave us the short version of what he'd been doing for nine months. When the announcement came for people to go home and shelter in place, the NSA had initiated its second-highest level of emergency protocol. About half of the daytime employees were sent home, but other high-level folks were called in. The emergency generators came on when the electricity failed, and work continued in an effort to produce actionable intelligence on the responsible parties. Charles stayed at the NSA building with an ever-dwindling staff for two months, until the food finally ran out and conditions became unlivable. From the NSA headquarters, he'd made his way to my place, trying to figure out where I was. Linda let him in, and he went foraging for food and water for the three of them all summer. But then the baby got sick with a horrible diarrhea, and there was nothing they could do to stop it. She died in mid-September.

After that Linda was a wreck and finally decided to try to get to her mother's house in Frederick, although they were both pretty sure that they'd find more bad news. By circling around to the west of DC, they'd picked up the Baltimore and Ohio Tow Trail, which runs from DC all the way to Harper's Ferry at the far western tip of Maryland. It took them four days to get there, and they found Linda's mother's house empty. The road that she lived on seemed deserted, though people had obviously gone around to every house and taken whatever they could. Curiously, there were no bodies anywhere; either the occupants had gone somewhere else or someone had been diligent about collecting the corpses. After a few days, they'd found that there was a large group living at Hood College, but no one there remembered seeing Linda's mother. By then, Linda was getting nervous about the possibility that Steve would somehow come home and not be able to find her, so they made the trip back to Arlington.

When they got back to DC, assistance was starting to trickle in to some port cities from overseas. But the logistics of distributing it were almost insurmountable. People who could get to a few select and heavily guarded warehouses were given meager rations on certain days of the week, but there was no one to protect them from thieves when they left the area. With the weather turning cold again, people were becoming even more desperate.

"Even with a weapon, I wasn't any match when I was outnumbered," Charles told us. "At the end of October, Linda decided to join a group that's living at National Harbor. We'd run into an acquaintance of hers from college who was living there; we found her in the crowd at the port. She left a note for Steve and planned to check back every couple of weeks. For some reason, I felt better on my own. But after a while, it seemed like there wasn't a scrap of food left anywhere, so I helped myself to your camping supplies and headed toward the Appalachian Trail. Your survival book came in handy, but once I read it, I left it in a shelter near Front Royal to lighten my load."

It was an amazing story. An able-bodied hiker could have made it to my place from DC in four or five weeks, but having to stop in bad weather and scrounge for food along the way had slowed him considerably.

By the time he finished, we were all exhausted from the tale, and poor Charles hadn't even had a chance to take a shower. Then there was the problem of clothes. He only had the ones he was wearing, though he'd been lucky to find those in Harrisonburg when he left the trail and headed west. Edie volunteered to stay up and wash them after he had as much hot water as he wanted for his shower, and I retrieved a light sleeping bag from the cellar that he could wrap up in afterward. As he rose to head to the bathroom, Thomas stopped him with a question.

"So, did you figure it out?" he asked.

"Figure what out?" Charles answered.

"Who did this?"

Charles seemed to think for a minute, and then he said. "We're pretty sure, maybe ninety per cent. All the evidence pointed toward North Korea. But we won't ever know."

"Why not?" Thomas asked.

"We nuked them. Five days after the attack."

As I write these words, I am still in a state of disbelief. The house is deceptively quiet, both downstairs bedrooms are occupied, and I'm sitting at the front dormer desk, staring at the reflection of my book light on the window. Today was a jumble of stories: Charles accompanied me on my walk, and I told him about being run out of the cabin, my months living at the hut, and how Edie and Thomas came into my life. Charles has always exhibited what I regard as an unusual tolerance for not knowing all the facts of any situation, a trait that may have developed from the secrecy involved in his work. He'd noticed my limp immediately, but never asked, knowing he'd get the story eventually. I was still digesting his news about the strike on North Korea, trying to wrap my head around the idea that we could have done such a thing. And now I have so many new images crowding my mind: Linda living in a survivors' group at the National Harbor, hanging onto hope that Steve will eventually make it home; crowds of hungry people gathering at ports around the country, fighting each other for handouts; and Charles tromping through the woods, eating mushrooms, acorns, tree bark, pine nuts, and even grubs. I've spent months trying not to think about the outside world, but now it is once again crowding in on me and challenging what I've always believed about how things should be. Nuclear weapons were supposed to be a deterrent, not something anyone would ever dream of using. But they used them on us, Charles had pointed out. How many people have died because of the blackout? And if we hadn't retaliated, what might Russia have done? Or some other opportunistic power?

January 20

I've skipped some more days of writing, and so much has happened that it might take a couple of sessions to get it all down. We've stepped up our surveillance of the yard, and I'm writing from the desk upstairs that overlooks the front of the cabin. Edie and Thomas are cooking a batch of stew and doing laundry, while Charles naps in the front bedroom. The sky above the trees below me is full of dark, racing clouds, but so far, no snow. The bare branches flail and wave, reminding me of the night up in the woods when the oak fell so close to the hut. But I would welcome a bit of snow to keep us inside and discourage visitors, a day or two to kick back and not feel pressured to act.

On Charles's second full day at the cabin, I broached the idea of making a trip to the hut together. The weather was good, and I thought we could take advantage of the thaw to dig up some of the buried meat. In addition, I'd left my sketchbook and story map, and I thought it would be good to restock the stores there in case of an emergency. My foot had improved to the point that I'd put aside the crutches, and I was curious how it would do on uneven terrain. My only concern was that Charles might want to rest a little more from his journey, but he assured me that he was feeling better than he had in weeks. After a bit of discussion, we all agreed it would be best to leave Daisy at the cabin. With the AR-15, the Winchester rifle, and Daisy to bark a warning, we figured that Thomas and Edie would be fine if Charles and I stayed a night at the hut.

Yesterday we started off about an hour after daybreak. A chill fog had settled in the hollow overnight, but it dispersed before we reached the second hill, and the temperature climbed quickly. Charles was carrying all of the heavier supplies, leaving me with just water, a first aid kit, some food, and the pistol. It was liberating to walk along with so few encumbrances, feeling healthy and worry-free. Not that there weren't things to worry about, but being with a friend I could trust eased my burden in more ways than one. I hadn't realized until then how much of my exhaustion was due to the stress that came with taking responsibility for the survival of our little group. Having the companionship of Edie and Thomas was comforting but nothing like the relief of having another adult around.

When we got close to the hut, we detoured to the creek to get more water, and I related how I'd seen the bandana that day before I discovered Edie. My fear must have come across in the retelling because Charles stopped in his tracks and asked, "How long were you up here alone?"

"Six months, give or take," I answered, and I told him about my routine of setting traps and smoking the meat, and about the first time I saw Daisy and the coyote pups.

He shook his head, but all he said was, "Hmph…"

Nothing was disturbed at the hut. We brought in wood, lit the woodstove, and took out our lunches. I sat on a camp chair and ate, but Charles ate standing up, wandering from wall to wall, looking at the sketches pinned to the support beams and reacquainting himself with the general layout of the place.

"It feels different now that it's been lived in," he commented. "Not like an escape house. More like a home."

I found the map of my storage holes, and we spent the next couple of hours digging up meat, taking turns with the little trowel and swapping stories. Charles told me that he'd tried to contact Erica on the day of the blackout, just to make sure she had some sort of plan, but she hadn't picked up.

"You were out there for a long time," I said. "How much of the population do you think is left in DC?"

"I don't know…A third? Maybe less. Lots of people just walked out when it became obvious that the blackout wasn't going away anytime soon. Then older folks and babies and people with chronic medical conditions began to die off. Add the deaths from accidents, fires, murders, and everyday illnesses like the flu that couldn't be treated…I think people in towns like Wagner had a bit of an advantage just from being small enough to organize."

The temperatures had been erratic enough that the ground had never frozen hard, so the digging was fairly easy work. By the time we finished at the second site, we had about fifteen pounds of meat, ten or so of wild pork and the rest deer. I figured there were about thirty pounds left at the other locations, but there was no need to get it all at once.

After dinner, we sat on camp chairs in front of the stove and drank coffee with a dash of whiskey we'd brought with us from the cabin. Charles was looking through my sketchbook, occasionally asking a question, but mostly just scanning them with the intensity you'd expect if they'd been important documents, not just casual scribblings.

"This is amazing," he said, and I leaned over to see which picture he was referencing. It was the coyote pups, tearing at the deer.

He turned a few pages and came to the Christmas dinner scene.

"You guys really did this?"

"Yeah, Edie and Thomas brought the food up while I was recuperating from the infection. I didn't even know what day it was."

"They're good kids," he said. "You're lucky they came along."

"I know. Without them and Daisy, I might not be here."

"Do you think you could teach me to draw?"

"I don't see why not. To me, it's just a matter of how you look at things."

"Hmm," he said. "Isn't everything?"

That night we rolled our sleeping bags out on opposite sides of the bed platform, which wasn't as awkward as it might have been, owing to the fact that we were both exhausted, and it just seemed to be the logical thing to do. We headed down the mountain in the morning, and even though my load was heavier than before, I felt quite steady with my limping gait and my weight still on the outside of my right foot.

January 21

The snow started yesterday afternoon and came in microbursts like giant curtains being shaken across the yard. By dark there were a couple of inches on the lawn and by this morning about a half foot. Then the wind died and giant white flakes continued to swirl down like the ashes from a great fire. I have "first watch" tonight, so I should be taking a nap, but my mind is too full to settle down right now.

When Charles and I descended the hill to the house two days ago, Thomas came out into the yard, looked up the slope, and waved. He let Daisy out on his way back in, and she ran to greet us. There was something tired and deliberate in the way Thomas moved that immediately had me thinking that something had happened. When we walked into the kitchen and dropped our packs, he and Edie were sitting across from each other at the table, cradling mugs of coffee and looking dead serious.

"What happened?" I asked.

"We had a visitor," Edie said.

"Just one?"

"Hard to say," Thomas replied. And then he related the story.

They'd been asleep for a while when Daisy started to growl. We'd decided to give her the run of the house at night so she'd be more likely to hear noises. Thomas jumped out of bed and grabbed the AR-15. He found Daisy standing at the back door, ears forward. When he looked out, he didn't see anything at first, but then he made out a dark shadow crouching at the corner of the barn. The figure had its back to the house, and Thomas just watched for a minute, unsure of whether it was a man or maybe a bear. After a few moments, Thomas saw a bit of dancing light, and then the figure stood up, and Thomas realized he was seeing little tongues of flame, lapping at the corner of the barn.

"So, I ran out on the porch and started shooting," he said, "not really aiming, just trying to scare the guy. Edie was holding Daisy back 'cause we didn't want her to get caught in any crossfire. Anyway, he headed up into the woods. I ran out into the yard, but I didn't see anyone else. In the meantime, Edie'd filled a pot with water, and I covered her while she dumped it on the fire. It'd barely gotten started, so it only took the one pot. We've been awake ever since, waiting in case they come back."

"Damn," I said. I asked Thomas if he had any idea who it was, but he said that he thought the guy moved too fast to be Ray or Reese, and he couldn't think of anyone particular Ray would have sent.

"If they were just trying to lure you out of the house, you'd think they'd have shot at you," I mused. "Seems like they were just trying to scare us. But I think you probably gave them a pretty good scare yourself. I'm glad you two are okay."

After that we all had lunch, and then I sent Edie and Thomas off to get some rest. I was wondering whether the man or men had a camp in the woods; it was a long trip to hike from town to my house and back in one night, but he might have had a bike on the road. I even toyed with the idea of going to look for evidence, but Charles thought it wouldn't be smart for either of us to go alone, and we didn't want to leave Edie and Thomas asleep without someone to keep watch.

Since then we've had someone up all night, with first watch ending at around two and a second watch ending at six, when that person wakes someone else before turning in for a morning nap. The routine is still new and, therefore, not too grueling, but I can see how it could become tiresome really fast. What's already tiresome is living with the threat of Ray hanging over us all the time. The snow has given us a bit of a respite but also prevents a trip to town. By the time it melts off the road, though, I am hoping to have a plan in place for a visit to the sheriff, and perhaps this stalemate can come to an end.

January 24

Like most Virginia snows, this one has been disappearing quickly; the ground is showing through most of the front yard, and the driveway is a slushy mix from my traipsing up and down for exercise and to check the road. Within a couple of days, we should be able to make our trip to town. This evening after dinner, we started to make a plan.

The first question to resolve was who should go. We all wanted to, but it seemed unwise to leave the house unguarded. If Ray or one of his goons discovered the house empty, they might set up an ambush or even burn the place down. So, we decided that Charles would stay with Daisy and the AR-15, since Edie needed to talk to her mother and Thomas could direct me where to go and also accompany Edie. He would take Charles's pistol, a Glock 17, similar to my own. I'd visit the sheriff, carrying the 9mm. While I was visiting with the sheriff, Edie would try to convince her mother just to come for a visit. Our hope was that once we got her out of Ray's influence, she might think more clearly. Edie would tell her to pack a bag and be ready for us to pick her up in a few days.

Chances were that by the time we left town, Ray would know that we were there. It would be important to get in and out before he could react. Charles wondered whether he might even try to waylay us somehow.

"Suppose you took the truck. Is there someplace along the way that you could hide it?" he asked.

We looked at Thomas and Edie.

"How 'bout the Goads' farm?" Edie asked Thomas. "They left right after the blackout. It's just a bit out of town on 63 South. Ray would probably expect us to stick to the woods north of 42."

The Goads' place was about a mile and a half from town, Thomas explained, and if we parked up the driveway by the house, no one would see the truck from 42.

It sounded like a good idea to me. We'd have to run the truck and clean off the windows the day before. Peter had put a rechargeable air pump somewhere in the cellar; Thomas said he'd find it and plug it in before he went to bed. We talked a bit more about what we would take and some other minor logistics and then broke off the meeting. Edie has second watch after Charles tonight, so she and Thomas retired early, while I stayed up for a bit, playing cards with Charles. He's been teaching me to play Casino, a game he learned while he was shut in at the NSA building.

"What did everyone there think was going to happen?" I asked him. "I mean, you were just whiling away the hours until the electricity and food ran out, right?"

"Sort of. A few systems were running on the back-up generators for a while, but to preserve energy, we were recording a lot of stuff by hand. The most crucial people had been shipped to a bunker somewhere on the first day. They were doing the real work. It was no worse a place to be than anywhere else, though, especially for us single people."

"And the president? Is he still out there somewhere?" I asked.

"As far as I know. The people distributing aid thought so."

Charles won all four games that we played, and I took a cup of tea up to my bedroom soon after. As I gazed out the front window with my journal before me, I saw bare branches tinged with lines of silver trembling under the near-full moon. Orion lounged near the horizon, and something was moving quickly from east to west across the upper window panes. Not an airplane. Too fast. What else? Finally, I decided that it must be a satellite, a piece of technology I hadn't thought of for a long time. When it disappeared to the west, I sat pondering all the events that might be occurring in other parts of the world. Across the oceans, millions of people were going about their business, mostly unaffected by what happened here. The thought left me surprisingly unmoved; I didn't envy their freedom of movement, access to technology, or even their modern conveniences. In fact, the only aspect of civilization that I really missed was being able to communicate with the people I cared about, like my mother, and Aunt JoAnn, and Linda. And then, for the first time, I began to wonder what I would do when if society was ever restored to some semblance of normalcy. Would I want to go back?

January 27

Besides the novelty of being in a moving vehicle, the strangest thing about the ride to the Goads' place was the heater. The day before we left, Charles pulled the truck around to the east side of the house, and he and Thomas spent part of the afternoon readying it for the trip. Before we left yesterday, Charles started it and got the heater going, so that when Thomas, Edie, and I piled in, hot air was coming full blast from the dashboard. Thomas had found a little mouse nest under the hood, but the critter hadn't done any damage, and the only evidence of its existence was a slight odor of mouse droppings, in spite of Thomas's cleaning efforts.

Charles had taken the late watch, so the three of us were excited and fairly well-rested as we took off down the road, which was mostly muddy with slush in just a few spots. We arrived at the Goads' driveway in a matter of minutes, I backed the vehicle up next to the kitchen door, and we tumbled out.

After shrugging into our backpacks and pulling on hats and gloves, we started off together through the field to the west. We planned to circle the town to the south so that Thomas could point out the elementary school. After I split off to find the sheriff, they would continue to circle and approach Edie's house from the north. Ray's base of operations was an auto repair shop on the east end of the main street, Rte. 42. Thomas and I had our pistols concealed in our jackets, and we all had our walkie-talkies handy. The going was rougher over the pasture than I had imagined. I had to choose between walking on big tufts of dead weeds or in the soggy dirt in between, which was awkward to do while favoring my foot. I fell once and soaked a knee in the mud. When Thomas and Edie grabbed an arm on each side, I felt like the Straw Man being pulled along by the Tin Man and Dorothy.

"I'm okay. I've got this," I told them.

As we neared town, the field ran along the backyards of the houses on the south side of Main Street, which provided some cover. Finally, the school came into view on the right, and Thomas gave me a last review of its layout. One of the deputies always knew where the sheriff was, and he was usually no more than a short walk away. We agreed to meet down in the hollow we'd just climbed, out of sight from the town. I was wearing Peter's watch, and Charles had given his to Thomas. Both of the watches read ten-thirty. We would meet up at noon, and if anyone was more than thirty minutes late and hadn't reported in by radio, the others would go straight to the sheriff.

After Thomas and Edie set off, I slowed to better take in my surroundings as I walked. The houses to my right were mostly brick, with small back porches and yards where dead weeds poked up around bits of trash and debris. One of the houses toward the middle had burned to a brick skeleton, and a few stood with their windows broken and doors gaping. Closer to the school, though, stood a few that evidenced some care: one had several pots of dead flowers lined up on the railing, at another two plastic Adirondack chairs were arranged neatly on either side of a little plastic table. As I passed that house, I thought that I saw a flicker of movement behind the curtained door, but, as best I could tell, no one was out and about on the street, as though the whole town were in hiding or sheltering indoors.

The atmosphere around the schoolyard was a different matter. Inside the fence behind the school, cows lay in the sun, indifferent to the mud, and along the far side a few stood under an open shed. A man in coveralls was dumping water from five-gallon buckets into a metal trough through the fence. He looked fairly young, but it was hard to judge his age through his thick beard.

He looked up as I came around the corner and asked, "Can I help you?"

I introduced myself and told him where I lived. He gave me a hard look.

"And you've been living out there since this whole mess started?" he asked.

"More or less," I lied.

"Well, what can I do for you? I hope you aren't looking for milk because we're a bit short."

"Actually, I'm just looking for Sheriff Shaheen."

"Really. Well..." He turned toward the building and pointed to a set of double doors. "Straight down the hall and through the last door on the right. What did you say your name was?"

"Aurora. Aurora Scott," I repeated as I walked on. I wasn't going to try to hide anything from anyone I met, hoping that a degree of boldness would make an impression.

Inside, the building was dim and the floor caked with a few days' worth of mud. To my left were the cafeteria doors, flanked by glass walls that allowed me to see through the room and out the other side of the building. A few tables had been dragged out onto a patio of sorts, and I could see several people at work in front of a makeshift fireplace. A steel drum steamed on a grill above flaming coals, but I couldn't tell exactly what they were doing, maybe sterilizing jars? I walked on and found myself in a long hallway with classrooms on either side. Every door was closed, and they all had cloth or paper blocking a tall window beside the door. I thought that these must be the rooms that the deputies and farm hands were using. A pair of buckets sat outside of each room and, judging by the smell, at least one was the inhabitant's potty. I wondered whether everyone emptied their own or whether they had some kind of system for that chore. Either way, I was happy to see evidence of organization and planning.

When I came to the office, I could see the sheriff sitting at a desk, writing in a notebook. He was wearing a heavy jacket and fingerless mittens, in spite of the woodstove that had been rigged up against the outside wall. The floor in front of the woodstove was covered in cushions, which were bordered on three sides by three fifties-style sofas with wooden arms that reminded me of the office furniture in my doctor's waiting room when I was a kid.

I hadn't yet reached the door, so I had the opportunity to spy for a few seconds, trying to size him up. As I paused in the hallway, he stood and crossed to the back of one sofa, rested his hands on it, and stared out the windows that flanked the woodstove. He was of average height with a roundish sort of face and a large walrus-type moustache that mostly hid his mouth. Unlike nearly every man I'd seen from the town, he was otherwise clean shaven.

I walked forward and rapped on the door frame. When he turned, his eyes seemed to narrow a bit.

"Hello, I'm Aurora Scott, and I have a few things I'd like to discuss with you, if you have a minute," I started.

He pointed to a chair in front of the desk and told me to have a seat, taking his own with no attempt to extend his hand.

"And I'm Sheriff Shaheen, but you probably already know that. What can I do for you?"

"I live out on the Forest Service road, number 607, in the Bensons' old place. The one with the solar panels." I was having a hard time reading him, and it was making me nervous.

"How's that working out for you? Having electricity when no one else does?"

"Um...okay, I guess. The hot water is nice. I've taken in a couple of your people, Thomas Mabry and Edie Horton. And I have a friend from DC who's joined us."

"You're preppers, right? You and your husband? I've heard about you."

"Well, then you might have heard that my husband passed away before the blackout."

"No, sorry. I didn't. So, what is it that you need? 'Cause I gotta tell you, we have our hands full here. It's good of you to take on Thomas and Edie, but if you're looking for help, maybe you should just send them home."

"No, that's not it. In fact, I think that there are some ways that we could help you. But what I really want to talk about is Edie's uncle, Ray, and Reese and that gang. They're harassing us, and a lot of what he's been doing is clearly outside of the law. They ran me out of my house back in the summer in the middle of the night, stole everything that wasn't too big to carry, and they've been back several times since."

He took a deep breath and frowned.

"They said you'd left."

"When they busted in waving guns. A few months later, I found Edie in a tent in the woods. She'd just miscarried. And she told me that Ray raped her."

"So that's why those two ran off," the sheriff said.

"A few nights ago, they tried to burn down my barn, and all those old folks Ray's found dead? It seems like he's been helping them along. But how can you not know this?"

He pulled at his moustache and answered slowly.

"I've known Ray since he was a kid, and he's always been a no-count sneak, but he's also always managed to cover his tracks enough to stay out of real trouble. And what exactly am I supposed to do? Do you think I can arrest him? On what evidence? A while back I started sending a deputy with him whenever he went on his out-of-town visits, and, you're right, the body count seemed to go down. But most of those people he found were pretty frail, and they probably wouldn't have lasted much longer anyway."

"So, you let him kill weak, old people and steal them blind like he's doing them a favor? Come on!"

"I just can't do anything about it. I would have to catch him in the act. And then I'd have to chain him up somewhere, since we don't have a jail. It takes all the manpower we have to bring in wood, take care of the animals, and try to make sure that what little we have gets distributed fairly."

"Okay, then. Let's look at this another way. You know that Ray and his posse are dangerous, but you aren't equipped to deal with them. But if he were seriously threatening someone, you would agree that they would have the right to defend themselves, correct?"

"Virginia has never had a Stand Your Ground Law, but self-defense is self-defense," he answered. "It'd be hard to prove otherwise, on either side."

"Fair enough. By the way, Edie is trying to convince her mother to come stay with us for a while. In a few days, we're going to drive into town to pick her up in my truck. You might want to be on the lookout for us. Oh, and I have something for you."

By the time I finished showing Sheriff Shaheen the walkie-talkies and said we would be happy to arrange a schedule by which we could recharge the batteries for him a couple times a week, he seemed to have thawed considerably. I left the same way I entered and waved to the farmhand, who was now pitching cow manure over the fence onto a steaming pile that ran the length of the school yard. I had to admit that the meeting hadn't gone as well as I'd hoped, but, on the other hand, at least I knew better what I was dealing with, and, if anything, I might have made it a little more difficult for the sheriff to keep looking the other way.

Over lunch back at the cabin, we discussed the trip. Edie's mom had seemed open to the idea of a visit, particularly when Edie described some of our luxuries, like hot baths, decent food, and a washing machine. At this, Edie said, she actually got excited and asked if maybe she could bring her dirty sheets to wash. Edie told her to bring all the sheets she could find because we were a little short, though she avoided mentioning that it was Ray who was responsible for that.

Thomas has first watch tonight, followed by me, so I came up to bed immediately after our evening meeting. Charles volunteered to sleep on the couch when Edie's mom arrives, but then Edie and Thomas said they could just move back into the cellar. I am letting them work it out amongst themselves; I am uncomfortable enough already with the fact that I seem to have the final word on things just by virtue of owning the house.

My meeting with Sheriff Shaheen has left me with mixed emotions. It seems that he's taken the "to preserve" part of his job description much more seriously than the "to protect" aspect. But, as Charles pointed out at dinner, it's not surprising that he's overwhelmed and burnt out by the task of keeping the town going. And perhaps his hold on power is too tenuous for him to risk a confrontation. Still, I have to admit, I'd be more encouraged if I'd seen a stronger reaction to Ray's lawlessness. I continue to console myself with the idea that perhaps I have planted a seed, and that in the face of direct pressure, the sheriff will feel compelled to act. Ray must have heard about my visit, and that could go either way, influencing him to lay low or further angering him. I guess we'll just have to wait and see, but as we approach another night of round-the-clock watches, I am disappointed at our lack of progress.

January 29

Nothing of note happened yesterday other than Daisy bringing home a squirrel and me taking Thomas and Charles up into the woods to set some traps. I'm not sure whether the wild pigs come down this side of the mountain, but we see deer almost daily, and we shouldn't be missing the opportunity to get more protein. A couple nights ago, we went through all of the seed packets we could find in the root cellar. Peter was careful to choose varieties that produce viable seeds, nothing so altered as to be sterile. When the weather warms a bit, we'll start mapping out the garden and decide what to plant when. Thomas and Edie seemed particularly excited about this. They wanted to know if we can plant things like the Native Americans did, with corn and beans and squash together. Their spirit of adventure is refreshing, as though they see themselves transported into some Little House on the Prairie scenario where survival looks more like an adventure than the serious test it really is. It's as though they're immersing themselves in a second childhood. But I'm happy that they can shake things off the way they do, and their enthusiasm improves everyone's mood.

Today was another mild day, and I took advantage of it to hike up to the lookout spot with Charles for his first drawing lesson. Given the choice, he'd opted to start with landscapes. Sitting on foam pads with our backs against a tree with a double trunk, we studied the rocky overlook before us. The first task was to draw the horizon line, and I stressed the importance of just seeing the shapes, curves, and angles, and not thinking about what they were, like rock or tree. When I'd presented him with a sketch pad all his own, he'd protested, saying, "You should probably wait before you waste that on me. Don't you have some old copy paper?"

"Ah, but now you'll be more invested," I answered.

But really, he got off to a good start, beginning with the pointed rock at the center and working his way to the right, making me suspect that he wasn't as much of a beginner as he'd suggested.

"Good job," I told him. "Maybe next we'll draw a three-ring circus with a band and acrobats and tigers."

"Okay," he said. "I admit I studied drafting, and I might remember a bit about perspective."

I laughed and said I was just teasing.

We both drew in silence for a while, with me occasionally leaning over his shoulder and making a comment or two. For some reason, though, I stopped with my own sketch half done and found myself staring off toward the town. My legs were stretched out in front of me, and I was wearing my favorite jeans. I'd recently been able to fit both feet back into my own boots, and I felt comfortable and more like my old self than I had in months.

Charles caught me staring and asked, "Are you okay?"

"Yeah, just relaxing for a minute," I answered. "You know, you've made things a lot easier for me."

"And you've done the same for me, and Edie and Thomas."

"I suppose. But I was really in trouble for a while. Serious trouble, like what's-the-point-of-going-on trouble. And I was really angry at myself for not being strong enough to do this, especially after everything that Peter did to make it easy. I had food and shelter, and I still almost managed to kill myself."

"So, you're human. You knew that. Don't you think he did, too?"

"Yeah, I know. But there's more to it than that. When I think back on my old life, I'm ashamed. I thought I was a good person because I had Peter and because I had a job that helped people. But now I see someone who was really pretty detached from everyone around her, pretending to make a difference without really connecting. I know this sounds silly, but after a while I felt like being alone was a punishment for not caring enough when I had the chance."

Charles was quiet for a few moments, and I found myself just staring at the rocks, waiting for his response. Finally, he said, "I always saw you as a strong, independent person who did her best to do what she thought was right at the time, and that's still true. If your idea about what is right has evolved, that's called growth, and it's a good thing. At least, I think so."

He turned his head to look at me and when he saw the tears in my eyes, he put his arm around my shoulders and pulled me close. I let my head rest on his chest and realized that my memories of being held weren't anywhere close to the comfort of the real thing.

"I think you're going to be fine," he said.

After a while I straightened up and asked, "How do you think this blackout is going to end?"

"Well, we still have a president somewhere, and he has communications access to the outside world. So, little by little, pockets with limited communications and power should be established. But it will all be very slow and localized. Rural areas like this will be the last to see any of it."

"And do you think eventually everything will go back to the way it was before?"

"I don't know. Maybe."

I thought about all the suffering that resulted from the blackout and how there couldn't be a single person in this country who hadn't been profoundly affected. But I also couldn't help thinking about the town of Wagner and how it had happened that, with the exception of Ray's crew, they were pulling together as a community in a way they never had.

"I hope not," I said.

January 30

Last night I had the first watch, and I passed the intervals between rounds curled up on the couch with Daisy, writing and rereading my favorite novel from a course I once took in Native American Literature. It was Leslie Marmon Silko's Ceremony, and in it the protagonist, Tayo, comes back from WWII battling PTSD and the conviction that he is responsible for the deaths of his uncle and cousin, not to mention the drought that is plaguing his western New Mexico homeland. Tayo is half white and has never felt fully accepted in his family except by his uncle Robert. Over the course of the story, Tayo realizes that he must accomplish several challenging tasks to restore the natural order;

however, his illness, fears, and loyalties set him back time and again. The other students had a lot of difficulty with the novel; the flashbacks and insertions of Laguna myth take a lot of effort to integrate, but every time I read it, I find it more comforting. There is something soothing about the idea that a person who is totally lost can piece together a path from old truths reimagined for new situations, which I guess is what survival is all about and part of what Charles was trying to tell me yesterday afternoon.

I slept late this morning and then went with Thomas to check the traps after lunch. We'd caught an opossum, a first for me, and I wasn't sure how palatable it would be. But Thomas assured me that he could turn it into a tasty stew if I wanted to swap my turn to cook tonight. On the way back, we talked about ways to trap live turkeys. Thomas said that the cornfields the town planted should draw more turkeys now that insects are scarce, but out here, we would have to go to areas of moss, fern, and nuts up in the woods.

"Your hut should be a prime spot to trap from this time of year," he said. "If we set some traps under good cover where they're likely to go after a snow, I'll bet we could get a few."

I asked him what we would need to make some live traps, and he said that he thought he and Charles could work something out if they had enough chicken wire. Unfortunately, a need for chicken wire hadn't presented itself to Peter, so the only place to get it would be from the town, unless we started our own scavenging effort. So far, we hadn't needed to do that, and it presented another moral dilemma for me, since it wasn't a matter of direct necessity. I had to remind myself that everyone in the country had lived by scavenging for nine months now, and I was probably one of very few exceptions. Nonetheless, I decided that it was a decision to be made by the group, and I put it on the agenda for the evening meeting.

As we talked, we rounded the side of the hill behind the house and saw Charles angling toward us. We yelled to him and he stopped and waved.

"The Sheriff is here," he called, and then he turned back down the hill.

Thomas and I exchanged surprised glances and hurried after Charles. When we entered the kitchen, Sheriff Shaheen was sitting at the table with Edie, holding a mug of coffee, and Daisy was lying nearby with her head on her paws, watching the proceedings.

After we exchanged greetings, Sheriff Shaheen said that he'd ridden out just to "check out" our place and make sure that we hadn't "gotten off on the wrong foot."

"I appreciate your gift of the walkie-talkies, and they have already helped a lot, so I thought I should return the favor," he continued, and then Edie blurted out, "He brought chickens and milk!"

"Not much," he clarified, "and just a couple of pullets and a rooster, Rhode Island Reds. They're just a few months old, so it'll be a few weeks before the hens start laying."

I thanked him and said that we had a good chicken room in the barn, but we could use some chicken wire for an outside run and a couple other projects, and he said he thought he could find some for us.

"If you don't mind, I'd like to have a look around," he said.

"Sure," I answered, even though little alarm bells were starting to go off in my head. Charles was feeling the same; he looked at me with raised eyebrows as we donned our coats. I couldn't blame the sheriff for wanting to see exactly what we were working with, but that didn't mean we had to show him everything.

The chickens were on the front porch in a box under a blanket, and a horse was tied to the front porch railing. He was a smallish bay, a little shaggy looking and pretty calm, judging by the way he let Daisy nose around his hooves. Either that or he wasn't going to be distracted from chomping on the dead weeds in the overgrown flowerbed. The sheriff picked up the box, while Thomas and Edie went ahead to throw some hay down from the loft.

We'd left the truck in the front of the barn, since we were going to use it soon to fetch Edie's mom. The sheriff was impressed and asked how much gas we had.

"Not much," I answered. "We're going to need the truck for our next trip to town, but then we'll put it back into storage."

As Thomas and Edie spread hay in the nesting compartments and over the floor of the chicken coop, Charles and I showed the sheriff the back-up water system. He wanted to know how the water got from the pipe up into the tank, and I showed him the little solar panel on the outside of the barn.

"It's hooked to a couple of car batteries, and they run a water pump that we took from an old RV," Charles explained. "But with the well pump working, we don't have to use it."

Of course, we didn't show him the root cellar, and when we walked around the solar panels, he just shook his head.

By then, Edie and Thomas had the chickens settled in their new home, and they were scratching around in the hay. The sheriff said that they'd eat all the seeds out of the hay, but they could also eat table scraps if they weren't moldy. Any raw or green potatoes and onions were on the NO list, and beans only if very well cooked. Once we had a yard for them and the weather warmed, they'd find lots of bugs, and feeding them would be even easier. At somewhere between three and four months old, they were more than a foot tall, and I wouldn't have guessed they were so young if the sheriff hadn't told us. But they had shiny, auburn coats that looked plenty warm, which helped since we didn't have any heat lamps, and the sheriff assured us they'd been living outdoors for a few weeks.

After watching the birds poke around for a few minutes, Charles, Sheriff Shaheen, and I headed back to the house while Thomas went off to skin the opossum, and Edie stayed in the barn.

"I spoke to Ray," the sheriff said. "He denied everything you told me, but when I said I knew about Edie, he got really mad and said she was a little tramp and she'd tricked him. I told him it was rape either way and he'd better watch himself because the rumors I'd been hearing couldn't all be lies. He just shut up after that and stomped off. We were standing in the street right in front of the school, so I'm sure there were folks watching out their windows."

We'd come around the side of the house and stopped next to the horse. The sheriff released the bridle from the railing and hoisted himself up with a grunt.

"I still haven't gotten the hang of this horse thing," he said, as the horse took a step back. "Come by the office when you get to town. It'll show Ray that we're on the same team; plus, I have something else I want to give you."

Charles had stepped up to the horse's head and was stroking its muzzle while the sheriff spoke.

"What's his name?" he asked.

"Bonfire," the sheriff answered, "and, by the way, you can call me Paul."

Thomas's stew turned out well, and we used some of the milk that Sheriff Shaheen brought to make biscuits, so it was a better-than-average dinner. Edie and Thomas were in good spirits because of the chickens and speculated on how many eggs we should try to hatch instead of eating, although we all agreed that it would be awesome to save up enough for an omelet as soon as the hens start laying. Looking across the table at Charles, however, I noticed that he was staring into his plate, and I guessed that, like me, thoughts of our trip to town were already weighing on him.

After the dishes were cleared, we settled around the table to make a plan. Edie's mother should have had time to prepare a bag, and if we were going, there was no reason to put it off. Although we'd left Charles home the last time, I thought that we should all participate in this trip, even though we couldn't all fit into the truck. For the trip in, we decided that I would drive, and Charles would sit in the bed with the AR-15. After we picked up Edie's mom, two of us would stand in the bed of the truck, watching for trouble. At first it seemed to make sense for Charles to drive with Edie's mom sandwiched between him and Edie. Thomas had been taking more target practice than any of us lately and was probably the best shot. But the more I thought about it, the less comfortable I was with putting him at such a risk, so we finally decided that Thomas would drive home with Charles and me in the back. Thomas seemed excited at the prospect of driving the truck, which made me think that perhaps he hadn't been too anxious to stare at Ray down the barrel of a gun.

It felt strange to go from a celebration of milk and chickens to planning a covert operation. But by bringing Edie's mom home, we were again challenging Ray, and it seemed wise to be prepared for anything. Barring bad weather, tomorrow will be the day. Edie and Charles have watch tonight, but I doubt any of us will sleep that well.

After the meeting, Thomas and Edie went out to check on the chickens, and Charles and I did the dishes. Edie had taken a plastic container, printed "Chicken Scraps" on the outside, and set it next to the sink, but there was hardly a scrap left, and we'd decided to keep the birds vegetarian. Charles washed, and as I dried, I had a sudden thought.

"Hey, Rocket Man," I said. Rocket Man was the moniker he'd chosen to use with the walkie-talkies. "Why didn't you just radio us when the sheriff came, instead of coming out to get us?"

"Well, I guess I could have. Edie made us some coffee right away, and we'd been sitting for a few minutes before I went to get you. I had the thought that it might be good for her and the sheriff to have some time to chat alone, in case she had anything she wanted to tell him."

He pulled the plug from the sink and the water started slurping down.

"Good thinking," I said. "I hope they had a good talk."

He turned toward me and leaned back against the counter, arms crossed.

"You know, this trip could turn out badly. From what you've told me about Ray, bringing Edie's mother here could be just the thing that pushes him over the edge. Are you sure it's worth it?"

"Sure?" I said. "No way. I've looked at this thing from every angle, but I keep coming back to one thing. When Ray raped Edie, he didn't just assault her, he took away her home. As long as Donna is with Ray, Edie might as well be an orphan. If I had taken Peter more seriously, maybe I could have saved my own mother. I don't know if Donna will ever snap out of the spell Ray has her under, but I'm not doing this for her. I'm doing it for Edie. You can pull out if you want to."

"No," he said. "I'm in. I just wanted to be sure that we're clear on what we're doing here."

After that, Charles fixed a cup of tea to take to bed. He had second watch and wanted to relax and maybe get a little sleep. I chose decaf with a slug of whiskey, loaded the woodstove, and headed upstairs. Before long, I heard Thomas and Edie come in and head to their room, and Daisy, who'd been out with them, came trotting up the stairs and jumped onto the foot of the bed. I called her up beside me and assured her that even though the new chickens were getting a lot of attention, she was still the number one pet.

I hope that we have done enough to prepare for whatever may happen tomorrow. It's comforting to imagine that we will drive into town quietly, deliver fresh batteries to the sheriff, and then swing by for Edie's mom without mishap. But Ray has already suffered several humiliations at our hands: Edie and Thomas running away, my forcing him off the property at gunpoint, and the sheriff calling him out on the street. Our convincing Edie's mom to leave will be yet another affront to his power. Charles was right in pointing out that Ray could be ready to snap. What if we go and it all ends badly? Do I have the right to put the others in harm's way? Maybe this isn't as much about helping Edie than me getting back at Ray for all the misery he's caused. I honestly don't know. I just have this deep-down feeling that he must be stopped.

January 31

We assembled at the truck right after breakfast. The sun shone dimly behind a thin curtain of clouds, and the temperature had risen to just above freezing. Charles huddled in the front corner of the truck bed behind me with a wool blanket around his legs and the AR-15 across his lap. I took my time easing the truck down the driveway and onto the forest road, as though I could slow our progress toward the unknown. Too soon, it seemed, we passed Ray's garage headquarters, where all seemed closed up and deserted, and I leaned on the horn in two long bursts to let the sheriff know we'd arrived.

The town exhibited a bit more life than on my previous visit: a man and woman were clipping laundry between the posts of their porch, and a group of men were splitting wood in the next yard. As we approached the elementary school, a horse cart pulled out of the parking lot and turned away from us, and I could make out a couple dozen milk crates in the back.

I pulled to a stop in front of the main doors of the school, and Charles jumped out of the truck and went in with a package of fresh batteries. He came out just a few minutes later, carrying a box around three feet wide by a foot tall. Behind him came another man with something long and skinny wrapped in blankets and all taped shut. It was too long to be a rifle, and I had no idea what else it could be. They placed the cargo in the back, and Charles clambered back into the bed.

Edie's mom lived on Elm, the first right turn past the school. When Edie pointed to the fourth house on the right, I drove by and then backed into the driveway. It was a neat bungalow, yellow with dark red trim. Charles jumped out and headed into the backyard while we waited outside the truck. Within seconds, he gave an all-clear sign, and Edie and Thomas entered from the front. I stood near the truck, watching the street and the front yards.

Thomas had left his radio on the dashboard, but the rest of us had ours, and I wasn't surprised when I started hearing voices, meaning that Edie must be holding her call button down so we'd know what was going on.

"You can't just waltz in here and take your mother away," said a man's voice.

"Reese, she's my mother, and she can come visit if she wants. You act like she's a prisoner or something."

"Certainly not," came a woman's voice. "I'm not anyone's prisoner. That's silly. Just tell Ray I'll be back in a few days."

"You better think hard before you do this." It was Reese's voice again. "Ray has had enough of people interfering in his business."

"My mother IS my business," came Edie's voice. "Ray seems to own a lot of people around here, but he doesn't own her, and he doesn't own me."

I don't know what Reese did then, but Edie's response came through loud and clear.

"Back off, Reese. You're making me uncomfortable."

At the signal word, I headed up the porch steps and pulled open the screen door with my left hand, holding the 9mm by my thigh in my right.

"Hello, Mrs. Horton," I said as I walked in. Thomas and Edie stood in the doorway to the living room with a short woman in a sweatshirt and jeans. They were facing Reese, who stood almost toe-to-toe with Edie. At the sight of me, Reese took a step back, and I thought I saw a flicker of uncertainty cross his face.

"Oh, you must be Aurora," Edie's mom said, turning toward me. "Please, call me Donna. I don't know what all this fuss is about. All I want to do is spend some time with my daughter."

"I don't know either," I said. "What's this really about, Reese? Is Donna a prisoner or not?"

He opened his mouth, closed it again, and looked from me to Edie and then back at me. Finally, he mumbled, "Ray has some stuff he needs her to help him with, that's all."

"Well, I guess he'll have to wait a few days."

At that Reese just stood there, looking indecisive. Then he said, "Don't think this is over," and headed toward the back door. He let the screen door slam behind him.

"Well, then, are you ready to go, Donna?"

"Why, yes, if Thomas and Edie can help me with my bags. I did pack up some laundry. I hope you don't mind."

"Not a bit," I answered.

As Donna pulled on a dirty, pink parka and leather gloves, I had a chance to look her over. She looked to be in her mid-fifties, but she had the paunch and posture of a woman much older. In spite of the doughiness of her skin, her eyes and thick hair made it easy to see her resemblance to Edie. But unlike Edie's rich brown, Donna's hair was streaked with gray. She wore it in a tight ponytail, with bangs cut about an inch above her eyes.

Edie and Thomas emerged from the bedroom with two pillowcases, stuffed taut, and a small canvas suitcase.

"Is this everything, Ma?" Edie asked.

"Yes, dear."

"Well then, let's go," I said.

We lifted Donna's bags into the truck bed and she slid into the front seat. Charles walked up from the back yard and said, "Reese took off running as soon as he was out the door. Three guesses where he was heading."

Edie climbed in beside her mother, and Charles introduced himself before we climbed into the back of the truck. We positioned ourselves on either side behind the cab, with a couple of hay bales between us to lean on. I bent toward the driver's window and instructed Thomas, "Just go easy, and stop if I bang on the roof."

He nodded and let out the clutch, and the truck rolled forward at a pace that just allowed Charles and me to keep our balance. Before we even reached Main Street, my legs grew tired, so I half-kneeled on a hay bale with a hand propped on the roof of the cab.

Thomas made the turn, and we faced the three blocks of road that stood between us and relative safety. Most of the houses along the street appeared intact, but others squatted forlornly with broken windows and yawning doors that could be hiding anything. I glanced into the cab and saw that Edie was holding her mother's hand and talking, while at the same time, she looked from side to side, scanning the block.

We were maybe five houses from the garage when Ray rushed out through the office door in a pair of brown coveralls, clutching a rifle in one hand. I don't know whether he was drunk or high, but he seemed unsteady, and he stumbled on the cracked concrete. For a split second, I almost felt sorry for him and the way he grasped the rifle as though he could squeeze from it some slight measure of dignity. Then he straightened, walked into the middle of the road, and raised a hand to stop us. "Hold it right there!" he yelled, as he lifted the gun to his shoulder.

I slapped the roof and Thomas stopped the truck. Then I stretched my arms over the top of the cab with my pistol trained on Ray and shouted back, "Ray, get out of the road!"

Charles was half lying on the cab with his rifle trained on Ray, and I thought that he couldn't possibly think he would survive against the two of us.

"Ray, MOVE!" I yelled again.

"Give me Edie and Donna!"

"No WAY," I yelled back. "THEY DON'T BELONG TO YOU! Now MOVE!"

At that, Ray tightened the rifle against his shoulder and that slight movement was all I needed to tell me that he wasn't going to back down. I squeezed the trigger and there was a burst of gunfire that seemed to come from all around but lasted just a few seconds. The last thing I saw, before the truck lurched forward and stalled and I fell back on top of the boxes, was Ray crumpling to the ground.

Somewhere in the confusion Edie and her mother had ducked under the dashboard, and someone was screaming. As I picked myself up, they raised their heads to look cautiously around.

"Is everyone okay in there?" I yelled.

Thomas looked over at the others and called back, "I think so!" Donna had stopped screaming and Edie was holding her head to her chest and saying something in her ear.

I turned toward Charles, but instead of standing beside me, he was sprawled on Donna's laundry bag with a hand to his forearm, watching the blood ooze out between his fingers.

"Damn! Charles! Is it bad?" I dropped to my knees beside him.

"I don't think so," he said, as I tugged at the sleeve of his jacket.

I ripped open his shirt where the bullet had entered. The gash was maybe a quarter inch deep and a stream of blood trickled down his arm. I rummaged around to find Donna's other laundry bag and that's when I saw Sheriff Shaheen approaching from the yard beside us, a rifle dangling in his hand. I grabbed a towel from the laundry bag and pressed it against Charles's arm.

"Everybody okay?" he asked.

"Pretty much," I answered. "Just a flesh wound, I think. When did you happen along?"

I didn't mean to sound sarcastic, but the sheriff didn't seem to take offense. "Oh, I've been around," he said.

"I don't know who shot him," I said. "Could've been either of us."

"Or all three of us," he answered. "And no ballistics to tell." He looked down the road toward Ray's body. "Self-defense all around, I'd say."

A smile crossed Charles's face at that. "Is there anything you need us to do?" he asked.

"No. Just be careful getting home." At that he walked toward the body, giving a half-wave toward the others as he passed.

By then a few folks had ventured out onto their porches, and most of them stood quietly with their arms crossed and none of them seemed too surprised that there had been a shootout on the street in front of their houses.

Ray had fallen backward and rolled onto his side. When we passed his body, I could see that a bullet had torn open the left half of his neck, and it looked like too much damage to have been done by the 9mm, but I didn't know for sure, and I thought maybe that was a good thing. He was motionless, and the blood had slowed to a trickle, but the puddle under his head spread out equally in all directions like a sticky, red halo. Edie still cradled her mother's head against her chest, and I was grateful that she'd thought to spare Donna the image.

Just outside of town, I banged for Thomas to stop, and all of us except Donna stood in the road, trying to put together exactly what had happened. Thomas said, "I looked in the mirror to see if Reese was around, and I saw the sheriff on one of the porches. Then the shooting started, and all I could think to do was to take cover. Sorry for stalling the truck."

I took another look at Charles's arm. The bleeding had stopped, but it would need a good cleaning.

"Well, I guess the sheriff's right. There's nothing to do now but go home," I said. "Go easy, though. We don't want that gash to start bleeding again."

When we got to the cabin, Donna still appeared dazed, and Edie suggested that she lie down for a while. She showed Donna to the back bedroom and brought her a cup of tea. In the meantime, I gathered some supplies to clean Charles's wound. Edie helped by cutting bandages and handing me things as I needed them, and it occurred to me that we'd been playing a weird first aid version of musical chairs these last months.

When we finished, it was only midday, and no one seemed to know quite what to do with themselves. Eventually, Thomas and Edie headed out to the barn to watch the chickens, and Charles and I sat on the front steps, sipping coffee and not saying much until he decided to get Thomas to help him unload the truck. I'd forgotten about the boxes the sheriff had given us, and I was still too shaken by what had happened in town to really care, so I headed up here to my desk to try to clear my head.

You shot at someone today. The thought keeps echoing through my mind. *You shot at a living, breathing, human being.* Something I never thought I could do and the reason I abandoned the cabin the night Ray first showed up.

Even if Sheriff Shaheen's shot actually killed him, that doesn't change the fact that I aimed my gun and pulled the trigger, in which case it might as well have been me. Shouldn't I feel sorry?

But you probably saved someone, too. I can hear Peter, once again making sure I look at both sides of the issue.

Peter's voice brings a new thought. He knew all along that it might come to this—that under the right circumstances, I could hurt someone to protect myself or someone else. Sure, he'd set things up so that we could be separate and mostly sheltered from the actions of desperate people. But he had to have known that we would eventually reach out and connect with others. He just wanted to make it on our own terms. And when there were people in our lives that we cared about, good people who were trying to make things better, we would help and protect them, no matter what it took.

Do I regret shooting at Ray? No, what I feel is not regret. Just sadness that it had to come to this and that Donna had reality forced on her in such a brutal way.

February 2

Dinner that night was pretty somber. To have the Ray problem suddenly erased left a void that couldn't be filled with any real celebration out of consideration for Donna and the raw fact that we'd left a man dead on the street.

"When he raised that gun, I knew that everything you'd been trying to tell me must be true. But if I had just had the chance to talk to him…" she said.

"Mom, there's a lot about Ray that you still don't know. And that's my fault. But he was beyond talking to. Please, believe me."

"It was the darned blackout," she said, staring into her plate. "It changed people."

After dinner we had our usual meeting. Edie had decided to sleep with her mother for a while, and instead of keeping our watch schedule, Thomas would sleep on the couch with Daisy nearby. None of us thought the remnants of Ray's band would continue without him, but we decided that it would be prudent to be vigilant for a week or so, just in case. Then Edie and her mom started on the laundry, and Thomas went to tend to the chickens while I did the dishes. As I finished up, Charles came in and said he wanted to show me what the sheriff had sent.

Out in the barn the overhead lights were on, and Charles had laid the items directly under the bulb. There were a bunch of aluminum rods of different thicknesses, yards of electric cable, and a metal box with a bunch of dials like an old-fashioned radio.

"Is that what I think it is?" I asked.

"Only if you know what a ham radio looks like."

"Damn," I said, and the outside world took a giant step closer.

After further investigation, Charles figured out that the antenna was actually two antennae in one, something called a di-pole, which was apparently good news because it meant that the radio would be able to send and pick up transmissions from at least a hundred miles away with no repeaters. All of this was a little out of my range of understanding, but the main point was that it really didn't take much more than a day to get the antennae up. Since Charles was the logical person to run it, we put the base unit in the downstairs front bedroom and ran the wires a short way from the window to the corner of the house. I say, "we," but it was Charles and Thomas that did all the work.

This morning, while the guys drilled holes and ran wires, I decided that I needed some alone time, and I called Daisy and headed up into the woods. From force of habit I took a sketchbook, some snacks, and the pistol. Though I still walked on the outside of my foot, I'd gotten good enough at it that my limp was barely perceptible. Instead of foraging ahead as was typical, Daisy trotted along behind me, perhaps sensing that something was off in my mood.

When I reached the lookout point, I sat with my back against the same tree where Charles and I had done our sketches not so long before. I took out my sketchpad and a thermos of tea, but I didn't draw or drink the tea, just stared across the hollow at the side of the next mountain. Daisy laid herself down at my side, and I stroked her head and tried to figure out where this great sadness had come from and what I was supposed to do with it. It would have been easy to blame it on some kind of delayed reaction to the trauma of our showdown with Ray, but I knew that it had nothing to do with the past and everything to do with the future and the black box that was sitting on the desk in Charles's bedroom.

The truth was that my world was as big as I wanted it to be. It was enough for me to keep our little family going and help the sheriff here and there. Communication with the outside world would mean knowing firsthand about the struggles of people that I was powerless to help. It would mean worrying about who was in charge out there and whether their eventual encroachment would be a blessing or a curse. And what if Thomas and Edie decided to go back to town?

But they don't belong to you any more than they belonged to Ray.

Is that what I was really afraid of? Losing my new family?

I sat until my butt was numb with cold and Daisy had risen, stretched, and wandered into the woods. It couldn't have been much past noon, but the sky was an opaque gray, and I wouldn't have been surprised to find that I'd been gone for hours and that dusk would overtake me any time. I had my headlamp, of course, but the others were probably waiting for me to try out the radio, and besides, I'd promised Donna that we'd cook supper together. So, I stood, whistled for Daisy, and started down the slope.

Ingram Content Group UK Ltd.
Milton Keynes UK
UKHW020603250423
420706UK00007B/97